SHADES OF PURPLE

NIKI DOMINIQUE

 RIZE

Shades of Purple
text copyright © 2023 remains with the author
Edited by Laura Huie

All rights reserved.

Published in North America, Australia, and Europe by RIZE.
Visit Running Wild Press at www.runningwildpress.com/rize Educators,
librarians, book clubs (as well as the eternally curious), go to
www.runningwildpress.com/rize.

Paperback ISBN: 978-1-955062-82-4
eBook ISBN: 978-1-955062-83-1

For Dad and Derrick

CHAPTER ONE

I've always hated churches. The fact that I stand before one right now, cold, wet, penniless, and alone has to be some sort of cruel joke crafted by the big man himself. A big "fuck you" aimed right at me and my hubris. I can hear the organ whining through the door as I stare down at the water pooling into my dainty, overpriced flats, my fists clenching and unclenching as I try to muster the courage to simply push open the door, prostrate myself on their cheaply carpeted floor, and beg their mercy. "Respect my authority," their colored glass windows and rows of orderly pews will say down to me, mockingly. And respect them, I shall. Partially because I have no one and nowhere to go, but mostly because my mama always told me so.

I don't come from religious people. I mean, if you asked my dad if he followed a religion, he'd claim to be Christian, but we're Christian in name only. We're Christian in the way that all black people are Christian, you know? We always praised the Lord for getting us out of a bind and bowed our heads to say grace. But we weren't really religious. We didn't go to church, we celebrated Easter only with baskets of candy, and Christmas was always all about gifts and Quality Time.

Although I wasn't raised religious, I was raised to respect other religions. My mother would hiss at me when I'd ask strangers naïve questions about communion or bar mitzvahs, pulling me to her side and clutching my fist in a tight grip. "Whatever you do," she'd say through clenched teeth, "you'd better not disrespect anyone's religion." Her words were blazed into the depth of my brain, right along with the searing glare that went along with them. Maybe that's why I'm here, pressing my forehead to the wooden door of a Catholic church, staring down at my broken shoes, as I shiver in the rain. Maybe that's why I've chosen this location as the place to gather up my strength and find some sort of shelter, even if only for a minute or two.

Respect.

Tit for tat. I respect you if you respect me. I respect this place. Perhaps it will show me the same courtesy.

And so, I gather up all my strength and push until the heavy door gives way and grants me an audience. The doors shut behind me, cutting me off from the cold. And I stand there, shivering silently, forcing my teeth shut to prevent their chattering as I scan the large, open space. Candles line the walls, and my eyes are drawn to the grotesque image of Jesus Christ hanging on the cross, dying for your sins and mine. My eyes alight on the confession booths pressed up against the wall and I feel drawn to them. I walk over to one and allow my fingers to dance across the mahogany. But I dare not enter, respectfully. Instead, I wander down the aisle, towards the front of the room. I slowly march to the first pew and slide down into the seat, aware that I am soaking the velvet cushion beneath me, but not sure what else to do.

I stare at my hands, surprised to find that I am still holding my oversized Louis Vuitton. Something about looking at it in all its overpriced glory, makes the reality of my situation that much more heartbreaking to me. When I had packed it this morning with my last remaining dollars and a leather folder overflowing with resumes, I had known that today would be the day I turned it all around. That I would finally land a job and that would be my first step towards a new beginning.

How wrong I had been.

The bag falls from my fingers, and I hunch over myself. I watch the tears fall silently from my eyes feeling detached from them as if I were not the one they were coming from.

And now what? I wonder. The words bouncing around inside my head, begging to be set free to be answered. But the part of me that usually answers the questions is gone. Curled up in a ball crying and sucking its thumb, wishing this could all just be over already. I don't have the answers, it screams at the question. I have no more answers to give. Please, just stop. And I press my hands to my ears in a futile attempt to silence the voices in my head.

This is how the world ends. A line of poetry snakes its way through the noise. By who? From where? It doesn't matter. I don't care. All I know now is that this is how I lose myself and become a person who is lost to the world. Now I know. Now I see. Well, okay then. So be it. Let it be.

"Ma'am?" a voice says, and I jump.

I look up. A pale priest with kind eyes looks down at me.

"Can I help you?" he asks, his hands clasped in front of his white robes, his voice dripping in concern.

Please.

CHAPTER TWO

The room that the priest shows me to is not even as big as the walk-in closet that I used to share with my husband. He shows me the room then takes off to retrieve some sheets for the small cot that the room is barely big enough to hold. I sit there, staring at the blank, bare walls, and wonder if I would have perhaps been better off just wandering the streets all night. I mean, it's just cold and dark and dangerous, not to mention I'm a female and there are all kinds of perverts. No biggie, right? I shudder at the thought and wrap my arms around my body.

When he returns with clean sheets and a heated blanket, he hands me a bag of toiletries including, oddly enough, a bottle of purple nail polish.

"Um, Father?" I ask, pulling out the small bottle.

"Oh, that," the priest shrugs, "my wife put this bag together for you and I guess she just thought you needed some sort of pick me up."

"Your wife?" I ask, confused, "You're allowed to get married?"

"Loopholes," the priest says, and his grin is so wide it changes the entire shape of his face. For a moment I get a glimpse into the mischievous boy that I am sure he used to be. It reminds me of Darrius and my heart stutters to a stop just long enough for me to lose my breath. I push his face out of my mind by focusing on what the priest is saying to me.

"... lucked up and met my wife when I was five. Always knew I wanted to be a priest but I also always knew that I needed to make Gertrude my wife. That she would do nothing but enhance my service and my life. So, I found a loophole and I exploited it. You can't get married once you're a priest, but if you're already married..." he winks at me mischievously, "Now every church is a bit different, but I happened to find the right church and the right circumstance and, bam." He slaps his palms together, startling me. "Here we are." He folds his hands back together in front of his robes. "I got everything I've ever wanted in life. You can too."

I snort at him but avoid his eyes as I grab the sheets and start to make the bed. He grabs the other side.

"What?" he asks. "You don't believe in happily ever after anymore?"

"I used to," I say, forcing the words out. I don't dare look at him as I fold the sheets under the mattress. "To be honest, Father, I believed I could have it all. Everything I ever wanted. That all my dreams could come true. That I could make them a reality. I believed in every single fairy tale they ever sold to me. And I did everything I could to make it happen. I gave it my all. I gave it my heart and soul."

"And?" he asks, stuffing the pillow into its case.

"I lost it all," I say, in a voice barely above a whisper, "everything that has ever meant anything." I gasp from the pain of remembering. "It's all gone." I clench the sheets harshly. "And it's all my fault." I'm crying again. This is a thing that I do all the time now, apparently.

The priest hands me a handkerchief, then drapes the blanket over the newly folded sheets. I wipe my eyes and snotty nose, but the tears continue to fall silently. He walks over to me.

"You have a choice to make, my dear." And I cautiously look up to meet him in the eye as I await his answer.

"You've messed up, I get it. You've lost everything, I get it. But there are two types of people in this world, my dear. The kind that get knocked down and just stop. The kind that lay there, at rock bottom, bleeding on the stones, bemoaning their sad fate, woe-is-me-ing forever more. You know those people. The bitter and broken ones. The ones that accept their defeat like a badge of honor and display it for all to see."

I nod at him, biting my bottom lip.

"But there's another type of person too. The ones who realize how far they have fallen and see the bottom for what it is—an opportunity." He holds my gaze. "Which one are you going to choose to be?"

"Choose?" I ask, feeling confused and empty.

"Yes. We all choose who we are each day. These choices they pile up, one on top of the other, and they make us who we are. If we make the right choices today, we can have a better tomorrow. And those better days, piled one on top of the other, can lead to a whole new life."

He leans over and presses his forehead to mine, an act so intimate that it throws me off guard, but I force myself to live in the uncomfortable space.

"One day at a time. One step at a time. You'll figure it out." He backs away from me, squeezes my hand. "You've already come so far," he says, nodding down at me.

CHAPTER THREE

H e had been up all night that night. And I had too. Lying in bed, in the dark, listening, listening, listening to him pacing the length of the sitting room of our hotel. A room we couldn't afford in a hotel that we shouldn't be. But there we were, splurging for the last night with each other. His last night free. I'd wanted to get up and go to him, wrap my arms around his waist, press my face into the middle of his back, and tell him that I love him over and over again and hope that he would finally collapse against me, stop pushing me away, and let me in.

Let me in.

Ever since the day I had confessed my sins to him (some, but not all, never all, never everything) he had held me at arm's distance. He stood up; he took the blame. He protected me for reasons I will never understand but that just boiled down to an unapologetic and unconditional love. At least that's what I figured it to be. He never quite told me.

By the time he came to bed I was delirious with sleep. Fading in and out, in and out. Trying to find the strength to hold on until the moment I felt the mattress shift beside me, so I could reach over for him, wrap myself around him and exhale onto his skin.

So he could know, so he could know, so he could feel. My never-ending, undying love for him and knowing that it was real.

Julien.

It's real.

CHAPTER FOUR

The first night is long and hard. Not because the bed is uncomfortable, but because I can't find a good way to quiet my mind and allow the sleep to come. I sleep so lightly, waking up every so often to chide myself for not sleeping soundly. I look out the slit of a window and sigh as the world shows no signs of waking up and I return to trying to sleep. The sun is just beginning its slow ascent into the sky when I finally decide to just get up already. I creek down the hall to the bathroom where I brush and wash then pull on the shapeless clothes laid out for me, taking a moment to bask in their clean, laundered smell, a scent that reminds me of my mommy. And I stutter a bit at the memory. My mother loved the smell of laundry detergent. She would pour entirely too much into each load so the clothes would smell extra laundry-like. It drove my money-conscious father crazy. All the money she was literally pouring down the drain. I take a second to wonder if they will ever forgive me. I take a second to question it, then I release it into the mental pit in my brain where I have dumped all the wonders I have wondered and may never actually know.

I follow the scent of coffee to a large cafeteria. I grab a bagel, smear a glob of cream cheese all over it, and happily fill two mugs of coffee with cheap, black coffee.

I try not to think as I pick at my bagel and sip slowly. I don't focus on things that will make my heart stop and cause my bottom lip to tremble and that watery stuff to fall down from my eyes. I've cried enough already.

And yet... his name still calls to me from the void. It still wafts up from the nothingness to haunt and taunt me.

Curtis.

"Excuse me, Miss," it's a female voice and I look up to find a middle-aged white lady with stringy blonde hair smiling down at me like a smile has been plastered on her face ever since 1963.

"Yes," I say, trying to sound as devoid of emotion as I can.

"May I sit with you?" she asks, her voice more of a command than a question.

And I hesitate before gesturing ostentatiously at the chair directly in front of me.

"What are you doing here?" she says, eyeing me up and down. "Did daddy cut you off? Your husband dump you for a younger, thinner, prettier model and you had the unfortunate luck of signing a prenup?" She dumps way too much sugar in her coffee as she continues to badger me. "Or was it some sort of get-rich-quick Madoff scheme? Come on, spill the beans, I'm dying to know what got little Ms. High-and-Mighty down here with the common folks."

She grins at me as she stirs her coffee. And I simply cock my head to one side, refusing to respond, knowing she is simply trying to goad me. She continues to eye me, taking a small sip of her coffee before leaning in towards me, a half-smile dancing on the lips.

"Oh no, no, no, no, no," she says, now, shaking her head at

me, "I've got you all wrong now, haven't I? No one got over on you." She squints her eyes at me like a fortune-teller trying to read me. "It was just you, destroying yourself, wasn't it?" Her voice has lost its playfulness and she reaches out a hand towards me as if to caress my cheek. I jerk away from her, breaking the connection, the air still electrified by the sudden shift in energy. She shrugs and chuckles softly to herself.

"No matter," she says as she begins digging in a big hobo bag that she wears across her body. "I gave you the polish, but I forgot to put the remover in there," she says, pulling out a small bottle of the stuff and sliding it across the table towards me, "And I want to give you this." She pulls out a small black book tied up with a black string. She places a purple pen atop it and slides it towards me.

She stares until I reluctantly reach for the notebook but grabs my hand just as my arm begins to extend. I try to pull away, but this little old lady proves to be much stronger than me. I look at her, anger and confusion in my eyes.

"You are more than your circumstance," she says, and I stop trying to pull myself from her grasp. "You are more than your bank account. You are more than the car you drive. You are more than your job or your mistakes or even your accomplishments. You were destined for greatness. And great is what you will be."

I look away from her. Who is this lady kidding? I am a terrible human being. I'm as far from great as a person can be.

She shakes my hand in her grip.

"Look at me," she orders. Her voice drops when I don't turn to meet her eyes. "Look at me."

And my head turns slowly.

"So what your path is a bit harder than you thought it'd be? You're still here. You're blessed enough to have your life and your health and your heart."

"My heart?" I ask before I can stop myself. Because my heart has long ago abandoned me.

"Yes, your heart. Listen to it, and you can find your way out of this, find your way back to you. Start here." She gestures with her head towards the notebook on the table, purple pen poised atop, just waiting for me. "Write down the kind of person you want to be and find a way to be that version of you. You owe yourself this at the very least."

She lets go of my hand, nods at me, stands up, and leaves.

CHAPTER FIVE

"Hey," Jill had said, grabbing my hand, "I know it's scary, but..."

I'd eyed her quizzically, her eyes all ablaze.

"I think that we are underestimating ourselves," she'd said, nodding at me as if trying to instill in me her same level of energy.

It wasn't working.

"You," she'd said, shaking my wrist, with a Tony Robbins level of intensity, "are an outstanding, gorgeous, vivacious, African-American creative genius."

I'd tilted my head to the side in a half-shrug, acknowledging the truth of her words.

"But am I a creative genius for an African-American? Or are you just describing me as African-American?" I'd pondered aloud.

She'd rolled her eyes at me and sighed.

"And if it's just a description, was it necessary given the topic?" I'd continued, half-serious and half just to exasperate her.

"Okay, okay, I'm sorry, Jesus," Jill had said, exasperated, shaking my hands. "You are an amazing, outstanding, gorgeous, creative genius—period."

"You forgot vivacious," Gabe called from the kitchen.

"And vivacious, or course," she'd rolled her eyes, "vivacious, creative genius."

"That's better," I'd said.

"And Gabe," she'd let go of my hands and gestured over at Gabe, who'd stood up, stuffing a cold piece of pizza in his mouth, "is the most amazing engineer I've ever met."

"Well, how many engineers do you know, really, Jill?" he'd said, talking with food in his mouth as he'd closed the refrigerator door.

"I know... quite a few..." Jill'd said, sounding flustered.

"Yeah," I'd grinned, walking over towards Gabe, "Besides, you forgot to mention how handsome he is!" I stroked his chin as if he were a puppy. "Who's a handsome boy?" I'd asked.

And he'd swatted my hands away, but grinned at me nonetheless.

"Ugh, I can't be with the two of you!" Jill said, flopping down on the couch. "Can you guys just listen to me for once?"

We'd looked at each other, shrugged, then nodded.

"And you," I'd said, sitting next to Jill and motioning for Gabe to sit on her other side, "are the glue that holds us all together."

"You damn right about that," she'd said, crossing her arms and trying to hold back a smile, "But that's the point guys." Jill looked from one of us then to the other. "We are like the three musketeers."

"More like Charlie's Angels," I'd said.

"Hey," Gabe said, sulking, "I hate being best friends with girls."

We'd both ignored his whine.

"We can do whatever we want to. We could take over the goddamned world if we so choose. All we have to do is decide to be the best versions of ourselves that we can be. The artist," she'd nodded at me, "the engineer," she'd nodded to Gabe, "and the business genius."

"I don't know that I'd call you a genius, per se," Gabe had said.

"Shut up, Gabe," I said, throwing a couch pillow in his face.

"What?" he said, tossing it right back at me.

"Asshole," I said.

"Like I was saying," Jill said, getting in Gabe's face and forcing him to be serious, if only for a minute, "If we decide to be the best versions of ourselves, the best artist, the best engineer, the best businessperson, every day and week and year, we can do anything we want to."

"Like be rich?" Gabe had asked.

And while I had sighed exasperatedly, Jill had simply said, "Exactly."

CHAPTER SIX

I pace my cell-like room for hours. The length of it is so short that it takes only two strides for me to reach the wall, so I pace slowly. One, two, spin. Pause. One, two, spin. Pause. My feet make a steady rhythm that I focus on until my head clears of all thoughts. And then I focus on the nothingness. Float in it. Revel in its beauty. And then it comes. The answer floating out of the void in a misty cloud that bounces around in my head as nothing but a gentle whisper that slowly becomes louder.

And it surprises me because it's not about money or notoriety or power or even him. It's them. Things one, two, and three. Not the ones I've hurt the most. But the ones I have hurt the longest. The ones I have pushed aside time after time. And yet, somehow, the ones I know will be quickest to forgive and forget.

And so, I take a deep breath, sit down on the bed cross-legged, and slowly open the notebook. I glide my fingers, freshly painted with lavender nail polish, across the pristine first page, gearing myself up for the courage to take this first step towards change.

What kind of person do I want to be?

I hesitate, playing the words out in my head over and over again before I finally pick up the pen and write in small, neat lettering:

I am a great mom.

Not mother, not ma, not mommy—mom.

When I was pregnant with the first one, TiTi, my beautiful little angel who looks and acts just like me, and my stomach just started popping out to the point that I couldn't button my pants anymore, I stood in front of the mirror frowning like every goddamned pregnant woman has throughout all of history. My husband came up behind me and placed his hands over mine and said all the things a good husband is meant to say. How beautiful I was. How I had never been sexier. How grateful and happy he was that I was carrying his baby. And he asked me what I wanted to be called. Which version of a mother would I be? And I said, Mom. So simple. So plain. So small. The tiniest of all the titles that had ever been bestowed upon me. And one that I had never taken all that seriously.

This is what needs to change. This is the first title I need to finally reclaim.

And so it begins.

CHAPTER SEVEN

Julien wanted to have kids, I wanted Julien to be happy. And so, we've had TiTi, followed by the twins. I wasn't a good mom. I was the mom equivalent of a 1950s dad: always at work or talking about work or falling asleep in front of the TV. I didn't like being pregnant, hated dealing with babies, and rarely listened when my children would talk to me. By the time I'd given them over to my parents for safe keeping, the big one wasn't talking to me at all and the two little ones just ignored me mostly. The only time they acknowledged my existence was to enquire as to the whereabouts of their daddy.

It is these relationships that I need to fix. The ones that had always been broken. The ones that have always been the most important. The ones that I had always failed to truly see.

I am sorry.

CHAPTER EIGHT

I find the priest easily. He's in his office. A door with a small, simple marker that bears the name I hadn't bothered to ask for yesterday: Father Frederick Von Wilkins.

"Father Fred," he tells me, when I knock tepidly on his door and am welcomed into his space with a warm embrace.

"I need to get my kids back," I say to the matted green carpet at my feet.

"Okay," he says softly to me, "Did you give up your parental rights?"

"No."

I look up at him slowly. He leans forward in his seat, hands entwined. He looks like he wants to speak, but instead he waits for me.

I clear my throat. "I left them with my parents when I lost everything. I thought that I would be able to turn things around. That it would be temporary. But it's been at least a year since I've seen them and I'm not sure where to begin."

I lay my problem at his feet and pour all my hope into his willingness to assist me. He opens a drawer in his desk and pulls out a cell phone. He places it in the space between us and lets its presence fill me.

"You can call them right now. I'm sure you know the number."

"I do." I stare at the phone, willing it to disappear with the power of my mind. "But, I can't," I say, hoping that my measly answer will be sufficient enough.

"Why?" he asks, his voice low and gravely.

And we sit in a silence that becomes uncomfortable. My mind keeps wandering. Nothing coherent, just images that flash across my brain. My kids, each one of their faces the last time I saw them—the look in their eyes. My parents. Their voices when I called to tell them that, no I wasn't coming back to get the kids, I wasn't sure if I would ever be ready to get the kids, and, by the way, I had fucked them over too. I shake my head forcing myself to be present in this moment with this priest whose eyes are watching over me so closely.

I clear my throat and close my eyes as I force myself to speak. "I don't think that I can face them like this."

"Like what?" he says slowly.

I gesture at myself. "Broke, homeless," I let out a sharp laugh. "Surviving on the kindness of a bunch of people whose religion I don't even subscribe to."

"Well, whose religion do you follow?" he asks with a half-grin.

I shrug, shaking my head at his absurd question. "Does it even matter at this point, Father?"

"Precisely, it doesn't matter. None of what you said matters. Your kids are your kids. I guarantee if you gave them the option between no mom at all or a mom who maybe doesn't have all the fancy knick-knacks that she used to have, that they'd pick you, every time. Show up for them, and they will show up for you." He leans back in his chair, waiting for some sort of response.

"I know all of this," I finally say, "but my parents, they're a part of this, I have to deal with them too."

"Listen," Father Fred says, leaning forward in his chair, eyes stern like a dean staring down at a thief caught red-handed, "I can only help you," he says, pushing the phone closer to me, "If you decide to help yourself."

I pull my eyes away from him and stare down at the phone. Its presence is so heavy.

"What kind of mom do you want to be?" he says, his voice steady, words slicing at the soft spots I'd thought I'd calloused over long ago.

I press my lips together to keep from crying, then I close my eyes. I picture each one of their smiling faces. And I pick up the goddamned phone.

CHAPTER NINE

I saw my kids last about a year ago. Maybe a year and a half. Things with the hubby were getting dicey. Yelling matches damn near every night. Money was getting tight. We were late on the mortgage and had to make decisions like, food or the electric bill. We choose food. The day my kids walked into our house, flipped the light switch and nothing happened, was the day I decided to take them to my parents' house. I expected it to be nothing. Excited hugs and kisses when they walked through the door like they did every time we dropped them off for a weekend or to go on a week-long business trip. No big deal. But instead the three of them stood there, eyes wide, clutching their belongings, trying not to cry. They didn't return my hugs when I doled them out, just kept asking me how long they would be there and when I was coming back.

There was a time when I went to pick up my daughter when she would pretend I wasn't her mother. I overheard her say snottily to her bitchy little white-girl prep school friends that, no, that wasn't her mother. Her mother was taller, prettier, drove a nicer car. She was too busy and important to actually pick her up from school. This was her mother's other assistant. The one that usually picked her up must be sick or something. The girls standing around with her, all equally waiting for their mothers, nannies, and assistants to come pick them up from the bougie ass elite school that I paid out the ass for my daughter to attend, shrugged, saying that she looked a lot like me, and my daughter had basically accused them of being racist, thinking all black people look alike. Really? And with a swish of her hair she had bounced towards me, walking past me with a mumbled, hello, and gotten into the back seat of my Porsche SUV, my "mom" car.

I had climbed into the driver's seat slowly, unsure of how I was feeling.

I sat there for a minute, repositioned my rear-view mirror so I could look at my daughter without turning around to do so, and I watched her as she sat in the backseat texting, scrolling, giggling at this and that. She was, what, 14? That was the last birthday for her, right? And there she was. Looking every bit just like I did when I was her age. She'd used to look much more like her father. And his influence was still there, in her cheekbones, her hazel eyes, her height, but her overall effect was mine. She had my gestures all of a sudden. Quirky movements that I recognize as only mine. Half smiles and the tendency to run my tongue over my teeth when I'm thinking about something. Me. My mini-me. My daughter.

It had taken her a few minutes to realize that we weren't moving. She looked up and caught my eyes in the rearview mirror.

"What's up, Mom? You forgot the way home or something? You can just put it in the GPS." She said, a sliver shy of having an attitude, but disparaging, nonetheless.

"I heard you," I said, ignoring her stupid comments.

"You heard what?" she'd asked, but the glimmer in her eyes told me that she knew exactly what I was talking about.

"Why?" I'd asked, as I watched her try not to cry.

"I don't know," she'd said, shrugging, trying to play it off nonchalantly, "I just thought, I'd maybe sound cool." She looked away from me, out the window, "Can we just go? Everyone's going to think it's weird that we're just sitting here."

And I'd bit my lip and wanted to push it, to push more out of her, to strangle the real truth out of her overly glossed lips and force it all to come up to the surface. To make her be real with me. But it felt impossible. An insurmountable wall up between us that I had played a big role in helping to build, so I just threw the car into reverse and drove off in silence.

And so when she answers her cellphone, questioning, hesitant, since she doesn't recognize the number, and I respond by simply saying her name, it is this same familiar silence that I am met with. And so I sit with it, and wait for my daughter to do what I could never manage to do with her—break the silence.

But she doesn't.

She is truly her mother's daughter. After several seconds of silence, I hear the sounds of voices in the background, and then all of a sudden I am bombarded with the high-pitched squeals of children screaming in my ear.

"Mommy! Mommy! Mommy! Where are you? When are you coming to get us? What are you doing? I miss you! I got a new truck. I got a new truck too." The voices of my twin boys assail me, two voices blurring into one, layered overtop of one another. I smile into the phone and wait for an opening to speak.

"Darrius. Parris. How are you guys?" I ask, hesitantly. My voice was loud and excited.

"Mommy, Mommy, Mommy, I told Parris that you were

going to call us soon and I was right! Now he owes me a whole dollar, Mommy." Darrius shouts in my ear.

"No, no, no, Mommy. I never said that! I knew you were calling!" Parris shouts in return, trying to drown out his brother's protestations.

"Mommy, he promised! He promised!" Darrius wails.

The twins must be six years old by now. I missed their birthday. It was about a month ago. Why didn't I call them? What kind of mother am I?

I hear someone scolding the twins in the background, and my stomach automatically begins to tie up in knots. The twins' whines subside and then suddenly I am assailed with my mother's voice.

"Adrienne?"

CHAPTER TEN

He wanted another kid. The first one was so great, so beautiful, so perfect. I had all the help I needed, didn't I? The bilingual nanny who taught the kid Mandarin. The bilingual cook who taught the kid Spanish. The in-house tutor who taught the kid ABC's and 123's. All the help in the world. Let's have another one. What's the worst that could happen?

I went to the sonogram by myself. No biggie. I'd told my husband. We'd done this shit before. Seen the sonograms and had the conversations. Not much can change in a few years, right? Go to the meeting with the very important people. I'll be fine. But as the lady rubbed the cold gel on my belly, I had the sinking feeling that I was wrong. That moment was one he needed to be there for. That a hand to hold was exactly what I needed right then and there at that moment in time. But I didn't call him, and I didn't call Jill, and I didn't call my mom, and I sat there in that cold room with a total stranger as she rubbed that thing on my belly and said, "Oh, wow, look, there's two of them in there. Did you know you were having twins?" and felt the entire world spin all around me.

Twins. Boys. Look at their penises. Look at their heartbeats. Here's a three-dimensional printout of their faces. Oh, look, they have your nose and your chin definition. Look.

But that was then and this is now, and my mother is saying something to me...

"... are you going to do it? What are you doing now? Why now?" Her voice is crackly, pained, and I want to hang up the phone. Push the red button. Be done with this conversation and this moment in time. Fast-forward to the moment when this has all worked itself out and everything is fine, because that moment is coming, right?

I want to ask her how she's doing. How she's managed with my three little angels. I want to ask her about dad and his health, and how they are faring after I have stolen their money and their future and their wealth. I want to ask her if she will ever forgive me for all the pain and the sins I have committed against them.

But instead I say what I always say when my mom calls me and asks me about my day, "Hi, Mom."

CHAPTER ELEVEN

It is dark and cold, but there is a soft yellow light in the distance, a flickering yellow light. I feel the pull immediately. Come this way. Come this way. Come and see what you need to see. But I hesitate. Something inside me tells me that what that light has to show me is something I would rather not see. Something that I don't need to see at all. Something wrong. Something bad.

A stone falls down in the pit of my stomach and the hairs stand on the back of my neck. I frown. And down down down I fall. The floor gives out beneath me, but I land softly. The world rippling around me in cascades of blackness. I spin around slowly and there is nothing, nothing, nothing. But in the distance, the light slowly comes to be. The same dull yellow glow, flickering. I don't want to go towards it. Every fiber of my being screams out in protest, but the darkness is cold. I feel it, seeping up from my feet. A creeping sensation that is pulling me down again. So I move away from it and towards the flickering light. I inch, slowly, knowing that what the light has to reveal to me is something I don't want to see, but the darkness also pulls at me.

The cold feelings at my feet grow, and my footsteps increase their pace. I can feel the darkness coming to life around me, turning itself into fingers that grip and pull at me, tugging on my jeans, on the hem of my shirt, on my body. And now I'm running. Running more so away from the darkness than towards the light. The ominous light flickering, growing steadily as I move closer. I slow my pace as I get closer to the light, but the darkness is still pulling at me, tugging me back, trying to engulf me in its coldness. I can't let it. I won't. And so I continue forward, at a slow jog now. The push pull. The light pulling me to it, the darkness tugging me back, me fighting against both of them, wishing I could just be. I am close now. And I see a doorway. The flickering light within. A bulb hanging on a wire, swaying to and fro, within the doorframe and out. A dancing bulb swaying to a rhythm I know all too well. Why do I know this melody? Why is this song so familiar to me?

I step up to the doorway and the darkness pulls away from me all at once. The hands withdraw, recoiling from the light in disgust. Pulling away with a soundless screech. I cross the threshold tepidly, eyes on my feet, scared to look up but compelled to nonetheless. I am compelled to look, and I obey like the little girl that I have always been inside. Follow the rules. Know what they are so you can break them properly, Adrienne. And so I look up, and I see.

CHAPTER TWELVE

"Adrienne," a voice had called to me.

I'd opened my eyes slowly.

"Come here," he'd said, "come closer." And I'd climbed onto his body and entwined my limbs with his and rested my face on his chest and listened to the familiar sound of his heartbeat.

And this is it, I'd thought then and I think intermittently in random moments to this very day, this is the place that I should always be. Here with him and he with me. I'd inhaled his scent and allowed myself to wonder if it could always be just like this. Every day. Him and me for the rest of eternity, together. It's a possibility, right?

"I love you," he'd muttered softly into my hair.

"Always," I'd replied.

Him and me.

Me and he.

CHAPTER THIRTEEN

I t is colder outside than I thought it would be. Cold and dark. The sunlight is still thinking about creeping up into the sky, wondering if it has the energy. I pull my gray hoodie over my wild mane of hair and shove my hands into my pockets as I walk over to the place where Father Fred told me that I needed to be. Honeydew Farms, a sign smiles at me. An urban garden. I weave my way through a path lined with trees and spot an older woman stooped on one knee, examining a row of sprouting plants, small and green and smiling as they dare to stand. Newborn baby plants, that have matured underground and now stand, weak and frail, yet refusing to bend to the chill in the air.

I walk over to the woman and wait for her to acknowledge my existence. She finishes doing whatever she is doing before slowly coming to stand and stare straight at me. I ask her if she's Esther and she nods, so I tell her who I am. That Father Fred sent me, but she continues to just stare at me. Her grey hair stringy and pulled back into a bun. A brown cap on her head. An oversized men's button-up shirt dancing around in the air, just past the tips of her fingers. Her skin is a beautiful and smooth medium brown, a shade lighter than my own. But it's her eyes that startle me with their grey intensity. The gaze of a woman who has spent her life sizing people up. I wonder whose grandmother she is. I want to see how her face breaks out into a smile of remembrance. I want to sit her down before a fire curled up onto a couch somewhere with handmade quilted blankets and listen to stories about her life and the places she's been and the things that only she has seen. But something in her gaze tells me that she has sized me up. That she has seen parts of me that are better left unseen. That she is already not a fan of me.

She gestures her head towards the path and I step back onto it, carefully maneuvering around the baby plants sprouting all around me.

She begins walking the winding path and I follow, silently.

"I know Father Fred well, and he has often sent people to me," she begins, not bothering to look back at me, "some of them have come for a while, stayed, moved on to their own things. Some are still here with me. Others," she says with emphasis, as if suggesting that these others are the category that I belong to, "don't make the cut. They come for a day or two and find the work too hard or too menial, and leave or are asked to do so." And the unspoken questions hang in the air between us. A silent asking, reminiscent of the question Father Fred asked me just days ago—which type of person are you?

I stand up taller, although she doesn't move to see this, some sort of physical response, confirming my own determination to not be the others that she spoke of, to withstand whatever she throws at me.

"We rotate jobs here. We all do a bit of everything, so you must be proficient at all things in order to last here." She gestures around her as she points at various areas and the job titles associated with them. Farming, planting, weeding, watering, organizing tours, taking phone calls, dealing with the buying and selling of things. I halfway expect her to ask me where I'd like to start, and yet I'm not at all surprised when she stops in front of a large barn-like building and points me toward a man hauling a huge bag, loaded up with something solid and weighty like seeds or manure.

"Hey," I say, walking over to him, fighting the urge to stuff my hands in the front pocket of my hoodie and look down at my shoes like the nervous little girl that lurks in the dark, cobweb-ridden corners of my mind.

When I introduce myself I don't say, "Hi, I'm Adrienne and I'm a terrible person, you should stay the fuck away from me." I just tell him who I am, that Father Fred sent me, and that Esther apparently wants me to start here, working with him.

He nods at me, a half-smile dancing on the corners of his lips, and I stand there, watching him take in every inch of me, very, very, slowly before he finally deigns to open his mouth and introduce himself to me.

He tells me that his name is Roscoe and immediately I start to look a bit closer at him. The name Roscoe conjures up images of a man standing in a jail yard, wife-beater on, tattoos up around his neck, rock hard body, cold steel in his eyes. But this man looks nothing like that stereotype. His eyes sparkle mischievously, but he has a petite frame. His skin is a golden brown and his hair is peppered with gray. He smiles at me, obviously thinking that I'm checking him out too, and although he's not a bad-looking guy at all, I have to check him real quick. I've had enough issues with love to last me a lifetime, thank you very much, I don't need any more. Besides, my heart still belongs to him. No matter how big I messed up, no matter how fucked up things got between us two, my heart belongs to him, pure, plain, simple, and true.

"You ever been to jail, Roscoe?" I ask, knowing the wince will come before it shows up on his face.

Instead of answering, he turns and begins walking, talking to me over his shoulder.

"Did anyone ever tell you, you are a heart-breaker, Adrienne?"

And this makes me laugh. A real laugh, a deep down in the pit of my stomach laugh that takes over my entire body. The first real laugh that I remember having in a very, very long time.

CHAPTER FOURTEEN

"AK47," he'd said, attempting to run his finger through the tangled maze of a mess on top of my head. "I have to go," he'd said, before leaning over to place a kiss tenderly on my lips.

I'd reached out to him. Don't leave me, the message my fingerprints imprinted on his body.

"AK," he'd said, "AK47, you're killing me."

"Marry me," I'd said.

And he'd leaned down and kissed me and whispered into my mouth, "But we're already married."

"Marry me again," I'd said, pulling him back down into another kiss. His lips on mine—so delicious.

And he'd leaned back, and he'd looked up as if thinking over the scenario, as if he could see something in the ceiling, some aspect of the future, what our life would be, before finally opening his mouth to speak.

"So, let me get this right, you want to divorce me, split up the kids, figure out custody, child support, all that bullshit, just so you can marry me yet again? That seems like a bit much, no?"

And I'd scrunched up my face, as if pondering the ridiculous situation, and I'd climbed slowly out of bed, and pressed my naked body to his, fully clothed, in a fucking sexy ass blue suit nonetheless, before I'd finally said, "But aren't I worth it?"

And he'd smiled at me, and kissed me gently, and told me, "You are, Baby. You are worth anything. But I'll be damned if I risk losing you. You are mine, for all of time. Till death do us part and all that. I'll fucking kill you before I let you divorce me, and I don't give a fuck that you want it just so you can remarry me."

He'd been so serious. So fucking serious. So delusionally in love with me, that I had laughed and laughed and laughed, because it was so funny, imagining him trying to kill me for wanting to marry him again.

But he had lied. He had been the one to file the paperwork. He had been the one to say he was done. He had been eager, thrilled really, to get rid of me.

Lying piece of shit.

I hope he's happy.

CHAPTER FIFTEEN

My husband once told me that I was a fucking flake. That I liked to order people around, to ask them to do things I was incapable of doing in a timeline that was impossible. That I had never taken anything outside of work seriously. That I would make promises and promises and promises and never ever keep them, yet nail employees to the wall for doing the same.

"Do what you say you're going to do," he'd yelled at me once when I'd missed yet another promised recital or some other such kid bullshit. "Or stop making these shitty promises."

I could say the same to him now, ironically. You said you'd never leave me. What happened to that, huh? What happened to forever?

But then again, maybe it was me. Maybe I'd had a negative influence on him. Maybe I had warped and twisted him into becoming the man he is today. Maybe I had broken his heart one too many times in one too many ways.

Or maybe this is just who he had always been.

And the truth shall set you free.
Maybe.

CHAPTER SIXTEEN

During the day, I'm fine. I go about life mechanically like an empty robot programmed to do and say the things a person is supposed to do and say, but at least I'm functioning properly. I hold banal conversations, I show up to work early, I work hard, I stay late, I take on extra responsibilities, I throw myself into the minutiae of every aspect of my job. Roscoe takes me home most days when he can. A bumpy ride in his pickup truck, but he doesn't like to talk and that suits me just fine. Other days I walk back to the church slowly. Meandering walks that remind me of how I found the church in the first place, staring down at my shoes watching my feet move with little effort, with no guidance, going all on their own.

I live this life with no problem. I do these tasks with no problem. I empty my mind with no problem. No problems.

During the day.

But night is different. I eat dinner with everyone else, slowly, silently. I offer to help clean the dishes, sweep the floors, wipe down the tables, and prepare the space for the next day. For the next day. For the next.

But eventually it all ends. And when all the tasks are done and my teeth are brushed, and I pull my stiff excuse for pajamas on and the door closes and I hear the sound of the lock- I fall apart.

I used to hear my mom crying sometimes. A muffled sound late in the wee hours of the night when I would get up to pee. I don't think I'll ever find out why. If I ever dared to ask, I don't think she'd be able to tell me. Maybe it's something that happens to us all. Maybe we all cry in the dark when we think no one is listening. Because when else would we cry? When else is it acceptable? No one but babies are allowed such a liberty as crying in the light of day, out in the open, for all to see.

All I can do is hope that no one has to walk by my room late at night in order to pee.

CHAPTER SEVENTEEN

It takes me a month of working for Esther to build up enough money to put down a down payment on a small cabin that Esther rents out to people she trusts on her huge property. It's a two-bedroom cabin, fully furnished with a pullout couch. The boys can take one room, and my baby girl can have the other. I will have the luxury of sleeping on the couch. Oh joy. But at least I can finally retrieve them, at least they can finally be with me.

I showed up a bit earlier than I said I would be. I have to prove myself to be reliable and consistent, a pillar of dependency.

I force a grin at my mother when she opens the door, but all she does is lean in towards me, her breath hot and stinky of moldy cheese as she says to me, "You have to earn your children back, do you hear me?"

And so I nod and I smile and I look around her to usher the kids towards me. The twins run at me, all hugs and sticky fingers, before running past me, outside onto the lawn with bookbags bouncing behind them. The girl moves much more slowly, nonchalantly. Eyes on her phone as she walks past me, careful not to touch me. But she comes. And for that, I am grateful.

"You don't even have a car," my mom says, snidely, looking past me at the nothingness parked in front of her house.

"People have been known to survive without cars, Mom. They will be fine." I try to not grit my teeth as I speak, but I'm not sure how great of a job I actually do.

She scoffs at me, "You spoiled these children quite soundly. It took the larger part of the first year to tone down their expectations, and now you show up here with no car, thinking that you're going to take them and never return?" She lets out a harsh, bitter laugh, "Well at least you won't be able to ride off into the sunset this time."

And all I can do is continue to hold my forced smile. All I can do is take the bullshit she's dishing at me. Accept it, because I have made her into the person standing before me. This travesty of a parody of my mother standing before me.

"I'll have them back to you Sunday night, Mother, but don't you worry, I will be taking them off your hands completely soon enough." I turn to walk away, and she laughs at me.

"Don't think I wasn't there when you gave birth to TiTi, don't think I don't remember how you handed her off to the nanny the second you walked through the door. You haven't spent a single 24-hour period being their mom. What, now you're broke I'm supposed to believe in you? Supposed to be rooting for you? Supposed to want you to get your shit together and take your kids back and be happy?" She lets out another harsh laugh.

I stop walking, but gesture at the kids to go on. Something inside me tells me that they don't need to hear what she has to say, but that she has to say it, nonetheless.

"You know what, Adrienne? You know how I got through

all this bullshit you put me and your father through?" she pauses for emphasis I guess, and I just wait, not bothering to look back at her like I know she wants me to. "I thought of you as dead. I took a day off of work and held a whole funeral for you in my head. I cried and I cried and I cried and I buried you, dead. And I wish your ass would have stayed there, underground where you belong."

I allow one single tear to trickle down my cheek. There, I think, we're finally even, my mom and me. And I jog after my children who are now halfway up the street.

CHAPTER EIGHTEEN

When I was a little girl, my mom had once grabbed me on the playground and pulled me aside right after I had slid down the winding, big slide. Her hands were hard, dragging me behind the trees.

She had bent down, bringing her face close to me, her eyes hard and red with fury. And I had recoiled inwardly, yet still met her gaze as was expected of me.

"Stay away from that boy," she'd said to me, through gritted teeth, "you hear me? You stay far, far away from that boy."

And it had taken every ounce of strength held within my little body to avoid looking away, glancing at the boy I had left, the dancing smile and exuberance that he had held only for me. And I nodded at her.

"I understand," I'd told her.

And from then on, when I'd see him, I'd kept my distance. He'd attempted to talk to me again and again. But no, I'd told him simply with a shake of my head. No.

That's what my mama said.

CHAPTER NINETEEN

The first night was a little crazy. The boys are loud and excited, talking a mile a minute. The girl, though, is reticent. She wanders from room to room, touching things, unsure if this is real. I see it in her eyes. Unsure if this is a safe place to be. Here in this little house with me, her mommy.

I find her, curled up on the couch, huddled around her phone, like a wolf in captivity, yearning to be free, and I curl up next to her, close enough to touch, yet those last inches seem so far away from me. A distance she needs to travel on her own.

I am here, I hope my nearness is conveying to her. Her and me. Me and she. My daughter. My love. My TiTi.

CHAPTER TWENTY

When we hit the first million, we were so excited. Exuberant. We'd told everyone. Every. Body. The parents, the friends, the aunts, uncles, and cousins. We'd bought a loudspeaker and drove around town blasting it to the world. He'd hosted parties and mentioned it fake-nonchalantly with a hint of hoity-toity. What's new? Oh nothing, we just are millionaires, each, independently. Jointly and separately. Millionaires. No biggie.

I had told my husband in the early days of our love, casually one night while watching something we were obsessed with at the time on my big box TV, that I was going to be a millionaire so if he wanted to marry me, maybe we needed a prenup because I've seen the shit that happened to people on TV. And he'd told me, no. He'd said he planned to be a millionaire right along with me. Both of us—independently and together, worth millions. So, no prenup was needed.

So, when we had achieved our goal, we needed to tell everybody.

We learned from that shit real quick. New money brags on

it and learns quickly to regret it. Because once you tell people how well you're doing, people start treating you differently. Friends start with fake smiles, talking shit about you behind your back. Family comes out from out the grave, with hands out. Gimme, gimme, please please please. Such-and-such is your cousin and he has needs. Can't you just... please. And the takers never stop talking. They are a bottomless well that never fills. And so we pulled back. And so we pulled in. To him and me. Us against the world. No, no, no. We don't have anymore to give. We have given, enough.

We pulled back and away and focused on making more and more and sharing our successes less and less. Yeah, we're doing okay, but not that well. Millionaires? Maybe, but the taxes are crazy and the car note is real and the mortgage on the house is like a heavy weight tying us down, so, no, I don't think we have it to give.

No.

CHAPTER TWENTY-ONE

He kisses me. So softly. A kiss. So simple, so effortless, and yet it pulls me all the way in. No, no, no. That was then. Be present, be here. I have missed out on being here. I shake my head and focus on my sons' soccer game. I have picked them up and we have ridden two busses to get here. An adventure to them for now, but one that I can see them soon getting tired of, along with me. The stress of knowing that one missed connection could mean a missed game completely. But I need to show them I can be a mom, I think.

My daughter lounges on the blanket spread out on the damp grass next to me, looking up intermittently from her phone to cheer her brothers on. Darrius, ever the showman, weaves and bobs, knocking into the other kids in his determination towards the goal. His stance is so aggressive. Never losing focus. His brother is much more calculating. He keeps up with Darrius but he is much more aware of others: weaving and bobbing, avoiding contact if he can, making himself seem like the lesser threat when he has always been the more athletically talented of the two. Glad to let the other team think Darrius is the star, so he can have the space and opportunity to really shine when he needs to.

Parris. My baby. My last-born child. When I was in labor with the twins, Darrius came right out. He didn't even cry, just looking around with the same quizzical eye of his daddy. Parris took a minute to come. The doctors wanted to cut me open and pull him out of me.

"He's taking a mighty long time Mrs. Louden, we think it'd be best to just get him out of there, so we can make sure he's safe."

But my entire body rejected that notion. No, no, no. My baby was fine. He was just taking his time. They'd see.

And so we waited. Hours we'd waited. The doctors got more and more insistent. They were worried. Usually, the twin comes out after such and such amount of time. He could be having some sort of issue. He could be struggling to breathe. But I stood my ground and my husband got them to back down by threatening to sue the shit out of everybody. Was our son under duress? He'd asked. Was his heartbeat steady? No. Yes. Okay then, leave us be. Or he would have a team of lawyers here to oversee the harassment of his wife and family.

I don't think I've ever smiled so brightly.

And then, only then, when his father had stood up for him, did I feel little Parris move inside me.

"Doctor," I'd grunted, gripping the frame of the hospital bed fiercely, "I think he's ready."

And less than one full minute later, they were placing him on top of me.

Parris. And when he'd looked up at me, I'd grinned, and I'd known right then, that he would be just like me. And even though we'd had their names before they came, clearly laid out and ready to go- Darrius for the first-born son, Parris for the second, it was strange how those names seemed to fit them perfectly.

Darrius, my show-boating star who always shines so bright it's hard not to stare, is just like his father- handsome, debonair, good at everything he does and knows it, with a killer smile that can just melt your heart, and tons of energy. The goddamned life of the party. Everyone knows him. Everyone loves him. Everyone wants to be his friend.

Parris is much more silent, but deadly. Just as much in the limelight as his brother but for a much different reason. There's a quiet confidence in his walk. A reservation to his words. He is calculating and thoughtful, but with a warmth that I never possessed. He knows the right way to approach everyone, and while his brother will dump buckets and buckets of words on people, Parris will step in and just know the right way to approach each individual- a look, a touch, a word or two, and people just fall all over themselves to be around him.

Darrius and Parris. Parris and Darrius.

I used to hate having twins. Someone was always grabbing at me, demanding ownership of my body. Pulling at my breasts, rubbing jelly-smeared hands on my designer suits, crying, screaming, fighting, throwing things. I used to pry them from my legs and push them on a nanny, on their sister, on their father, anybody. Someone please take these boisterous boys away from me, can't you see I'm busy?

But now I am here. Now I can see them for who they are. Or at least I can try.

Darrius passes the ball to his brother and he jumps in the air, his leg swinging with the perfect arc as it connects with the ball, sending it directly into the goal. The ball moves so fast that no six- or seven-year-old goalie could ever stand a chance. This one doesn't even try. He stands there, mouth agape, watching the ball wiz by. I see his face fall as he realizes his mistake, but he is not my child. His heartbreak is not mine to soothe. Instead, I turn to my boys and see them grinning right back at me.

Did you see? Their eyes shine at me.

I nod and follow it with a yell of exuberance.

I am here. I am present. Finally.

CHAPTER TWENTY-TWO

I AM A GREAT DAUGHTER.

The voices in my head had been demanding more of me. Reach out to him. Reach out to him. Believe in him. He believes in me. Always. And yet I wasn't able to make the call.

He calls me first instead.

"Adrienne," he says, after I greet him with the standard hello, as if he is not my father but someone I don't quite know.

"Yes," I say, forcing the question out of my voice. I know better. I've been raised by the best.

He clears his throat. "Your mother tells me that you still don't have a car. That you've been running your kids around on the..." he hesitates before stumbling over the final word, "bus. Is this true?"

"Yes, Daddy," I say, automatically, the response, crisp and clear.

"I know you're broke and all, Buttercup, but there's no reason for all that."

"I've been working hard, Daddy. I'm going to get one soon,

I promise. As soon as I can, your grandchildren won't have to ride the bus for very long." My mind races over my response as I speak it. Yes, good. I took responsibility. I didn't make a single excuse. Yes, good.

"Now I know that you messed up our retirement a bit, but there's no reason for all of this. We have more than enough money to help you-"

But I cut him off right there. "No," I say.

"What," my dad replies, full of a stuffiness that I am not at all surprised hasn't in the least bit diminished since I was a little girl.

"It's not even that I don't want your money, although I don't, it's that I simply cannot take it. I cannot take a single dime from you and Mom. I don't deserve it. I..." and here I stumble, but I clear my throat and quickly recover, "I don't deserve a single dime." And that sentence makes me smile.

"You know what, Dad," I say, and my heart fills up with joy at the words that I'm about to convey, "I've been getting some help and advice from a priest and his wife, and she asked me a couple months ago about the kind of person I want to be, and I've been telling myself, all the different ways I want to act in the world, and," I chuckle to myself softly, "The kind of motherfucker who loses the majority of her parent's retirement money and then asks them for more, is so far off from the person that I'm trying to be that there are no words. No words strong enough in all the world, in the entire dictionary, can convey my feelings more accurately than this." And I sigh, leaning back in my chair, and smiling up at the ceiling. "No. Just no, Dad. I love you for still trying to help me, despite everything, but no. I will find a way and we will continue to ride the bus until I do. That is all. And look, it's the truest truth, Daddy, and it's beautiful."

"Okay, Buttercup," he says, after a long pause. "Have it

your way."

CHAPTER TWENTY-THREE

"Love me or let me go," I'd screamed to Curtis all those many moons ago. When things were just starting to unravel in every part of my life and I was left standing holding onto the threads, trying to keep everything together.

He'd laughed at me, pulling up his jeans, picking up his ridiculously expensive watch off the nightstand along with his cufflinks.

"I do love you, Adrienne, but is it enough? Is it ever enough? Look at what you have done to me. You say all these things like you love me and only me, but time and time again all you have done is devastate and hurt me. Love you? What the fuck do you think that I have done? What the fuck do you do? Do you even love me? Or do you just love the idea of me? How can you say that you love me when all you do is lie and take, take, take everything from me?"

I'd rolled over on the bed, naked, running my hands up my belly, across my breasts and through my hair. I'd grasped my hair into my fists and stared up at the ceiling, the pressure stopping me from screaming.

"Was it ever real?" I'd asked, finally, more to myself than to him. And I'd run down the trajectory of our love story in my head. All the way down to that very moment, just before. Him inside me, filling me up with every ounce of himself, his sweat dripping onto my body, mingling with mine, his secretions becoming one with me. Him and me. Me and he.

He'd walked over to me then, towering over my naked body with his, fully clothed, but I could see the erection pressing up against his trousers. He still wanted me. He'd just had me- up against the windows, in the bed, fingers in my hair, lips on my lips, eyes glued to mine. Tell me whose it is. I'd said it was his. But it'd always been mine. Just mine. To give as I saw fit.

"Love me or let me go," I'd said again, up at him. Taking in the lines of his face, the shape of his eyes, the grace in his stance, the way his fucking presence took over mine. "This is the moment, Curtis. This is it. Love me now, or end it. I can't-" at this my voice had broken, a tear had stolen away from my right eye and trickled down my face, melting into my hair. I didn't dare swipe it away. "I can't do this anymore. It's been too long. It's been too much hurt. Too many things have gone wrong. I will give it all up for you, if you say that you'll love me right now. If you promise to give your all to me right now. If you say that this is what you want to do. I will give up everything for you."

The words dance off my lips and hang in the air, and I see in his eyes that he is contemplating it. Weighing all his options. Looking at every angle. Seeing everything there is to see. Deciding if he wants to have a future with me.

He opens his mouth and closes it. Opens and closes it. Opens it again. The words come slowly, forced. Hard and stagnant.

"I can't." He backs away from the bed. "I'm sorry, Adrienne, but I can't."

And with that, he'd left. And I never spoke to him again.

CHAPTER TWENTY-FOUR

Winning my dad over is like massaging a sore muscle. It takes a little patience and a lot of fucking energy.

I've known since the day I started down this winding trajectory of an apology and a second attempt at life, the exact way that I would find myself back in his good graces, and yet, it takes that phone call from him to propel me into action.

I know my dad. I know him better than I know anyone. And although he has never quite understood me, he has always given me the space to be exactly who I am. And for that, I have always both appreciated and hated him.

And so, the very next day I finally manage to get my ass up at 4 am so I can ride the bus across town and be standing outside his house, clutching my old rusty bicycle as I shiver in the cold, when he opens the garage door and steps outside, wheeling his bike alongside him. He stops for a second when he spots me, and I just nod at him before throwing my leg over the bike and waiting for him to take the lead and show me where he wants to go.

It takes him a few seconds longer than I think it will, but he eventually begins riding, his long legs moving with the ease and grace of someone who is in his element doing the thing that he both excels at and loves to do. I take a deep breath, hoping I have it in me to keep up before hopping on the bike and following along closely behind him.

There is something about this. This inhale, exhale, pump, pump, pump, uphill, glide, and coast. This physical exertion that forces you to remain fully present in every single breath flowing through your body. This.

I pump my legs as hard as I can, doing the best I can to keep up with my dad. And I do a halfway decent job, partially because I don't let my thoughts wander from moment to moment, or thought to thought, but mostly because I know that my dad is taking it easy on me. I haven't ridden a bike in at least three years, he rides almost every day. I'll be regretting this in the morning.

After an extremely long patch uphill in which it takes everything in me to not get off my bike and walk it up- the slow, trudging uphill walk of defeat, he finally stops on a small patch overlooking all of the city. He disembarks from his bike and I have to bite down on my lip to prevent myself from shouting "hooray" for this much needed break. He carefully props his bike up on the kickstand, but I just let my rusty bike fall to the ground.

"Twenty-three years," he says as I walk over to him, wiping beads of sweat from my forehead, "Twenty-three years your mother worked for the government."

"Yeah dad-" I start to say, but he cuts me off.

"She put in her time, good time, the best years of her life, doing soul-crushing work, day in and day out, so that you and your sister would have a good life, with the hopes that one day she'd be able to retire and devote her time to doing only the things that she really cared about. To finally fulfill her heart's desires. And she was doing just that. She was spending time with her grandkids, she was tending to a flourishing garden, she was working part time with the elderly, she was exploring more in the bedroom-"

"Dad! Ew! Too much information!"

He ignores me and continues. "But then, one day, her eldest daughter came to her and asked her, begging her to put her money in her company. To help her to make it grow and expand. She'd get it back three-fold. More money than she'd know what to do with."

I say nothing to this. I know, more than anyone, what I had done and the levels to which I had sunken.

"And now she comes back around, not a penny to her name, to try and steal the one good thing left in her life," he turns away from me, looking out over the expanse of the city, "her grandchildren. How do you think that makes her feel?"

It takes me a second to respond. This is not what I was expecting. This long diatribe about how I have wronged my mother instead of how I have wronged him.

"Dad," I finally say, "I can talk to mom about all that, but I'm here right now to talk to you. Because I hurt you and betrayed your trust. Because I lied to you and caused you to lose a large chunk of your retirement plan too. I didn't just do that to mom, I did it to you too."

My dad continues to stare out at the land before him, the darkness fighting to keep hold of the ever-approaching day. I watch as his hands clench and then unclench. Clench and then unclench. And I wonder if he is thinking of them wrapped around me. Clenching tightly around my neck, squeezing and squeezing. The Homer Simpson to my disappointing Bart. Except with me, my dad wouldn't just strangle me half-play-fully out of frustration, never meant to actually maim or do serious harm. With me, my dad would wrap his big hands around my neck and never let go. Squeeze until the very last breath becomes my very last breath and hold on for a couple seconds longer just to seal the deal and make sure there was no coming back for me. Then release my body and let me rot right here in the middle of nowhere, to be ravished by the elements and wild beasts.

I let the idea settle in all around me. Picture it. Feel it. Imagine my death at the hands of my father. And I let it consume me, as if it's the only thought I have ever had. As if it is a real actual moment that is happening somewhere in an alternate reality. And I surrender to it. I don't fight against it. I don't struggle. I listen closely and hear my heartbeat stutter and then slow to nothing, and I look up at my dad with the same curious eyes that I had when he first held me in his arms. Hello, I had been saying then in my head if I had words to express my emotions. And now I say goodbye. Goodbye, Daddy. If I have to go out this way, I'm blessed that it was you who had the gall to release me.

"You hurt your mother," my father says, in a voice harsh and gravely, "And I find anyone who hurts your mother to be disrespectful to me."

I open my mouth to speak, but he continues before I can force the words out.

"And you lied to me, which I find to be disrespectful to me."

At this, I sigh inwardly.

"So, you have disrespected me dually. And I am not sure what to do about all this. I'm not sure how to treat you, because in all my 67 years, I have never in my life been disrespected twice by the same person. And in such close succession." He shakes his head. "This is unprecedented. And by my own child nonetheless. I was unprepared for such a deception."

I bite my bottom lip to keep from speaking. A long heavy silence hangs between us.

"And now, you're back," he says suddenly, with a sorrowful chuckle. "And what the hell are we supposed to do with you now?"

He laughs a bit more loudly.

"What in the world do you want from us now, Adrienne Destiny?"

And this I have the answer to. This is what I have been thinking about since the day I decided to turn my life around. This, I know.

"I'm just asking that you approach me with an open mind. That you look at me that I am each individual moment in time and that you take each moment and stack them up one upon another and use it to paint a new, updated picture of me. That's all I could ever ask anyone. Especially you, Dad."

My voice lowers with the last sentence I speak, and I let the words hang in the air between us. And I wait.

"Come on," he finally says to me, "There's something I want to show you." He walks over to his bike, his legs long and muscular and sure, and I follow along behind, a hobbling mess of uncertainty.

He climbs on his bike, and I follow suit. One pedal and then another, I remind myself, as my overworked muscles groan in protest. We don't go further uphill as I'd expected, but instead my father turns down a narrow path that I never would have noticed had I not been with him. Low-hanging tree branches swipe at my arms as I follow him, focusing on the muscles of his back bending and flexing with each turn.

My dad.

I let my mind drift to another ride at another time, a time before I'd destroyed our relationship.

"This way, Destiny," he'd said all those years ago when I

was all but thirteen or so, the only one willing to go on these long winding bike rides with him.

I'd followed him, like now, panting to keep up, but determined. Through a winding path through a flatter wood, a skinny path that weaved its way through the trees. One, I had thought correctly, that was a path of which he himself had made. Laid out. Had weaved through the tress day in and day out until a skinny bike path had been made clear enough for thirteen-year-old me to traverse. Until, bam, we had emerged out into a clearing of flowers and sky and nothing else. The flowers blooming at the time were red and yellow and purple. Swaying gently in the breeze. And he had wound his bike around the clearing in a slow circle.

"See," he had said.

And he had dropped his bike. And wandered out into the clearing, arms outstretched, reaching, reaching.

See, he had said, see.

See me.

But this path he is taking me down now does not lead to a clearing of flowers blowing softly in the breeze. While I duck my head to avoid the branches swatting at me, I wonder what exactly my father has waiting for me.

"Come on," he yells back at me, picking up his pace.

My legs are crying, whining at me, but I'm afraid that if I lose sight of my dad I'll not only be lost in the woods, but I will lose him. That he is challenging me right now, and if I were to fail he might not give me another chance. And I can't afford to lose him.

I grit my teeth and force myself to pedal harder, duck my head further down from the branches scraping at me, and I narrowly avoid hitting a skinny tree.

You can do this, you can do this, you can do this. I chant to myself as I continue to push myself. One, two. One, two. One, two. Adrienne, you can do this.

I lose sight of my dad as he turns into a thick set of trees, and my heart jumps into my throat.

Oh no, I think, I have failed. But as I make the same turn I find him standing six feet in front of me, pulling off his helmet at the side of the road. We'd somehow wound up right back where we had started, at the base of the path we had just ascended.

I grasp my side as a cramp enflames me there, and I wait for him to make whatever point he has brought me here to make.

"There are many ways to get to the same destination, Adrienne. But the fastest way, it isn't always the best one. Sometimes it's better to take the long way."

He digs in his bag, pulls out a bottle of water, and tosses it to me. I attempt to catch it and fail miserably. I get off my bike, and scramble to pick it up, chugging the entire contents of the bottle in one long swig.

"It might take longer," my dad continues, "but that time gives you a chance to evaluate your surroundings and make informed decisions based on those evaluations. Plus, it also won't leave you quite so scarred."

I just stare at him.

"You don't have to do anything, Adrienne. I forgave you already. Just make it better with your mom, and never ever lie to me again." He mounts his bike and nods at me to do the same.

"Rest time's over," he says, "Time to go home."

CHAPTER TWENTY-FIVE

"You have broken my heart," he'd said, "into a million tiny pieces, and danced on the shards, carelessly."

I'd looked away from him, then. Looked down at my feet. But he'd called me out on it.

"Look at me," he'd demanded with such ferocity that I could do nothing but comply.

"Look what you have done to me."

CHAPTER TWENTY-SIX

I was a child once. I had hopes and dreams, the way a child does. I had hoped, known, believed, that everything always worked out for me.

But where is my happiness now? Where is my sense of peace?

It has died. And now? And now this is all that is left of me.

And I am empty.

CHAPTER TWENTY-SEVEN

I asked my mom about my birth once.

"It was long," she'd said, as if that was supposed to answer all my questions, "Unlike your sister's," she'd added. Always a qualifier, always a comparison, "She came out so easy, so effortlessly, we didn't have time to make it to the hospital."

"Mom," I'd said, interrupting her, "I heard the story before, of how Camille was born on the kitchen floor, with three-year-old me, confused and bothering you."

Her eyes take on that dreamy faraway look that her eyes always take when she talks about my dear baby sister. The one she had wanted and planned for. The one she was happy that came to be. Her baby.

And then there was me.

"I was so worried, so worried. I held her to me, umbilical cord still attached as I called for an ambulance and you-"

I'd cut her off, I had heard this story already, so many, many times. I wanted to hear about me.

"I tugged on your leg and annoyed you, I know, Mommy, but I'm asking-"

She cut me off this time, "She was so tiny and warm, curled right up against my body and started sucking right away on my breast. Like she was born knowing how to feed. Did you have that with the twins Adrienne? Did they just latch on to you and understand you like Camille understood me?"

And I had stopped listening then.

I had had all three of my kids by then, one of the twins sucking the milk out of me, the other one in her hands, sleeping contentedly. TiTi playing at our feet silently, as if she knew, the conversation happening right then was one to be silent for. TiTi, my TiTi, knowing in her knowable way when to be silent and when to speak.

"But what about me?" I'd asked, a whisper, lost in the sea of my mother's nostalgia about Camille, her real baby. Her favorite.

What? What about me?

CHAPTER TWENTY-EIGHT

My parents had two children.
      The replacement rate.
One for daddy. One for mommy.
One a daddy's girl, the other for her mommy.
Guess which one I was.

My parents met at a corner store. Daddy ordering a bagel with eggs made scrabbled lightly with cheese, salt and pepper and ketchup, please. My mommy ordering a sandwich on rye mixed with wheat. I had heard the story so many times it had become a part of me.

Daddy had seen her. Radiant and effervescent. Waiting for her sandwich to be made and had to say something, had to introduce himself in some way, 'cause when you see your queen you know it, immediately. Mom being all shy and coy. Do you come here every day? Yes. But usually I'm a bit earlier and I'm a bit later and, hey, I like the way that your face looks, do you like me? Yes. I will see you again, and yes, you have just made my day and my life so happy.

Daddy and mommy. Mommy and daddy. The famous day

that led to my accidental creation, to the conversation, to daddy stepping up and claiming what he would have one day anyway.

Or so they say.

I have always felt resentment there.

A question floating in the air. A bit of my mother that has always wondered if I didn't pop up and come to be, if she would have truly found a way to make it work with my daddy. For no "meant to be" story is the whole story in its entirety. And as such, my birth has always been tainted with the truth behind the story. My existence is a reminder of a moment of uncertainty.

Hello, I am here!

Mommy.

I am here, and I am me, Mommy. Why don't you love me?

CHAPTER TWENTY-NINE

I AM THE PERFECT WIFE.

He had been on my phone when he had found it. Evidence. He had saved a picture, a funny meme or something and had gone into the bowels of my photos to retrieve it and his eye had been drawn to an image of me. Me. On a bed I had never seen, wearing a nightgown that I had never worn for him. Me.

And something didn't feel right. Some rock had fallen into the pit of his belly as he looked at the photograph- the nightie, the angle, me, smiling coyly, giving the look I give when I want him to come fuck me.

And so, he had gone hunting. Searching, sifting. Flipping through pictures on my phone, emails, text messages, anything that looked suspicious. Everything.

I had walked in on this. My husband, huddled on a corner of our bed, his entire body curved around a 6-inch screen, searching.

I had slowed, toweling my mane of hair, still dripping wet

from my long, hot, shower, and I had approached him cautiously, hand reaching out for his shoulder, so as not to startle him completely.

"Baby?"

And he'd jumped, spinning around in a whirlwind at me, his entire body shaking with anger, furiously.

"Who are you fucking?" he'd said between gritted teeth. His words spraying spittle at me.

I'd flinched at him. "What are you talking about?" I'd said, arms outstretched towards him, a zookeeper carefully approaching a spooked elephant, knowing a single misplaced word or step would be the death of me.

"I saw the picture!" he'd screamed, eyes wild and red with fury.

"What picture?" I'd ask, confusedly, "What picture?" And as I spoke my mind took its own mental inventory.

What picture could he be talking about? I have always taken great care not to leave a single trace of anything. He had to be mistaken.

"Just show it to me," I'd said, shrugging at him innocently.

"Fine," he'd said, hunching back down over my phone until he'd found the photo that had led to turning my faithful, smart, and devoted husband into the crazed man standing before me.

"This!" he says, shoving my phone at me.

I'd taken a step back because he'd shoved the phone so close to my face that I couldn't even see the image presented before me.

And it was me.

I'd laughed at him then.

"Ohhhhh," I'd said, "How dare my wife take a picture of herself in a sexy nightie. She must be cheating on me." I'd mocked in a deep male voice as I'd said the words.

"No," he'd said, shoving the picture back in my face, "I've never seen this nightgown before."

I'd pushed the phone away from me and resumed my after-shower routine, toweling my still damp body off briskly.

"Baby, I have a gazillion nighties. You think you've seen all of them? You think you can even remember half of them?" I'd opened one of my lingerie drawer and pulled out a nightgown at random.

"Seen this one before?"

My husband had looked sideways at it, had squinted.

"Yeah," he'd said finally, "I remember this one."

I'd reached in my drawer and pulled out another one, a similar shape and shade as the first, "Think you can tell the difference between this one and this one?" I'd asked.

And he'd walked over to me, examined each pair of lingerie distinctly.

"Yeah," he'd said, but he sounded uncertain, his voice a deflated parody of the anger he'd expressed before.

"Baby, I have tons of nightgowns that you haven't seen. Some are for you, but some are just for me." I'd shrugged, squeezing a big squirt of lotion in my hands before I started the long process of moisturizing my entire body. "I like to put on some lingerie and walk around expensive hotels, drinking wine and feeling sexy." I'd turned to catch his eye, "It makes me happy," I'd thrown my hands in the air like he was a police officer who had caught me, "Now my secret's out! Don't tell anybody."

I'd winked at him, then bent down before him, giving him full view of my goodies as I'd lotioned my feet.

He'd cleared his throat before continuing with his line of questions, almost fully deflated by then.

"Well, what about the angle of the camera? How'd you get that kind of shot by yourself?"

At that, I'd cocked my head at him like a cocker spaniel listening out for her owner to call out dinner being ready.

"Let me see the picture again," I'd said, reaching out for it, but my husband, dear sweet soul that he is, had grabbed it and handed it to me before I could snatch it up myself.

I had scrutinized the picture thoroughly before finally deducing the words that I'd needed to speak.

"Ah," I'd said, "I think I remember this one. See, look at my hair," I point out the braids that I'd had pulled up into a big sloppy bun, a style I had been rocking a few months ago, "This is when I went to Costa Rica to get that new contract. That's back before Darrius-"

And at this he'd cut me off, looking at me with a sheepish grin on his face, "Had broken your selfie stick."

I'd raised my eyebrows at him. "So yeah, can we drop this bullshit?" I'd finished rubbing lotion on myself before I had turned to look at him.

"Something still doesn't feel right," he'd said, coming over to me and wrapping his arms around the small of my back, then bending down to rest his head in the crook of my neck, a movement that always made me go weak.

"If you did all this to take this super sexy picture," he'd said, "why didn't you send it to me?"

He'd squeezed me more tightly then. I could hear my own heart pounding against my eardrums. Thump thump. Thump thump. Thump thump.

"Just tell me the truth AK," he'd said, his words so soft and tender they'd nearly broke me. "Tell me," he'd said, stroking my back softly, the tenderness of his words and his touch, breaking through the barriers that his angry words could not.

"Baby," I'd said, as a tear fell down my cheek before I could stop it.

The words had come out before I knew what I was even

going to say.

"I did," I'd said slowly, "have a moment of weakness. A moment when I'd questioned you and me of you and me."

He begins stroking my back, slowly, gently, tenderly, telling me it's okay, it's okay with every ounce of his body.

"I'd thrown myself at him, offered up to him my body."

"Who?" he'd asked, so, so softly. His voice had been barely above a whisper.

"Curtis," I'd breathed out his name, reflexively, my mouth so used to formulating the name as his body had ravished me.

And with that, my husband had tensed, but I'd grabbed onto him, holding his body close to me.

"Don't worry," I'd said, the lie coming so easily, "he rejected me."

I'd laughed.

"The silly attempt, by a silly girl, at a moment when I was weak and he was there."

I'd run my finger down the length of his spine, reassuringly.

"He'd pushed me aside, shut me down profusely." I'd let my eyes drift up then, looking up at the ceiling fan, lost in the whirlwind of the blades spinning, spinning.

"He'd said, he could never do that to you. That he could never do that with me."

I'd felt my husband relax back against me. His body releasing all the pent-up emotions and letting them fall down besides our feet. I'd felt him smile against my neck, felt him there, my husband. He is mine. I am his.

I had taken every precaution. Dotted my I's and crossed my T's, and there was nothing left for him to see. The affair as nonexistent as I wanted it to be. A fleeting blink of an eye in our love story.

Him and I. I and he.

Always.

CHAPTER THIRTY

M y daughter had grown up when I wasn't around to see. A grown woman in a pint-sized body.

Who is she?

Who am I?

Here in this life, breathing within this body.

And she holds my hands, and takes a deep breath, before asking me about her daddy.

CHAPTER THIRTY-ONE

My husband is in prison right now.

A sad, shell of a man. Covering for me and my lies stacked on top of lies to hide the truth from everybody, including him, and including me.

"I'll take the blame," he'd said, when the police had come for somebody. Someone had to be at fault. He'd rather it be him than me.

I didn't deserve him.

I don't deserve his love or his loyalty.

And yet, there it is. And yet here I be.

"Be happy," those were the last words he'd uttered to me.

"Just live," he'd ordered, "and be happy."

CHAPTER THIRTY-TWO

I knock on Father Fred's door. It isn't him I'm looking for, but his wife.

Where is she?

Somewhere being her own person in her own body.

I smile at his wrinkled, knowing face.

"I believe you will find her here," he tells me, sliding a slip of paper across his desk towards me, an address scribbled there haphazardly.

I nod at him and thank him for all he has done for me. He just waves me off, dismissively. And I leave as quietly as I came, closing the door silently behind me.

It takes me two busses to get to the address the father has given me. And when I arrive at the shelter for the homeless, I am not half as surprised as I thought I'd be.

"I'm looking for Gertrude," I tell the man at the door, and he leads me down a maze of hallways until I find her in a large room organizing boxes of things, a clipboard in hand, a slight smile of her lips that welcomes me as a friend.

"Hey," I say, folding myself into a chair near her, "I was hoping to speak with you."

"You have found me here, so I guess it is important. Shoot."

I take a deep breath and force the words out with my exhale.

"I would like you to accompany me," I say, twiddling my thumbs nervously, "to see my husband."

"Ahh, the husband. I thought he left you."

"He filed the papers, it's true. But he still belongs to me, the actions haven't quite been... followed through."

"You haven't signed yet, then I see," she says, and her words are so true I wonder who she has been talking to.

"No, but..." I hesitate, "I will, if he still wants me to, after I see him and talk to him and find out if he still loves me at all. I... he... I would like to make it work, that is, if he will still have me."

The air between us lies heavy. The frail, old, white woman with way more strength than I ever thought could be inside one body, standing next to me, scanning boxes while I ask her to be a crutch for me.

"Just say when, Adrienne, and I will make myself free."

And I grin at her. A grin that stems from my very soul and spreads throughout my entire body.

CHAPTER THIRTY-THREE

I wanted to call him so many times. So, so many times. After he went to prison, I thought that I could keep things afloat. But I didn't focus on the joys of life, the joy of living, as my dear sweet husband had asked of me, instead I keep grasping at straws. The business had to be sold, all assets liquified and turned over to the government. That was part of the deal, reduced sentencing for him, and I owed him that if nothing else. 3 years, out in 12 months with good behavior. And six months had passed already. I'd called every single contact I had ever made. Please, please, please, can't you just make me a VP or something? I promise you I will bust my ass for you, day in and day out. One day before another, one foot in front of another. One moment in time.

The papers had arrived the day they had auctioned off my 2.5-million-dollar home. The sheriff arrived just as the auction had ended.

"Adrienne Louden?"

I was smoking a cigarette in order to prevent myself from

crying, as I'd looked over at the sheriff hovering above me, his flat brown hat judging me with its straight perfection.

"That's me." I forced a smile, that he didn't return.

His eyes had looked sad as he'd handed the folder to me.

"Can you sign here please? You've just been served."

I'd scoffed at him. "What could you possibly be serving me with?" I'd taken the pen from him and signed haphazardly, handing him the slip of paper carelessly. I'd flipped open the tab, confused as to who could still be coming after me, there was nothing left to take. The cars, the house, the bank accounts had all be confiscated by the US of A, the only things left were the trusts we'd set up for the kids, and boy, was I glad we'd had the sense to protect their futures for them, protections that we should have also taken for ourselves, safeguarding our lives against each other. Safeguarding his life against me.

I'd pulled the papers out as the sheriff had finally answered me.

"Divorce papers, Mrs. Louden," he'd cleared his throat, "I'm sorry, ma'am. Are you okay? How are you feeling?"

And with this, the tears had broken free. I'd dropped the papers, the tears falling freely down my cheeks, a stream I'd no longer been able to tamper and hold at bay. And then the laughter had come. "I'm fine," I'd told the sheriff, "You picked a fine day to come serve me with this, sir." I'd said, between bouts of laughter as I'd wiped fruitlessly at my eyes, "They've just sold my house. And now here you come to deal the final blow and ruin me completely." I'd laughed harder, bending over at the waist to slap at my knees, coughing out the smoke I'd been clutching onto as if it were some sort of remedy.

"Mrs. Louden?" he'd said, taking a step back from me. "Are you sure you're okay?" his voice had been a little shaky.

I'd glanced at him and something in his eye told me that I'd better get my shit together. So I'd taken a deep breath and forced myself to stop laughing, but despite my best intentions, I could not stop the tears from coming.

My voice had been shaky as I'd spoken to him. "Honestly Sheriff," I'd said, glancing down at the shiny nametag on his lapel, "Bergenstein." I'd cleared my throat. "I hadn't been expecting this, and it's been a pretty shitty day, so I'd say that I'm feeling pretty shitty, but I think anyone in my shoes right now would feel like shit so..."

"There are counselors I could recommend-"

I'd cut him off, his good intentions and soothing voice disturbing me to my very soul. I couldn't believe that this man had thought I'd been really capable of killing myself or something.

"I have a therapist," I'd assured him, and I did, although I knew damn well that I could no longer afford her exorbitant fee. "And I do think that this is the perfect time to schedule an appointment with her, actually, now that you've mentioned it, and I will do just that." I'd extended a hand out to him, "I hope your day is a hell of a lot better than mine."

And to my credit, I'd forced a smile through my tears. He'd shaken his head at me and pulled me in for a big bear hug. I had tried to pull back.

"Your uniform." I'd tried to protest but he'd pulled me in, pulled my head against his big chest, and I couldn't resist any longer. I had cried all over that man and he had held me. Held me closely, exactly like I'd needed to be held at that exact moment in time.

He'd rubbed my head and let me cry for as long as I needed to.

Sheriff Bergenstein.

A kindness I didn't deserve in the exact moment I'd needed it most.

CHAPTER THIRTY-FOUR

I AM THE PERFECT WIFE.

A nd this, I remember. This, this-ness. This waiting,
waiting, waiting. This at his beck and call-ness. This.
Curtis.

It's the night before I'm scheduled to go and see the man I'd
pledged my life to, and yet, and yet and yet and yet, I can't stop
myself from dialing the numbers stamped permanently onto
my brain. Call him, call him, call him. The thought driving me
insane.

And I cave. I press the phone to my head and hold my
breath while listening to the hum of the phone ringing.

But he doesn't answer.

Of course, he doesn't answer.

Why would he?

And now the waiting.

And now the familiar feeling of nothingness. The antsy
restlessness. The uncertainty. What if he doesn't call back?
What if he no longer loves me?

Ha.

Impossible. He was made to love me, just as I was made to love him, just as we were never meant to be.

Curtis.

I. Must. Stop. This. I. Must. Stop. This. I. Must. Stop. This. We. Were. NEVER. Meant. To. Be. Me and Him. Him and Me.

And so, I turn my phone off. And I go to sleep.

CHAPTER THIRTY-FIVE

He comes out and I feel him before I see his face. The curve of his jaw. The sway in his gait. I look down and clutch Gertude's hand for strength. She clutches back, her touch saying, you can do this, I'm here. You can be anything you need to be. Strength. The wind. Brave and calm and free.

He marches past me, almost blending in like he's one of them, walking in time in a straight line. I can feel the effort it's taking him to not look over at me, to hold his head up, to keep his gaze straight. But I watch him openly. Freely. Unabashed. And I want to cry.

A buzzer goes off and the door slides open. I turn to Ms. Gertrude, I clutch both of her hands in mine, and I search her eyes for some unspoken wisdom. There was a time when I would not have deigned to ask for help. When I would have swallowed my true feelings and pretended that everything was okay. When I would have pretended to be impenetrable. When I would have put on my mask and lied.

I don't have the strength to lie anymore.

"Just speak your truth," she says, as if she can read my

mind, "If you do that you can live with whatever happens next."

I bite my bottom lip, squeeze her hands one more time, then take a deep breath and close my eyes. I ground myself, using her energy as an anchor, and I let myself in. I fill up my skin and a memory comes flooding back to me.

I had been standing outside in the lightly falling snow, staring down at the blanket of white, when I had seen his feet walking slowly towards me.

"Adrienne," he'd said as he'd neared me.

He'd cupped my face in his hands and forced me to look into his eyes. The ones that have always been able to see the real me. The brown pools that held a hidden depth I had always thought myself too stupid to fully understand, to fully comprehend. I'd blinked through my tears as he'd leaned in to kiss me. Wet kisses, salty.

"Julien," I'd whispered, "I'm scared," I'd said, and he'd smiled at me.

"It's just me. You and me," he'd said, pressing his forehead to mine. "Together, we can do anything. Together we are everything."

Julien.

He'd wrapped his arms around me, and I'd breathed him in, the smell of his skin.

"You," he'd said, pressing his face into my neck.

I had sucked on my bottom lip, trying to hold myself together.

"You have nothing to worry about. There is no need for this fear. I have always and I will always be in love with you."

And this, apparently, was what I needed to hear. I'd shut my eyes and finally allowed all the tension to release from my body. I'd collapsed into him and just stood there in the snow, allowing him to hold me, breathing in deeply.

And then.

And then.

And then.

He'd married me.

But that was then, and now is now, and now is the time to be the version of myself that Julien has always seen, the fullest version of me.

And so I open my eyes and I smile at Gertrude and I walk through the open door and I take the seat across from the love of my life.

"Julien," I say, as I start to reach across the table before I remember where we are.

No connections can be made here. No touching. No hand-holding. A metal table between the him and me that is him and me.

He is still refusing to look at me. I watch his jaw clench and unclench. Take in the rigidity of his body. And I want to wrap my arms around him, press my face into the crook of his neck and squeeze until he relaxes against me.

But instead I thread my hands on the table in front of me, and I force myself to speak.

"I got your papers," I say.

He nods.

"I heard," he says, with a laugh bitterly, "about Curtis."

And I wince at that, at the bitterness in his voice. Because even on my worst days, I'd never actually imagined this. Julien finding out. His response. Any of it. Because Curtis had only ever been a fantasy, a fairy tale, not someone real who could penetrate my life in the light of day.

And yet he had.

"It's nothing," I say, my voice a whisper, so faint it could be missed completely, "nothing but a stupid fantasy, a wet dream. Nothing like the truth of you and me."

"You shot your shot," he says, "I found that picture and you told me that bullshit," he spits the words out at me, spittle flying from his lips as he continues to look down at the table instead of at me, "and I believed you. I fucking believed you completely."

He chuckles to himself, a mean, deep laugh meant to hurt me; it does.

"In reality you shot a real shot. You offered yourself up to him, mind, body, and soul." His hands clench into tight fists. "You chose him over me," he laughs, "What did he have to offer you that was better than me?" He gestures as his surroundings. "Would he have done this for you?" he says, before finally looking at me.

He lowers his voice as he holds my gaze.

"Would he have lied for you and sacrificed his future for you so that you could go free? What the fuck did he offer you that could compete with me?"

And now I look away. I had been waiting for him, begging him silently to simply look at me, but when he finally does, I can't take it. Gone is the gaze of understanding, of everlasting love, of undeserved devotion. Instead what I see in his eyes is a mixture of anger and hurt so deep I don't think it has an end, just pools that flow one into the other and then back again.

Julien, I think, and I'm almost surprised when the first droplet of water plink-plinks against the metal table. Surprised, almost. I watch the droplets fall and splash and quickly reform into perfect semi-circles. Bravely maintaining their form against the cold, hard reality.

My mind races and there are so many things that I want to say, so many words fly across my frontal lobe, that I am left speechless. Paralyzed with possibilities. So I shake my head and take a deep breath and look up. Past my husband's dark and angry eyes, his mouth moving with words I can no longer hear, up, up, up, to the fluorescent light hanging from the ceiling.

And I allow myself this moment, this single moment, less than a fragment of a second in actual time, to allow all the possibilities, to see them all laid out before me, and to accept them all as possible realities.

I can lie. But no, no, no, this man deserves more from me. I have lied enough lies, I have done enough dirt, I have hurt enough people. And where has this brought me? What has this led to?

Nothing at all.

No. I am moving forward, I am growing, I am making the wrong things right, I am putting in the work. And right now, that all starts with the truth.

"You're right," I say, interrupting him mid-sentence, "I betrayed you. I betrayed our marriage. And I'm fucked up for treating you that way."

I meet his eyes and I hold the gaze.

"But I love you," I say, and my voice cracks on the word you. I swallow hard and hold back my tears so I can keep my voice steady. So I can keep my words clear.

"I have always loved you. This is an undeniable fact," I say, pressing my entwined hands into the table.

I am hoping that I am conveying seriousness. I am hoping that I am conveying sincerity. I am hoping that I am not conveying the desperation that I feel.

"And you can bash me Julien, you can do whatever you want to me, say whatever you want to me- I deserve it all. But at the end of the day there are only two things you can do. You can forgive me and we can fix this, this us. Or you don't. You say fuck me and leave me alone. The choice is completely up to you, and whatever you decide I'll accept, I'll have no choice but to accept whatever you choose. But the choice is completely up to you. I want to be with you forever. You and me. Me and you. Forever. But if that's not what you truly want,

I understand. I'll jump off a bridge or something, but I'll understand."

I look at him for a second, but I'm too scared to hold his gaze. I wait a long while staring at my hands. Listening hard for any signs of hope. I finally deign to look up at him. He doesn't meet my eyes. He clenches and unclenches his fist in front of me. I watch his jaw flex and release. Flex and release. So handsome, my Julien, even now, even here, even with this sadness encasing his entire being.

He speaks slowly when he finally decides to speak, "Are you still in love with him?"

Yes, I want to say. No, I want to say. Maybe, I want to say.

"I don't know," is what I finally say.

He stands up. His fists clench at his sides, his eyes bleeding, his mouth a fish opening and closing, opening and closing, then opening wide.

"Come back when you know," he says, and he turns and walks away.

I reach an arm out to him, but I stop before I call out his name. Instead, I place my hand on my knees and force myself to breathe. Breathe in. Breathe out, Adrienne. You can do this. You have to. You will.

Just breathe.

CHAPTER THIRTY-SIX

I was right on time as I'd stepped off the elevator onto the floor bearing my name. Jeremy was waiting with a grin and a steaming cup of black coffee.

"Good morning, darling," I'd said, taking the cup from him, with a grin that spread across my entire face, followed by an air kiss.

I took a sip from the mug bearing a carefully crafted signature version of my name and grinned at him.

"Jamaican coffee?" I'd asked, marching down the hall and nodding at people walking by.

"Yasss, diva. You know I got you," Jeremy said, handing me a portfolio containing the outline for my day, "You have a 10 am with the entire JJG,"

"Ohhhh, all three?" I'd asked, grinning, "Lucky me," I'd said, meaning every word. We'd each gotten so busy lately that we hardly saw one another. On any given day I'd be lucky to see one of my co-founders, so it was surprising that I would see them all. I'd wondered what delicious news or ideas they had for me.

"You have an 11:30 pitch," Jeremy had prattled on, "and a," he'd hesitated, raising an eyebrow at me, "a confirmed lunch appointment with a Mr. Simpson?"

"Sampson," I'd corrected him, with a roll to my eyes, "It's just business, Jeremy, as always."

"Well, Mr. Sampson had a sexy ass voice, and, I don't know, it may have been just the way that he said your name, but I'm pretty sure homeboy has the hots for a little Ms. Louden." He'd bared his teeth like a tiger when he'd said my name.

"That's Missus Louden," I'd said, emphasizing every sound in my title, "Put some respect on my husband's name."

And I had spun into my office to be greeted by my three closest friends. All waiting for me to toast to another successful quarter. Sales of the Julien shoe had continued to climb and our company as a whole was looking great. Julien himself popped open a bottle of champagne and poured us each a nearly over-flowing glass full. He grinned at me as he'd handed me a glass, the same sparkle in his eyes that drawn me to him the very first time I saw him.

"It was because of your wisdom and financial savvy that we were able to produce a single shoe," I'd said softly to him, before kissing him sweetly but quickly.

He'd grinned at me and said what he always says, "And none of us would be here without your brilliantly creative mind."

"Well, someone has to be the brains of this rag tag operation," I'd said, pressing his forehead to mine.

And we'd stood there for a second or two, breathing each other in. The smell of his skin seeping in through my nose and spreading from my head to my fingertips to my toes.

Julien.

But it was a brief moment, a long brief moment, but a brief moment nonetheless, before Gabe literally pushed himself between us, giggling as he's shouted, "Mommy, Daddy, behave!"

"Gabe, why don't you behave," Jill had said, pushing herself up on my desk, and crossing her legs like she owned the place, and since she sort of did and since she was one of my closest friends, I didn't bat an eyelash.

"The two of you," she'd said, taking a long pull on her drink and finishing it. "Always picking at one another like a pair of siblings." She'd grinned at us.

"Of course we argue," I'd said, "I mean Gabe is just Gabe," I'd said, eyeing him up and down as if he were poop stuck to the bottom of my shoe, "And I'm, well, me," I said with a flip of my hair, "There's just no competition." I'd said in an exaggerated snooty voice right before I'd wrapped my arms around Gabe's neck, and kissed his cheek.

"I love you snob," he'd said, kissing my cheek right back.

"And I love you more."

And that was the day that I decided to go in a new direction. Expanding in a new direction to keep us on top. Just as that was also the day that I met Mr. Sampson, an alias of course. For the man who destroyed my entire world. Or the one who at least tried to.

CHAPTER THIRTY-SEVEN

I decided to call him to find out the truth. Am I still in love with him? After all this? After his rejection? After everything.

I used to replay the events in my head. Our encounters. I used to replay them while I masturbated with him. His hands on my neck. His knee grazing the sensitive tip of my clitoris.

Curtis.

I haven't talked to him since the last time he rejected me. I haven't allowed myself to fantasize or even daydream.

And yet. And yet. And yet and yet and yet. There is something, still. Lingering.

I dial his number absentmindedly and listen to the ring ringring.

"Hello."

I pull the phone from my face and check the number. It is correct, but a female voice is speaking.

"Hello," I say, tentatively, hitting the speaker button so this woman's voice doesn't crawl into my ear directly, "I'm looking for Curtis." I say, flatly, and listen as she giggles, sounds muffle, and suddenly he's speaking to me. Curtis.

"Hello," he says, his voice questioning.

"Hey," I say, and wait for him to recognize me.

"Adrienne?"

CHAPTER THIRTY-EIGHT

The second time he'd been inside me had been on a whim.

"We should fuck," I'd said, laughing. Always laughing. Always joking. Always dancing too close to the edge, waiting to see if I'd fall.

But his face had responded, seriously.

"Okay," he'd said.

"Now," I'd said, and yet, I'd been surprised when his hands had found me. When his fingers had danced along the seam of my dress, when they had slid in between my thighs and found, me.

I had gasped for air, and my head had pounded its uncertainty, but my voice... my voice could not seem to find the words to make it all just stop. And so, the words remained pushed down, pressed down, stamped out by the pressure of his lips on mine melting me into a puddle at his feet.

Do with me as you will, Curtis, my body had said, bowing prostrate before him and opening itself up like a flower, first revealing itself to the light of a full moon. This. This was always meant to be.

And then he'd pushed himself, every last inch, deep, deep, deep, inside me, and I was... nothing.

CHAPTER THIRTY-NINE

"I love you," I say into the phone and wait.

"Adrienne, I...." And I can see him, running his fingers through his hair and then along his chin, contemplating.

I let the silence fill the space until it becomes deafening. His answer floating in the air, in the nothingness between the cell towers pinging, pinging, waiting, waiting.

The silence continues, I continue to wait for him to say with finality that he no longer loves me.

"It's okay, Curtis," I finally say, a tear teetering.

A lie, like the millions of others I've grown used to telling.

"I'm not in love with you anymore, I just... I just called, because I wanted to be sure."

He sighs into my ear and I hear the girl giggling in the background, her giggles drawing nearer.

"I love you," he finally says, his voice barely a whisper, barely a breath, barely anything.

And then the silence. The dead silence at the end of the call.

CHAPTER FORTY

I know what she's going to say before I tell her. And she, being the better, newer, improved version of me, enhanced with the best parts of her daddy, does not disappoint me.

"You don't deserve him," she says, not looking up from whatever concoction she is brewing up in one of my two new, fancy pots.

"So," I say, moving closer to her so her brothers don't over-hear me, "you don't want us to get back together?"

I know I shouldn't be talking to her. I know this is not what normal moms do, I know that there is a line, and I've tiptoed across it by even broaching this subject. I know that I am wrong. And yet, I cannot seem to stop.

And TiTi, being who she is, calls me out on my bullshit.

"Mom," she whines, "I'm not sure I'm the best person to talk to," she says, reminding me of what I already know as all know-it-alls are prone to do.

I roll my eyes as she continues, "Not about this. He's my dad. You're my mom. A part of me will always be rooting for you. And yet..." her voice trails off, and when she finishes her sentence it's in a voice barely above a whisper, "he deserves better than you."

Yes, yes, yes. I know this. They all do. Someone better than me. Someone less hurtful. Someone more caring, more giving, more loving, more. I lean against the counter. Whatever she's cooking smells delightful, and my stomach rumbles at the first hint of a carefully prepared meal.

"But I love him," I say, leaning over her shoulder to get a better whiff. "This smells delicious, by the way," I say, salivating.

"Yes, Mom, I know," she says, shrugging me away from her, "but love didn't prevent you from doing what you did to him, putting him where he is, betraying his trust, it's, it's..."

She doesn't finish her sentence, but I know. I know. It's unforgivable.

CHAPTER FORTY-ONE

My mom looks nervous in my apartment, like she doesn't want to be there, and I feel the same as I sit in the chair across from my mom, hands entwined before me, staring at my ragged nails, unkempt with bits of earth still clinging to their edges, and wait for my mother to knock my appearance down from head to toe.

Adrienne, a woman must always appear to have effortless beauty. Effortless, yet exquisitely maintained. You are failing at your duty. These are the words that live inside my head.

It is the twin's last day of school, and I want to ask her to keep them this week. The whole week. Mother may I, please? But the words stick in my throat, refusing to be said, hanging out there in the air where they can be studied, examined, and picked apart. Word by word. Yes? No? They are my children though.

I clear my throat and my mom bristles in her seat. Back erect, huffy, her peacock feathers up and threatening. She takes a small sip of her tea and peers over her cup at me.

I try not to slouch and instead sit up straighter, emulating her limited notion of a "lady".

"Mom," I say, instead of asking the question I came here to ask, instead of saying what I came here to say, "what are you up to today?"

She huffs at me, "Like you care, Adrienne. You never wanted to spend time with me."

But as soon as she says it, I know that with her is exactly where I want to be. I stand up and walk slowly over to her. I sit down cautiously. A gazelle approaching a lioness, hoping that this predator will take pity on me, because I, after all, get my keen ability to draw blood from her. I take the cup from her hands and place it on the coffee table, careful to use the coaster of course, then intertwine my fingers with hers, lay my head on her shoulder, and take in a deep breath of the scent of her- my mom.

"Are you hungry?" I ask after a long silence.

Her thumb slowly strokes the curve of my hand, runs along my thumb and back again. Then after a long moment in which I wait patiently, counting the tick tick tick sounds of the grand-father clock's rhythmic swishing, she finally deigns to speak.

"I guess I can eat."

CHAPTER FORTY-TWO

Bethany Brown. My best friend.

Bethany Brown was my best friend from diapers and sandboxes. From sleepovers and roller-skates. From braces and training bras. From first crushes and first heartbreaks. Bethany Brown was my best friend.

The shift happened when we went to college. I was always a bit smarter; she was always a bit full of herself. I went to Brown. She went to some school in upstate New York whose name I could never remember. I spent my freshman year trying to swim in uncharted waters. She spent her freshman year living up under her boyfriend. I remember her calling and sitting awkwardly on the phone for ten minutes before making an excuse to get off, to get back to my books, to focus on what really mattered. By the time we graduated, our friendship had changed. It had become surface, basic. Filled with boring conversations, group outings, things of that nature.

We didn't get close again until I got married. She was so happy for me. Thought that marriage was what I needed. A base. Someone to ground me and pull me back in from my obsessions with work and getting ahead and making something of myself. She threw herself into her title as Maid of Honor. Honestly, doing the majority of the work for the wedding for me. She was in constant contact with the planner. She showed up to the appointments I couldn't be bothered with. Tasted the cake for me. Picked out the decorations and such. I promised I would do the same for her when she got married. But that day never came. At least not that I know of.

Back before everything fell apart, I stopped by her house one day after work with a tub of ice cream in an attempt to cheer her up after her most recent heartbreak. I remember walking in on her curled up on her oversized couch, legs crossed Indian style, swaddled up in a huge furry blanket. She was trying not to cry because she was no longer comfortable crying in front of me. Or had she ever been? I sure wasn't comfortable crying in front of her. Never had been. No, we were strong women. We didn't cry. We brushed over our feelings. We glossed over the pain. We leaned on each other for help, but we didn't need anybody. Not us. Not Adrienne and Bethany.

She'd looked up at the ceiling, a signature move of all women the world over, trying to hold back tears. And she'd hesitated, her mouth opening and closing, opening and closing, like a fish swimming in open water, hesitating before finally allowing herself to speak.

"DiDi," she'd said, calling me by a nickname I hadn't heard come from her lips for years upon years "Tell me how you did it? Just tell me your secret, okay? I promise I won't tell anyone. It'll stay between just you and me."

"What secret?" I'd asked, confused, hoping her eyes would lower to meet mine. "Tell me, B-day." I'd said, reaching over to grab her hand, hoping she'd take the chance to be real with me. "I know I'm not the best friend ever. I'm late a bunch. I forget to text back. But you know I love you always. You know I always got your back, right?"

She'd finally lowered her eyes to meet mine, and I'd tried to convey all the love I felt for her telepathically, watching the curves of her face adjust as she crumbled in front of me. I'd pulled her to me, and she'd wrapped her arms around my waist, pressing her face into my shoulder, and cried in long, loud, rolling waves that seemingly had no end. I held her gently, rubbing her back, surprising myself when droplets of water fell from the tip of my nose into her hair, and quickly swiped at my own eyes, not wanting my best friend to see how much her hurt also pained me.

It took a while but eventually the sobs gave way to silent tears, and still I'd held her, swaying gently, rubbing her back patiently, until I'd felt her go limp in my arms. I'd offered her some tissues and waited silently for her to begin to speak.

"Adrienne, I," she'd laughed softly, "I have to admit, I don't understand how you got everything you have, I just," she'd looked away from me, but kept talking, "thought you were so focused on being Miz Business-lady that you wouldn't ever get married, that you wouldn't have the time to find love, but then, Bam! There it was. And you and Julien, just, work you know? You're not on some bullshit. You have a real thing going on." She'd said the last part with a hint of surprise, and I'm not going to lie, it stung a little bit.

"I was so excited when you got married. I thought that if you could find the love of your life, then anyone can. Especially," she'd shrugged her shoulders absentmindedly. "Me. I mean, I always wanted to get married, have a family, that was my whole life dream. But while love just fell in your lap, it never quite seems to find me. Year after year, guy after guy, moment after moment, time after time. One by one they all fall down. And now, here I am, almost 35 and, nothing. This most recent asshole just dumped me over a fucking text message. So, tell me, please, how did you do it? How did you find him? Tell me your secret."

I'd started laughing, until I'd realized that she was serious. She'd really wanted to know "the secret" to finding a man.

"Bethany," I'd said, forcing myself to stop laughing and catching her eye. "There is no secret," I say, "Julien was the guy I didn't know I'd always wanted." I'd smiled faintly as I'd thought of his eyes, his hands on my waist, his smile, the calming nature of his presence. "I'd just lived my life and focused on all the things I love, the business-shit as you call it, and he'd found me. Julien loves me for me. I love him for him. If there's a secret, that's it. Do what you love and love will find you. Does that make sense?" I'd squeezed her hands for reassurance.

She'd smiled at me and nodded, but not convincingly. I didn't tell her that my perfect marriage wasn't all it was cracked up to be. That I'd been cheating on Julien. That sometimes he stared at me like he was confused about why he'd decided to spend his life with me. That sometimes I woke up in the middle of the night, prompted by some unknown, unforeseen compelling something, and stood out on the deck staring up at the moon for hours, searching, searching, searching for answers, just beyond the edges of my mind. That I never quite seemed able to find them. That it was probably because I was trying too hard. That no answers ever come when you're trying too hard. That life is about ease and flow, not about pretending to go with the flow and pretending to be easy-going. I didn't tell her because I knew where she was, and I knew she wouldn't be able to hear me. I didn't tell her because she's my best friend, and I love her. I didn't tell her because some things cannot be told. Some things have to be learned on your own.

I stayed with her that whole night. Eating ice cream,

watching movies, talking intermittently. She'd fallen asleep in my lap, and I remember watching her, closely, tracing the lines of her face in my mind, knowing that there were few times we would ever be this close. Trying to revel in the moment that could very well, never again be. Trying to soak it all in.

Bethany Brown. My best friend. The godmother to my children. I wonder if she will ever forgive me. I wonder if I deserve to be forgiven. A friend is such a fragile thing. A glass statue standing precariously on the edge of a cliff during a storm, willing to brave the elements, but probably not made to last that long.

And yet... and yet... something about the way it all went down just made me very, very angry.

CHAPTER FORTY-THREE

"What about Bethany Brown?" my mother asks me while she sips her tea.

I shrug. "What about her?" I spin the spaghetti around my fork on my plate. I am devouring this food like I've never had a full meal in my whole life. The spaghetti I'd tossed together is chock full of seafood instead of meatballs and the combination of shrimp, lobster, and crab is seasoned perfectly, if I do say so myself. I inhale deeply as I bring each forkful to my mouth and the whole experience is damn-near heavenly.

My mother gestures her teacup in the air. "Have you made your way to her on your list of atonement?"

She eyes me in a manner that seems casual, but I know better. I have known this woman all of my life, so I know she is watching every single move I make, analyzing it like a computer trained to scan and evaluate every minute detail- processing, processing, processing. I know she is coming to some conclusion that I do not yet have the ability to see. I shift in my seat and try to pretend that I'm not uncomfortable under her watchful gaze.

"No," I finally say.

I want to say that she's not on my list, that she's not important. I want to say, fuck that bitch. She, of all people, should not be so angry. She, of all the people, lost the least amount of money. But money was never her end game. Money was never her goal. Money was just money to Bethany Brown. Money had always been there for her when she needed it, but she didn't put a lot of stock into having money for money's sake. She saw it as a means to an end. What did she want? What did she need? What did she want to do to be happy? Money could help, but it couldn't make you happy. She knew that better than most people. She knew it a hell of a lot better than me.

Bethany.

Thinking of her makes my food taste significantly less amazing. Why is my mind wandering to her when I have much more important people to appease? My mama being one of them, sitting here, right in front of me. And yet, my relationship with my mama has always been this weird, cautiously strange thing, whereas my relationship with Bethany used to be so easy and carefree.

"When did you stop talking to her again?" my mom asks. She looks up at the ceiling as she tries to remember the moment in time. "Was it before the incident or after?"

I flinch at the mention of the word "incident," an allusion to what I have done to all the people I hold most dear. My head starts swirling with thoughts. Harsh words that slice through me like daggers. Cutting back open the very wounds I have just started to begin to suture. I force the voices out of my head by thinking of this moment in time. The food in my mouth, the breath in my lungs, my mom sitting across from me.

"Hey Mom, I think I did a pretty good job with this pasta, but I'm sure you could have made it better. What do you think

I could change?" I ask, forcing a grin as I watch her continue to poke at the meal I had just been devouring.

My mom huffs at me. "What do you think, I was born yesterday? You're not getting out of this that easy." She puts down her fork and focuses all of her attention directly on me, her eyes intense as she stares into mine, unblinkingly. "What happened to you and Bethany?"

I shrug at my mother, and I'm about to brush her off, but then I remember that I'm trying to build bridges, not burn them. That these are the moments, the moments in time. And I swallow my pride and my ego and the pain that I have been ignoring for all this time, and I tell my mother the story of the last time that I saw Bethany Brown.

CHAPTER FORTY-FOUR

I went to see Bethany the night after Curtis rejected me. And as she'd opened the door, it dawned on me- my mistake. How could I talk to this woman about the man that I was fucking behind my husband's back, when she valued marriage and fidelity so highly? How could I tell her I was cheating on the best man that has ever been created with a guy who didn't see me as anything more than a good time? And yet, I stood there, ready to say the words, ready to tell the tale. Ready to confess to my confessor. For she was Bethany and I was DiDi. My best friend for forever and always. And so, I'd shaken off my fear and stood at her doorstep prepared to share all. Surprised, in fact, that it had taken me this long.

When she'd opened the door she'd had a sadness clinging to her that I had rarely seen on her before. She'd tried to shake it off, put on her familiar smile of happy contentedness, but it was too late. I'd seen it already, in all its open clarity. The sad, droopy, basset hound face, dingy robe with the faint whiff of despair, rounded shoulders, fuzzy slippers, and a look of 'why doesn't anyone love me' hanging from the corners of her eyes.

Once she realized it was me, she'd put on a big smile, ushered me in, turned the TV off and put on some upbeat R&B. She rushed off into the kitchen with the pretense of making us some big sugary drinks, but when she came back, the robe and slippers were gone, and she waltzed into the room wearing a cute tank-top and yoga pant combo. Her hair even looked like she had run a brush through it.

She'd placed the tray of drinks on the coffee table and expertly poured us each a big glass of mango margaritas like the closet bordering alcoholics we used to be in college. We'd cheered each other to our fabulousity, as usual, but instead of taking a sip, I'd decided to cut through all the bullshit and get real with my best friend. Because, after all, if we can't be real with one another, then who the fuck can we be real with? If she can't tell me why the fuck she spends her nights wallowing in self-pity and pretending like everything's gravy whenever other people come around, then what the fuck are we even doing calling ourselves each other's best friends?

I'd put the glass down, and she'd looked at me curiously.

"What's wrong? You didn't even taste it. It's our favorite." Her voice was flatter than I'd expected it to be. Not angry or annoyed or even curious, really, just a bit confused. A bit thrown off. A bit defensive. There was a warning there, I'd thought. A warning I'd acknowledged but chose not to heed.

"I have something to tell you, Bethany, and I think you have something to tell me."

And this got to her. She'd put her drink down as well, placed it slowly back on the tray in front of her, and looked over at me. She didn't confirm or refute the claim, she didn't say anything. Just stared at me, waiting, waiting, waiting, for me to tell my story.

And so, I'd curled my socked feet up under my butt and

snuggled back into the couch, taking my familiar, 'gurl let me tell you' pose from back in the day.

But I'd hesitated. For some reason I'd wanted to warn her. To preface my story with a "you should know that" or a "I didn't mean for it happen this way" or even a "I know I fucked up" but that thought made me angry. Why should I have to apologize for being me? For doing what I did? I didn't fuck her over. I didn't cheat on her. I didn't fuck her boyfriend. I'd been fucking around on my husband. Why would this hurt her? And so, I'd pushed the apology aside and started off at the very beginning. At day one. At the first time we'd kissed. How it had just happened. The gravitational pull that bought me to him. How I had melted under the feel of his lips, the entire universe spiraling then collapsing down all around me so there was nothing else and no one else and nothing but the two of us floating in space.

But as I'd talked, I'd seen her pulling further and further away from me. Had watched as her face started at first drawn, taut, confused, and had morphed into a hard, angry line. And so, I'd given more details. Tried to explain harder, but this had only seemed to make her even more angry. Until all of a sudden, I'd realized my tactical error. There was something she was not telling me. There was a piece of the puzzle that I was missing. There was something I didn't know. Something that was making what I was saying an affront to her entire life, existence, and beliefs.

I should have let her, forced her, made her, go first. I should have found out why she was wallowing here in smelly robes and dingy bunny slippers that no grown woman with any self-respect at all should not even own. I should have listened to her spill all of her tea first. I should have found out where she was coming from. It wouldn't have prevented me from telling her my truth, but it would have altered my delivery. And sometimes delivery is everything.

"Bethany," I'd said, cutting myself off mid-sentence, "what's... up?" I'd asked, cautiously.

She'd hesitated. And I'd seen her trying to fight her anger, trying to tone herself down, trying to tell herself to be calm and collected, to approach me carefully. I'd seen her try. And I'd seen her fail terribly.

"You don't deserve Julien," she'd blurted out at me.

I'd leaned back from her, insulted. Who was she to come after me like this? Wasn't she my best friend? How dare she sit here and defend Julien instead of me. But I'd held those thoughts in my head, taken a deep breath, and forced myself to heed the warning bells going off in my head this time. I shut my mouth and I sat there, waiting for her to continue burying herself in an early grave.

"Do you know what it's like for women like me? Do you have any fucking idea what it's like for women like me? The men out here." She'd shaken her head and her voice had broken a bit. I'd watched the trajectory the tear that had escaped from her left eye as it wound its way down her cheek, and I'd continued to force myself not to speak.

"Some of them are the scum of the goddamned earth," she'd said in a voice tempered back from a scream. "I dated a guy for three months before I'd found out he was married." She'd laughed at that maniacally. "His wife had shown up at my door and had casually asked me to stop fucking her husband, please, they have four children and she's really not trying to raise them on her own." She'd run a hand through her hair at that, pulling the hair-tie out, and I'd watched it fly, followed its flight, until it had landed somewhere behind her couch.

"Another motherfucker gave me a goddamned STD! An

STD, DiDi! I'm fucking 33 and some motherfucker gave me an STD."

I'd wanted to ask if it was the lifelong kind or the kind that went away with a shot. I'd never had one, and I was curious if it made her feel any different. Like an idiot or simply like she was unlucky. But despite the questions running rampant in my mind, I'd continued to keep my mouth shut.

"I've played by the rules, Adrienne. I'm a good girl. I cook, clean, give a mean blowjob, you have no idea how well I can suck a fucking dick. Motherfuckers have bowed down before me and worshipped my feet after I have sucked their dick. And yet, and yet, no one has ever gotten close to asking to spend the rest of their life with me." She'd closed her eyes and leaned her head back against her couch and I'd watched a tear wind its way down her cheek. "And here you are," she'd continued. "With the best goddamned man in the fucking world. Who worships the very ground you walk on, and you go out and fuck his best goddamned best friend!"

I'd flinched at that, turned my head as if she had slapped me. And I guess in a way she had, mentally.

"And you'd set me up with him!" she'd screamed, and I'd flinched again. I'd honestly forgotten about that. "Were you fucking him when he took me out then? Trying to pawn him off on me? Hoping he'd take a liking to me and then you'd have no choice but to stop fucking him, then? Can't fuck over both your husband and your best friend, huh?" She'd laughed at that. "Good thing I couldn't stand him. Sad motherfucker Curtis is, I really don't know what you see in him. But then again, maybe it's that sadness that you like. Maybe it's those sad, puppy dog eyes, that tortured soul, that someone please save me from myself quality. Is that what it is, DiDi?" She'd spat out my name in a way that was anything but kind. "Got the best fucking man in the world, and just couldn't stop yourself from going after the kind of shit-head that you always felt you deserved."

"That's enough, Bethany," I'd said through gritted teeth.

"Fuck that, DiDi, you wanted to do this. You wanted to talk to me, confide in me all your bullshit. Oh poor DiDi. Her life is so hard. Cheating on her husband and with his best friend and surprised that he won't run away with her, boo hoohoo." She'd cocked her head at me and twisted her fists in front of her eyes to belittle me. "Well, guess what, Adrienne," she'd spat my name out like a disease, "Unlike all this drama that you've created for yourself, I had the shittiest fucking year ever."

She takes a deep breath and leans back in her chair, her face scrunched up and she begins to cry before she starts speaking.

"I had a fucking abortion this year. A goddamned abortion. And guess what? It was by the same guy who'd given me the STD. The same guy with the wife and children. The same motherfucker who'd been telling me stories of love and marriage and buying a house on the goddamned Caribbean Sea. And where the fuck were you, my dear, darling bestie?"

"Bethany, I didn't know-" she'd cut me off.

"Of course, you didn't, you selfish bitch. You can't be bothered unless it's something important to you."

She'd stood up at this, so angry she'd been shaking visibly.

"Get the fuck out of my house."

And I'd stood up, slowly. A bit afraid of what she would do if I didn't just listen to her. I'd figured I'd let her calm down and come back over after a day or two. Find a way to make it up to her later. My mind was racing while I walked towards the door. Why had I not called her back? I'd seen the calls, I'd heard the voicemails, but they hadn't sounded like an emergency, so I had put off calling her back. But why? I'd asked myself, who wants to have to make it sound like an emergency for their best friend to be bothered to reach out and check in and simply be there?

Nobody.

I'd walked out the door and turned to her, tried to catch her eyes. It had taken a moment, but she'd eventually looked at me.

"I'm sorry, Bethany," I'd said, trying to send all my love to her with the force of my words.

"Fuck you," she'd said, "I hope he fucking destroys you."

And she'd slammed the door in my face.

CHAPTER FORTY-FIVE

Dad comes to pick up Mom and she has a big smile on her face when she sees him. Forty plus years and the man still makes her heart skip a beat. I wonder if it will be like that for me. I wonder if Julien will forgive me. I wonder if I really want him to.

My mother kisses my forehead and reminds me to bring the kids when I come every Sunday from now on into eternity. And I know this is her conceding that they should, in fact, be living with me. They are coming to stay with me, not one, not two, but all three. My father rolls down the windows and reminds me about our biking excursion this Saturday. Like I could forget. Like I would ever be able to forget either one of these two things. Biking with dad every Saturday morning. Dinner lessons with mom every Sunday afternoon. My life was getting full, and I still had yet to make a dent in my list. Time to start making a bit more progress.

"Oh," my mom says, leaning over my dad, and stopping him mid-way from rolling the window all the way up. "Camille's coming this weekend," she says, her smile way too wide and bright. "She has a new boyfriend," her voice mocking like a school girl. "Be nice, Adrienne, she is your sister after all. I never did understand why you two could just never get along. I always wanted a sister," she adds, "and you have one! You two are so lucky, you know, I grew up all alone, had to play by myself, make up imaginary friends, but you two always had each other. And you used to be so close when you were little, what happened to you?"

I scoff at my mom in my head because I am a good, respectful daughter, then merely step back from the car with a wave and tell her and dad that I will see them soon. Saturday morning, bright and early for dad. Sunday afternoon, kids in tow, ready to cook my ass off with mom. I salute them both and watch as they pull away. I catch my mom, leaning over to kiss my father on the cheek, and I push thoughts of my sister and my former best friend out of my head. I have to go pick up the twins. I have to help TiTi with her Chemistry project. I have to find a way to save my marriage. And yet. And yet. As soon as I take my seat on the bus and stare out the window, I feel the sadness taking over me. I see the anger in Bethany's eyes, envision Camille mouthing 'fuck you' to me. So, I pull my headphones out and I try to drown out my own thoughts with the hard bass of a hip-hop beat.

But it's not half as effective as I'd hoped it would be.

CHAPTER FORTY-SIX

I put on my purple nail polish and go to work. It's my turn to weed the garden, so it's Roscoe's eyes who I meet first thing in the morning. He takes me in, and I know what he's going to say before his lips move to form the words.

"What's wrong?"

And I hate that I have spent so much time with this man that he knows instantly when something is wrong with me. What am I supposed to tell him? That it's been three days and I don't know what to tell my husband? That a part of me is still holding out for something or someone else? That I fucking hate myself.

I shrug at him instead. Insulting the man who I won't let be my friend because I just don't see the point. Friends are shit, clearly. I'd proven that myself. Something so frail, so fickle, blowing like the wind. Inconsistent, up and down, high then low, then not there at all. Not something you can count on.

He's about to walk away, to give up on me yet again, but something in cracks open and I call out his name.

"I don't know," I say, pulling my glove off and leaning back on my heels, looking down at my bent knees clasped in knees pads. Protection from the laborious job laid out before me.

"It's my husband," I say, the words falling out before I have a chance to catch them. "I went to see him, to win him back, but he asked me something, and... I don't know what to do. I don't have an answer for him."

"Well, you say you want him back," he says, kneeling next to me, taking my hand and clasping it between his two.

I nod, because I can feel my bottom lip quaking and I don't want to cry in front of this man who I have never shared intimacies with. And yet, who, I am just now realizing, as he strokes my fingers with his thumb, is a real, actual, true fucking friend.

"What did he ask you?" he asks in a voice so low that I could pretend not to hear him. I could pretend like the words were never spoken. Like a tree that falls in the woods with no ears to hear the sound. Nothing.

But he is my friend, and I am trying to learn how to treat them.

And so, I tell him the truth, the whole truth, and nothing but.

"He asked me if I am still in love with another man."

"And? Are you?"

I start to shake my head. But who am I to lie to him? No one. No one special. No one who has any lies left to lie.

And so, I say, softly, stagnantly, "If love is real and true can it even really cease to be, Roscoe? I was in love with him wholly and completely, but I love my husband. And that is real too."

"I assume it didn't work out with him, this other man?"

I shake my head, no.

"Did he love you, this other man?" his voice is gruff, his grip getting a bit tighter on mine.

"I believe he did, but not enough. Never quite enough."

"So let me ask you this," he says, and I dare to look him in

121

the eyes, a look tight around the edges. "If the choice weren't between your husband and nothing, but between your husband and this other man, who would you choose?"

And this is the question, I realize that was beneath my husband's question. It was never about love or no love, it was between him and his best friend. Who do I want? Do I want him because I can have him and not the other man, or do I want him- just him, Julien over anyone else in the world? Do I choose him because he's there? Or do I choose him and only him?

I close my eyes and imagine life with Curtis. I had done this once before. Only once, or maybe a million times before. I chose Curtis before, or I thought I had at the time. Curtis and me and the kids, pregnant with his baby, walking down the street on a rainy day. Him holding an umbrella for me, his arm around my waist protectively. Looking up at him in awe that he was mine. I had wanted that life more than the life I'd had. More than the house I'd built on lies and concessions. More. But had I ever given my husband the chance he'd deserved? Had I ever fantasized about him in the same mundane way? Or had I just taken for granted the fact that he would always be there for me? I shift the fantasy. Julien and me. He is walking ahead of me. A twin on one hip, clutching the other's hand. TiTi walking with me, talking absently about some party she's trying to convince me is safe to attend. He looks back at me. A smile, a shrug, this is our life, you and me. And I love him for it.

It is just a thought, just a vision of what our everyday reality could be.

Julien. My husband. My best friend.

"I don't know," I say, through gritted teeth, annoyed at the ever-present uncertainty. "There's just something about him that doesn't bring out that ooey gooey romantic part of me.

Something that just seems so mundane and so bland and so safe."

I drop my head to hide the shame. "It didn't use to be that way."

"But," Roscoe says, gripping my hand tightly. "Are you just chasing excitement? Relationships aren't supposed to be a rollercoaster, Adrienne, they're supposed to be calm and steady. Love doesn't give you goosebumps because it's dangerous, like falling over a cliff. It is supposed to be exciting every day, but also a safe harbor to place your whole self and your whole heart and your whole being." He shakes his head at me and seems like he wants to let my hand go, but doesn't. "You don't deserve him," he says, finally.

And this is a truth that I do know and acknowledge. This, I know, is true.

CHAPTER FORTY-SEVEN

I asked my husband to marry me on a rainy day. I'd been on the verge of losing him. He knew it, and I felt it. I'd been disregarding him. Treating him like something secondary. Like something that would always be there and didn't need any care. Like my annoying little sister who was always waiting for me to be kind to her, to pay attention to her, to stop scoffing at her every misstep. A terrible way to treat a human being. A terrible way to treat someone you love. Especially when that person is not your sister at all and absolutely will not keep hanging around waiting to be loved.

I was about to lose him, and I knew it. Had seen the sadness creep into his eyes. It was only a matter of time before he realized it too. And that once that happened, there was no going back. There was never any coming back from that. Even I knew that.

I had picked him up in my beat-up Jeep truck, intending on taking him to the park for a picnic, but just as I placed the truck into park, it started pouring. We'd sat in the car and laughed at our luck. Look at us. Trying to do something romantic and free.

Trying to be like the couples we saw on TV. Holding hands and picnicking and shit. How dare we?

"I wanted this to be perfect," I'd said. "I wanted to sweep you off your feet with my seemingly effortless romantic-ness." I gestured towards the rain pounding out a beat on my windshield. "I guess, I've failed terribly."

But he just laughed at me, brushed his hand against my cheek, and brought my lips to his. His kiss was soft and warm and enveloping. It smoothed over my frustrated edges, causing me to let go. And so, I had broken all of the rules, discarded the lines I'd recited in my mind, and I had said the words that had floated through my brain exactly as they'd come. No filters. No buffers. Nothing but me.

"I love you," I said. A tear had fallen from my eyes and landed on the palm that was pressed against my cheek. "I'm sorry that I failed you in this way for all these months and days and weeks. I-" my voice cracked, and I'd leaned further into his hand. "Marry me," I said, as his thumb grazed my lips, the softness always a surprise to me. "I cannot imagine a day without you standing next to me. I cannot imagine a life without you living it with me."

And that was it. He'd married me on a beach right before the sun collapsed into the sea. And yet, I'd never quite believed it to be true. I never quite let myself give in to him completely. I never quite believed in him and me. Despite all the years and the kids and the business and the houses and the cars and the money, we never seemed to be quite... us.

I guess I never stopped failing him after all.

CHAPTER FORTY-EIGHT

"I should let him go," I say to Roscoe.

But as the words come out, I know that it will never be so. I know that I will never let him go. I know that I must never let him go. No matter the cost. No matter the price. No matter the pain. No matter the lies. He is mine and I am his. We must always be. I know what I will say to him and what he will say to me. I know that I must lie to him. A lie that he must always pretend to believe. I know that it is inevitable that he and I must always be.

Julien and me.

CHAPTER FORTY-NINE

He pushes himself inside me and I gasp. The pain. The pleasurable pain. My body floods with endorphins and my heart skips a beat. He is inside me. Heavenly. I say his name, say his name, say his name, say his name. An endless muttering stream. A rhythmic melody that flows with the movement of his hips as he slams up against me.

Curtis.

I reach out for him, my fingertips grazing his skin. The feel of him. How I have missed him.

I jerk awake. My alarm blazes in my ear. My daughter mutters something about how she needs five minutes longer. My vagina aches with the memories of the dream still clinging on to the edges of my consciousness, begging me to hold on a bit longer. Live in the deliciousness for a moment more. Nothing else. Nothing crazy. Nothing but a fantasy.

But this one bears a resemblance to an alternate version of the life that I once led, once upon a time. Or that once led me, really.

I absentmindedly go through the motions of the day. I make

the kids breakfast, send them on their way. How many lives do we lead, I wonder, as I board the bus to see the only man who has ever really loved me. But is that even true? Or is it just a lie, a version of ourselves that we make sure we try to believe. But isn't it just as true that there is another version of me? Was I the same me when I was with him? So separate. So carefree. My hair blowing in the wind, like nothing can stop me. Nothing. Except it was never real. I shake my head to shake the visions from it. They were never really real. Just snippets of bits of a fantasy. He was never in love with me. Accept it. And I have. I've moved on. I gave up. I'm better now, more capable, stronger. I am standing on solid ground.

I close my eyes and imagine myself standing on a beach, arms wide, hair blowing in the wind. My entire soul singing. Go, go, go. I know.

The bus pulls up in front of the prison and I stand in line, show my ID, sit at the same table, in the same seat. The movements are already all too familiar. I drum my fingers. I sing softly. I hum to myself. I count the seconds as they tick, tick, tick by. I close my eyes and imagine the sand beneath my feet, the waves washing over my toes rolling, rolling, rolling then receding. I miss you.

He clears his throat and stands before me. Julien. My husband. My heart skips a beat, but not like it did in my dreams. The truth is, I love him. The truth is, I have always loved him. The truth is, I will always love him. But love doesn't mean a thing. The truth is, my husband would be the man of my dreams, if only I had never met his best friend. I look up at him, and I take his hand, briefly, briefly, before the guards yell at me. I need to feel him, his hands on me, his skin on my skin. If only for a second.

He doesn't say anything, just stares at me intensely, so

fiercely I can feel him. I can see the heat-rays emanating from his skin.

"So," he says, finally, gruffly, forcing my hand, "What's the verdict?"

I hesitate. I love him. I want him. How can I keep him and tell him the truth? What will he do if he knows? How will he feel? Where can we go from here? An old song plays in my head, a melody.

I steel myself. Be brave. I tell myself. Be real. Be true. Be you.

I look him in the eyes. "I love you," I say, "I love him, too." He doesn't flinch so I continue. "You are the sunlight on a cold, rainy day. He is the sand beneath my feet, standing on the precipice where the land meets the sea. You are beautiful and so is he, in very different ways. I chose him once. I asked him to be mine and he said no, he said no. He said we could never, ever be. He said he loved you more than he loved me. And I was heartbroken for a long time. But amidst all that, I never stopped loving you. If a heart can love two souls, I am in love with both of you."

My words hang in the air between us and I stare at his silent tears, wanting to reach out and wipe them away. Tell him that it's okay, everything will be okay. But instead, I just wait.

He clenches and unclenches his fists. He does not wipe the tears from his eyes. He slides his hands beneath the table and sits up straighter.

Here he is. Here I am. Here we are.

I think of all the nights I lay on his chest. Of him rubbing my belly. Of him inside me. Filling me up. A part of me.

"And the truth, shall set you free." His voice is barely a whisper, barely there, barely.

"If I take you back you have to promise never to see him

again, never to talk to him or about him. He will simply cease to be."

"Okay," I say, my heart hopeful, dancing, preparing itself to sing.

"I love you, Adrienne. I dedicated my life to you. Can you dedicate yourself to me?"

"I can," I say, quickly, "I will. I will never betray you again."

"Okay," he says, smiling, finally wiping away the tears on his cheeks.

Okay.

But maybe that isn't what I say. Maybe I cannot be brave. Maybe I chicken out because I'm a coward, always have been, always will be. Maybe, instead, I lie.

"I love you," I say, looking him right in the eye. "And I may have loved him once upon a time, but that time is over. I have always been yours, just as you have always been mine. I choose you, every day. Every time."

He smiles, a tear trickling down in relief. His entire body relaxes, and I realize that he had been sitting tensely, unsure of me. Unsure of what he could take if I had said something differently. And I beam at him, sure of my decision. Adrienne, protector of all that is sacred.

A wave of doubt suddenly washes over his eyes.

"Did you ever think that it was him instead of-" but he cuts himself off, he shakes his head, he releases the thought from his body, and saves me, mercifully, from lying ever more to him.

A part of him knows, I think, a part of him understands, a part of him will always wonder, a part of him will never be mine again. And I can live with that. I deserve that. Penance, after all is what I am after. Penance for who I have been.

"I love you," he says.

"I love you," I say.

"Never ever hurt me like this again."

"I won't," I say, drinking my husband's beauty in. "I will never hurt you again."

A half-truth this time. He forces a grin. He accepts everything- me and all my sins. He nods.

"Okay," he says.

Okay.

CHAPTER FIFTY

I wake up early and go see Father Fred. He is standing in his office, a notebook in his hand, pacing as he mutters to himself.

I open my mouth to utter his name, but something stops me. I watch him instead. Father Fred. He looks nervous, worried, uncertain. This unnerves me. Whenever is Father Fred uncertain? He has God to guide him. He has always struck me as the real deal. A man who finds it easy to connect with the one we should all have the power to connect to. The kind who actually listens in all facets of his life. The kind of connection I have always aspired to. How can he be so unnerved? Who is he- me?

Instead of speaking, I walk over to one of the chairs facing his desk. I have a seat. I steeple my hands under my chin. I wait for him to speak. To acknowledge me. When he does, he stops in his tracks, he slowly walks over to me. He places a hand on my shoulder, then slowly eases into the chair next to me. I am not expecting this. I am expecting him to take his normal seat of dominance. Perhaps he too realizes that this will not be one of those times. That he will be the one receiving the advice, this time. He sits beside me, a quiet but physical reminder of our equality at this moment. I tilt my head, slightly confused, am I equal to this man? How? I decided it's time to find out.

"What's wrong Father?" My voice is strong and steady. "What's gotten you all out of your element?"

He runs a hand over his face. Am I that obvious? His gesture seems to suggest. I simply nod my head. He leans back in his chair, crosses one ankle over his other knee, stares up at the ceiling, and I smile, because he reminds me of me.

"I've been asked to perform a wedding."

He stops there, but I wait for him to continue. Something in me tells me that he needs to say what he needs to say in his own time. In his own way. Father Fred, confiding in me. I guess we really are friends now. Not just me needing him for something, but him trusting... me.

"I make everyone do a few sessions with me. Marriage counseling. And they completed it, passed every test and yet-" his sentence trails off in the air. I stare at the space between us like I can see the words hovering there. So cleary I can pick them up and discard them, place them in my pocket and carry them with me.

"I've married many people. Many, many people, and I feel like after all these years I can tell, I can see, who is really real, and who is just pretending."

I nod and know he can feel it even though he is not looking at me.

"They have all the things," he says. "Checked off all the boxes, taken all the tests. They are compatible on paper. So compatible that I had to delve deeper, press further, seek more. I had to push and push and push and finally, the cracks in their veneer broke open wide. Finally, I was able to see who they really were underneath. And they are a surface couple. Never a hundred percent themselves with each other. Not really free."

I understand what he is saying. I know this. I have known this. I have lived this. I have.

"They won't make it. A love this surface, at this stage, it cannot last. It will not last." He clears his throat. He sits up straighter. "I know what it takes to make a marriage last, Adrienne. I have seen it all. I have been privy to it all. I have seen-" his voice trails off, but he picks up the stream. "I have seen things people only write about in stories. Real life," he says. "Is always crazier than fantasy."

"So what are you going to do?" I ask, feeling that it's time for me to speak. "Can you stand there and marry them, even though you know it's not going to last, that it's not real, that it's not meant to be?"

He is silent for a long time. Silence. A comfortable silence, but a silence so silent I can hear his brain whirring, his thoughts conflicting.

"I told them what I saw. I told them what my experience has come to know. I told them. And they have promised that if I marry them they will give a large, substantially large, ridiculously large donation. The size of which I have been praying for."

He leans back in his chair.

"The work we do here for free, it costs. There are needs, so many needs, that require money."

"And," I say softly, "Do you think this is the way the Lord has sought to answer your prayers? Do you think this is the only way your church can continue to provide for people's needs?"

He opens his mouth to speak, but no words come out. He is rendered silent.

"Listen, Father," I say, turning my body to face him fully, and leaning forward in my seat, "It must be by divine intervention that I sought you out today, something in my head said, Father Fred, when I woke up this morning. It bought me here to you at this exact moment in time so that I could speak with you, because money is probably the only thing I can advise you on. Money is how I wound up in your confession booth that day, lost and confused and hoping to find a way. Money is how I blew up my life."

Father Fred says nothing, but after a second he catches my eye, his gaze urging me to continue to speak.

"We had a company, my husband and I. He was the money guy, I was the mastermind," I grin, remembering the feeling of stepping into a room of people that worked for me, whose entire lives depended on me, and how I could command a room. Prancing around in my heels, listening aptly to people's ideas. The hum of energy I would feel, vibrating through me. It was like being high on life. But then I remember those same faces, those same people, their eyes boring holes through me when I told them all that they no longer had a job. That the company would cease to be. That my husband had been arrested. That this was the end of my dream.

I shake my head out of my thoughts and refocus on Father Fred.

"The company was doing well, but not as well or as quickly as I thought it should be or that it would be if my husband wasn't so conservative with money. He was always meant to be a balancing force to me. The veto power to my autocracy. But after a decade I was starting to feel a bit like he was hindering our progress. You know the phrase, scared money don't make money? Our company seemed like it was flatlining. He kept pushing back dates for us to start new projects because the numbers weren't lining up in the way that he wanted before he was comfortable taking on new risks. We argued about it, but he would not budge or bend. He told me that one day I would thank him. Instead, I cooked our books. Took loans from friends and family to prop up our numbers, flat out lied about things so he would finally approve the new projects, so he would finally stop stunting our growth." I close my eyes and shake my head at my stupidity. "I was never a numbers person, is the problem. I did a few Google searches and talked to some disreputable people and thought I was so smart." I shake my head at the memory.

"I wasn't."

I clear my throat, forcing myself to get back to the subject at hand.

"The point is, I knew it was a bad idea. I had a sinking feeling in my stomach as I approached my first victim, the very same people who turned us in, and I should have trusted that feeling." I swallow and shake my head, look down at my feet and my mind drifts back to that day. To that walk in the rain that led me here. And all the myriad of decisions that got me there. "It was just one time. Just one lie. No big deal, right? But it matters, Father. Because one thing led to another and another until eventually I had built a house of lies."

I straighten my back and catch the Father's eye.

"You know that it's wrong to marry this couple you don't believe in, Father. Stand by that feeling. Don't give in. Because not only will you be doing this couple a disservice, but you will ultimately be disserving yourself. And the worst thing you can do in this world is to fail you. Because at the end of the day. You are always your last defense."

I watch the father. His eyes are closed and he nods softly to himself.

"You are right," he says, slapping a hand on his knee before standing, "I already know all the answers that are right for me. I already know what to say and do, I just need to have the courage to face the consequences for following those actions, for in life there are always consequences."

He walks around his desk and takes a seat in his chair. Back, securely in his position of authority. Back, rightly, exactly where he should be.

He asks me about me, how I am making amends. And so I start with the good stuff. I tell him about my mother and father. I tell him about my children. I tell him about my husband. But he stops me, he cuts me off.

"How do you feel about that?" he asks.

"How do I feel?" I ask, pouring on the confusion. "What do you mean? I got everything I always wanted, I mean, maybe not everything, I still got a few people on my list to make amends with, but I got all the heavy hitters."

"Did you?" he asks me, raising his eyebrows at me suggestively. "What about the guy that you loved? Did you really stop loving him, did you really want your husband over him? Or are you just going through the motions, Adrienne?"

"I love my husband," I say.

"No one's denying that," he says, leaning back in his chair, fully back in his element, "but is it enough?"

And at this, I have nothing to say.

CHAPTER FIFTY-ONE

I'd been tossing and turning all night, so at 5 a.m. I decided to finally give up the goose and get out of bed. I leave a note for TiTi asking that she please take the twins to camp, and telling her that I love her. I lace up my sneakers and start walking. I don't know where I'm going, but I walk. I wind up in a park. I wind up on a path. I wind up climbing, climbing, climbing up a hill. I wind up at the top, standing on a boulder, overlooking the park. I stand on the edge, toes hanging off the ledge precariously. I clench my fists and look out over the expanse of grass and trees, and I scream. I scream. I scream until I cry. I collapse on the boulder, curl up into the fetal position, and cry until the sun starts to rise. I watch the sun as it crests above the horizon, spewing an array of colors across the sky, and I finally feel calm. An ease falls over me. I wipe my eyes then close my eyes and wait for something to jump out at me.

It does.

A name.

The one name I hoped that it wouldn't be.
Curtis.

CHAPTER FIFTY-TWO

Curtis lives in a part of town that is not easily accessible by public transportation. So, I order a ride through an app. An older man with a bright smile and a salt-and-pepper beard picks me up in a mid-sized black car. I stare out the window as he drives, watching as the landscape changes, pulling me back into my memories of another life. Another version of me. I place my hand on the window and allow myself the luxury of reminiscing, opening up a hidden closet in my mind that had long ago been locked up.

One night, back before I destroyed my company, blew up my family, and lost my integrity, I had been a beautiful woman with a head full of dreams. One of them was Curtis. There were times when dreams of me and him would keep me up at night. On one such night I popped up at 1:33 and crept out of bed. I checked on my babies sleeping in their beds. Then I went in search of my husband and found him asleep on the couch in his study and threw a blanket over him, kissed his forehead softly. I'd tip-toed out onto the back deck and stared up at stars. So many bright lights burning so far away, so many millions of light years away that we can never even be fully sure that they exist. Stars with their own planets revolving around them with their own beings, standing, looking up at the night sky wondering the same things- who they are and who they were born to be. What's the answer for me?

I grabbed my car keys and drove slowly, thoughtfully, a smile plastered on my face, practically holding my breath for the entirety of the drive through the night. My heart fluttered up into my throat as I drove up his driveway and rang the doorbell incessantly. It took him a bit longer than I'd imagined, almost so long that I wondered if I made a mistake, if I should not have taken that drive, if he was not home, if he would not wake, if this moment was not meant to be. But then the door slowly opened for me and there he was. Hair flattened on one side, eyes half-open, glowering at me.

I'd thrown my arms around his neck and kissed him fervently. I'd kissed him like I have never before kissed anybody. I'd kissed him like he was the last somebody I would ever kiss. I. Kissed. Him.

And more importantly, he kissed me.

Remembering that moment now makes me feel nauseated, so many mixed emotions swirling around inside me. There will be no kissing during this visit.

The driver pulls up to the front of his curving driveway and asks me if I want him to drive up to the front door, but I tell him no. I thank him and wait for him to drive off before I begin the long, slow walk. I focus my mind on the house, the door. I envision my hand pressing the doorbell, but don't allow myself to image what happens next, what happens when and if he opens the door.

The sun is just beginning to brighten up the sky when I walk up the small mound of steps leading to his oversized front door.

I ring the doorbell, then wait. I stuff my hands in my pockets, rocking back and forth from the balls of my feet to my heels and back again. And right before I'm about to ring the doorbell again, it opens.

He is dripping sweat, freshly interrupted from his morning workout routine with a look of annoyance on his brow. He doesn't say anything, but his expression is asking me what I am bothering him for.

I jerk my head for him to come and take a walk with me, and he steps out of his house wordlessly. We walked silently for several minutes, winding our way back down the path I had just trudged my way up. I reach out for him, and his fingers entwine with mine, and I almost sigh out loud.

He speaks first.

"I heard you got back together with Julien. I heard he forgave you. Congratulations."

His words lack emotion, yet and still they make me angry. My fingers tighten around his. And then, all at once I want to let go of them, pull away from him, back down, phone a friend to come and get me and take me away from him and all that he has ever meant to me. I force myself not to. I came here for a reason. There is something I have to do.

"Yeah," I say.

He scoffs at me, and it's like I can hear him breaking, hear him cracking beside me, the hard-shelled veneer of bullshit he puts on in front of me.

"I love you," I say.

And he lets go of my hand and stops walking. He spins towards me. "You can stop with the bullshit," he says through gritted teeth. "Geez, Adrienne, you called, and I almost believed you, I always almost believed you. I get so close, so close, pulled into your bullshit, but you're never going to leave him, are you? You just don't have it in you! Even when the man gives you a 'Get Out of Jail Free' card you go and beg him to take you back," he practically yells, "What is wrong with you? Can't you leave well enough alone?" He runs his hands over the top of his head.

He always talks like this. He always talks this bullshit. He always speaks in roundabout ways, in hope and myths. I could if you would. I would if you could. Can't you see, A? Look what you do to me?

But he's the one who always says no. He's the one who always says never would I ever. He's the one who rejects me. And then he spins it around like it's something I do to him. Something I have done to him. Some trick I am playing, some game I am playing, some fucked up way that I will always be.

"Look at me," I say, standing with my arms by my side, palms facing him, open, blank, free. "I asked you once, I begged you practically. Love me or let me go. You choose the latter. We haven't really spoken since then. And now you're here spouting all this bullshit. Now you're here acting like I'm doing something to you when all I did was love my husband. And I have never lied about that. I loved him then. I love him still. I always will. But you, you were always just a dream. Someone that I knew I could never have and that never would be. And you proved my greatest fears to be true. You rejected me flatly, no explanation given, now, today is the day that I've come to get an explanation from you. So cut the bullshit Curtis, and just be real with me, finally."

He throws his hands up in the air and growls at me. "What was I supposed to say, Adrienne? You're married to my goddamned best friend. You have three children." He turns away from me. "I love him too, you know. I love them too. Who am I to break up something so beautiful?"

"Who are you not to?" I ask, leaning into him. "I thought I was special," I say, catching his eyes and holding them, "I thought it would be you and me. I thought I was your goddamned person. And your saying no was a flat-out slap in the face to the dream I thought could finally be a reality."

My voice cracks at the end, and I take a step back from him.

"How dare you," I say, trying to prevent the sob from rising, "I gave my entire life to you, and you couldn't even stand beside me. How much of a bitch ass punk can you be?"

He looks away, up at the sky, now a bright, light blue with clouds floating by. A picturesque view.

"Go, Adrienne, be with him. Your family will be happy and full and complete. Forget about all the things we've ever said to one another. Forget about me. Live your life, Adrienne. Be happy." His voice is dead. His eyes are dead. His expression is dead. He refuses to look at me.

I want to slap him, but I ball my hand into a fist instead. I want to shake some sense into him, but there's nothing left to shake out of him. I wanted the answers, and as I stare at his face in profile, his jaw clenching and unclenching, some piece of the puzzle snaps into place for me. I suddenly realize that he is wound up so tightly, trying to contain himself, curled up in on himself, trying to keep himself to himself. And now I understand, something that a part of me has realized long ago, but that my brain has just now come to understand.

This man is a direct reflection of the person that I thought I was. Self-centered. Manipulative. Wanting money, power, praise, and willing to get it by any means necessary. Shortsighted and secretly ashamed of who he is and who he is willing to be.

I take a step back from him.

His name, his name reverberating in my head, it was not about him, it had never been about him. It was all just about me.

I want to reach out to him. To offer him aid, in the way that Father Fred had helped me. But something inside me shouts out at me. I had sought out Father Fred. I had wanted help. Help had not been forced upon me.

"You don't deserve him," my daughter had said to me about her father. My daughter parroting my own thoughts back at me. And this man with his vacant expression, his empty words, his broken soul, was what a person like me deserved. My love for him a reflection of the love I wanted to be able to give to me.

I deserve better. And I'm not sure if I say this aloud or just inside my head, but the words snap the invisible thread between us. The rope I had been holding onto mentally. And I feel so light suddenly. A weight lifted off me.

I board a bus for work and pull my notebook out when I sit down.

I am enough.

I write in my purple pen, tracing the words with my fingertips, hoping they seep into my skin.

CHAPTER FIFTY-THREE

I AM A GREAT SISTER, I GUESS.

I know I'm going to struggle with this one before I even write it down. Being a great sister was never something I really strived to be. After all, being a sister was a role literally forced upon me. I didn't ask to be one. I didn't even agree to it begrudgingly. One day she was just there, and a sister was something I was forced to be. And being Camille's sister has always felt like something meant to hamper, hold me back, prevent me from doing things. Watch out for your sister, DiDi. Take care of your sister, DiDi. Get off of your sister, DiDi. And on and on and on. A whole life of responsibility, but no one ever was there looking out for me.

Maybe that's why my sister was the first person I thought of when I decided to borrow money.

I'd asked her to brunch, a rarity between her and me. Let me take you out dear sister, tell me all about your life and what you want to be. My sister is a flight attendant. She'd always had such lofty goals. She'd picked that occupation just so she could travel for free. So she could see the world and everything in it. So she could find herself and continue on her airy-fairy path of bullshit. The path of no responsibility. No one is a flight attendant forever. It's a pit stop job. It's a "You know I used to be" kind of job. But I'd held my tongue. The nature of her flighty job meant that she was always working. She had few possessions; she hardly ever slept in the bed of the house she owned outright and shared with an ever-revolving door of other people, mostly young professionals, who were just as flighty. Her earnings, for the most part, were purely hers. She didn't have a car. She didn't have kids or even student loans. After buying food and random shit, she was banking most of her paychecks. I knew this. I'd had Julien help her set up her savings account, her retirement plan, her investment portfolio. He'd helped her buy her home and encouraged her to pay off her mortgage before she'd turned 30. Her portfolio was downright amazing for a flight attendant who had barely graduated from high school. But that was how it always worked out for Camille.

So when I'd sat across from her munching on overpriced salads and sipping on even more overpriced mimosas, I'd casually mentioned the idea. She was already invested in all these other companies all over the world, why not put some of her money into her darling older sister? I hadn't really had to sell myself at all. She didn't ask many questions, just shrugged at me.

"How much do you need, Adrienne?" she'd asked dismissively.

I'd promised her a return on her investment plus stock in the company. I'd emphasized how we were doing so well that we were practically bulletproof. She had looked at me a long while, before nodding. She reached into her bag unhurriedly and written the check slowly, so slowly, and handed it to me.

The first of many. Money she'd lost completely. I picture her face that day at the restaurant as I absentmindedly rub Parris' knee. He's sitting on my lap as we ride the bus over to see his granny, his granddad, and his only fucking auntie. The look on her face that day haunts me. The way she had looked at me. Her eyes holding mine when she handed check over to me. What was she trying to say to me? What was she trying to see in me? What was she trying to convey?

Julien had taught her well, too well actually. She'd been watching the stock markets and seen our company take a hit. She'd called me and asked me to tell her all about it. She'd invested a lot of money, and she was starting to get worried, she'd been beginning to think that she should have taken this investment more seriously. She'd asked for a printout of her quarterly. She asked for a prospectus of how we intended to make up for this set-back, and what exactly I had done with her money. Sure, I'd said, sure, Camille. Anything for you. I sent her the same bogus bullshit I'd sent the other stockholders, but my sister had seen through it. My sister had known immediately that I was doing something illegally and she'd called me out on it. Some people will always have the ability to see right through you. Some things never change. I should have seen it, caught it, recognized the error in my deceit. Revised a copy just for her. Different bullshit for her to critique. But instead, I'd been lazy. Too busy trying to find actual solutions to the fires popping up all around me. Trying to find more money to quell the leak. But with the dip in stock value, people weren't as open to helping me. They asked too many questions. They wanted to give, but have a voice, have a say in the workings and doings of what we did every day. And my pride wouldn't allow that. I needed to be the one to figure this out on my own. I know, I know. So stupid. So naïve.

And in the end, it was her, my sister, the person I least

expected, who ratted me out. And now here we are, headed to spend some time together as a family. Mom, Dad, Camille, the twins, TiTi, and... me. One big happy, happy family.

I'd been wrestling all morning with the idea of what to do when I saw her. Do I sit down with her and have a grown-up conversation like an adult? Do I give her a big hug and pretend like everything is cool? Or do I punch her in the face? I want to blame her for ratting me out, but I also blame myself for fucking her over. It used to be so simple, so easy. I blamed her so unapologetically. As if she had been the only wrong person in all of history. But it wasn't her fault I'd lost my company. Back then I'd been knee-deep in a sea of denial. I'd been carrying the company with siphoned money I'd taken from my house and my own family. The very fact that we were still functioning at all was as a result of sheer willpower and charisma. It was all going to fall apart and soon. But at the time, the only thing I could think of was the fact that I just needed one thing to go right in this sea of things that had gone wrong. I just needed one thing to pan out, and we'd be good, we'd be fine, we'd make it, we'd get over this hump. I could have been right, I guess. But looking back now, all I see is how blindly all my actions were shaped by ambition. I picked things that I thought would happen, that would pop, that would wow, instead of focusing on the small minute details, the reason behind the sale, the motivating factor that makes a person choose this over that. I'd lost that. I'd been drunk on the prospect of more and more success, so drunk that I'd been willing to risk everything for more of it. I'd risked it all, and everything is a hell of a lot to lose.

My sister had made a phone call because she was concerned.

And, oh, how I'd hated her for it. The days, the bottles, the tears I'd wasted lamenting over that phone call. Such a waste.

The bus screeches to a halt and we clamor out.

"Mommy," Darrius says, grabbing my free hand. "Are you going to get a car soon?"

And I smile as my heart breaks inside my chest.

"It's just," Darrius says, looking up at me, and the fact that he's actually being sweet about this is all the more heart-breaking to me, "that it takes forever to get everywhere. It was fun for a while, but now... it just feels... long and boring."

I look over at Parris, clutching my other hand, but he just stares down at his feet. I'm scared to face TiTi, but I force myself to, because once you cave into fear in front of your teenager, they will never ever again respect you. I catch her eyes and she nods, so faintly that if I would have blinked I would have missed it. Miss TiTi-loudmouth-McGee, silenced out of a sense of propriety? Something hard breaks off inside me, and I look up to the sky to stop the tears from falling from my eyes. I want to ask my kids if they would like to go back to living with their grandparents, but I bite my cheek before I let the words escape from my lips. I've already failed them once. I've already dropped them off at my parents' house without a second thought, without a second glance, for years on end. I've already treated them like they were unimportant. I can't do that again. I just got them back, I can't take a chance that they won't forgive me again. Time to step it up, Adrienne.

I kiss Darrius' hand, squeezed tightly within my own, then kiss Parris' hand, just as irreverently, and I make a silent unspoken promise to them that I will find a way to build a life that they can be proud of. That they can stand beside and look at as something to see. Gather around here, children, let me show you what your mom can be.

As we walk the few blocks to my parents' house, I take six deep breaths and let go of all my inadequacies. I am doing things the way they are supposed to be done, but I've gotten comfortable in my mediocracy. Am I living? Yes. Am I making an honest living? Yes. Do I have my children? Yes. Am I working on being forgiven? Yes. Forgive me, forgive me, forgive me, everybody. But this just getting by shit has never been me. I have to find a way to make more money, but not like I'd made it previously. It's time.

CHAPTER FIFTY-FOUR

My sister isn't there when we arrive and that suits me just fine. I'm not here to see her after all. She just happens to be here incidentally. Although she is on my list, too. Probably the next one I should confront and face head on. Probably. But I don't want to. And so, I rejoice like a small child who has just been excused from completing her chores and can finally just go outside and play. I hum to myself softly as I start cooking with my mommy. I don't even mind her admonishments of me. I lean my head on her shoulder and watch as she explains something that I only half pay attention to. I will get this cooking thing. I can do it. I can figure it out. I can understand it. I can.

The door bursts open, and with a big whoosh of air, my sister storms into the room, arm in arm with her new beau, and a bright smile lighting up her face. Did I mention that my sister is beautiful? I mean, we're all beautiful. The women in my family are all beautiful. I hail from a beautiful people. My mama was drop dead gorgeous in her youth, still is, even now in her mid-fifties. And I am beautiful, too, but I have that kind of slow beauty. That kind that creeps up on you. The kind where you have to just look at me for like 30 seconds and it will dawn on you, that yes, oh, she is quite beautiful. But my sister, my sister has that knock-you-over-the-head kind of beauty. The kind where she's walking down the street and men turn their heads to watch, even with their wife or girlfriend standing right next to them. The kind where her friends' boyfriends will hit on her the second their girl leaves them alone. She's that kind of beautiful. And she walks into our parents' house with a man that's just as fucking beautiful. I mean, there are few men who I have seen in this world who have made me think, goddamn, Jesus broke the mold when he sculpted him, and this man, this man standing beside my sister, looking at her like he would literally swear fealty to her until his dying breath, looks better than them all. I quickly scan him. He's about 6 feet 5 inches tall, built like a fucking football player with broad shoulders and chiseled arms. His skin is a flawless caramel complexion, and his locks are pulled up on top of his head in a goddamned man-bun. He flashes his 100-watt smile at me as he extends his hand in greeting.

"You must be Adrienne," he says, his deep baritone twinkling in my ears as I tentatively take his hand. "I've heard so much about you."

I glance over at my sister, who is actually smiling joyfully at me, then I look back at the man, just as he lets go of my hand. I force myself not to say that I'm sure he has heard a lot about me, in a voice cold enough to freeze water, like I want to.

Instead I say, "And you are?" doing my best to say it as pleasantly as possible.

"Oh, forgive me, I'm Travis, Travis Herald McCoy."

And as soon as he says it, I recognize him. I spin my head

around to my sister, now I understand the reason for her fucking grin. The bitch done snagged herself a real-life goddamned football player.

CHAPTER FIFTY-FIVE

When we were little girls and weren't ignoring one another or mad at one another, we liked to play this game. We called it "One Day" and we would lay on the living room floor ear to ear, bodies lying in opposite directions and take turns saying what our lives would be like one day.

"One day," I would always say, "I will have a business and be rich and successful and everyone will simply want to be near me."

"One day," Camille would always say, "I will marry a football player, and he will worship me, and I will be happy."

How silly, I would always think, but never say. Those were the rules of the game after all. No commenting on the "One Day" wishes. They were sacred and meant only to be heard but not commented on, especially negatively.

But I did ask her about it one day, pushing the boundaries of our game and inviting her to do the same.

"Why a football player?" I'd asked nonchalantly.

She'd shrugged, but refused to look at me as she responded,

"I don't know, they just always seem so strong, like they would protect me."

I'd been stunned by this, my sister was the vivacious, outgoing one. She had a gazillion friends and everyone loved her, including our mother, who loved her much more than she'd ever loved me.

I tried to stop myself from asking any more questions, but I just could not let it rest. "Camille," I'd asked in a voice barely above a whisper, but that I knew she could hear. "Who do you need protection from?"

And I'd watched carefully as she'd bit her bottom lip, her mind working so hard I could practically hear it. She was quiet a long time, but I'd stood there, silently. Knowing that if I had the strength to wait, she'd eventually get the courage to tell me. And after all, what are big sisters for?

"I always feel like I have to put on a mask for the world," she'd said finally. "I don't want to have to do that all my life. I think if I had a big football player besides me, I'd be able to take the mask off, because he'd protect me, from mean people, from nasty people, from everybody."

There are very few times we touched, my sister and me. The few times our parents had had nasty arguments, when one of us was having nightmares and couldn't sleep and crept into bed with the other, when we stumbled upon something scary on TV, and this time. We had been standing in the kitchen after playing the "One Day" game, mixing chocolate milk powder into overflowing glasses of milk, carelessly. And she had stood there, stirring, stirring, stirring, the spoon clinking against the sides of the glass, milk sloshing out onto the countertop, and I had grabbed her hand, stopping the stirring, and I had wrapped her into my arms, and she had collapsed against me. Through sobs she'd told me about the girls at school that had been bullying her quietly, so quietly that nobody knew. Nobody could see. They would follow her into the bathroom and block her from leaving until it was empty and pull down her pants and mock her body. They would whisper words in her ear, calling her fat, stupid, ugly. They would trip her, pinch her, tug at her hair when no one was looking. They did everything in secret, stealthy.

"No one will believe me," she'd said, hiccupping her words out.

"I believe you," I'd said, rubbing her back, softly. "I'm walking you to school tomorrow," I was in middle school, but she was still in elementary. "You point these girls out to me, and I'll handle the rest."

"There's a lot of them, A." she'd said, warning me, but I saw the hope started to spark in her eye. "There are six of them."

"You let me worry about it," I'd said, and I'd meant it.

The next day, I'd walked Camille to school, hand in hand, my thumb rubbing against her skin to remind her to calm down, that I had it handled. And when I'd got there, five of my closest friends (including Bethany Brown) had been there waiting for me.

Bethany cracked her knuckles as we'd approached them. "Show me where these little witches are, Camille, we'll handle them," she'd said grinning warmly.

Camille had nodded in their direction. They stood on the lawn of the school, huddled in a bunch, eyeing a group of boys that were all staring at Camille. That's when I'd understood. They were bullying her because she was the object of all the boys' attention, and they weren't. Camille seemed not to notice the boys ogling her, which probably infuriated the girls all the more. Camille was in the fourth grade, if we didn't nip this kind of jealous bitchy shit out now, it would only get worse.

I'd known exactly what to do. I nodded at my girls and we'd marched over to the little brats who had been torturing my sister secretly. I went up the tallest one and pushed my face right into hers.

"I heard you've been messing with my sister," I'd said, practically spitting the words out.

My friends chorused me with similar comments aimed at the other girls, each one zoning in on one younger bully.

"You jealous of her cause she's prettier than you are?" I'd said, mockingly, "All the boys want her, wahwahwah."

My friends fake-cried in the other girls' faces.

"Let me tell you something, you little brat," I said, blood rushing to my head, adrenaline pounding through my body. "You so much as breath in my sister's direction the wrong way, and you'll have to answer to me." And I slammed a fist into my hand right in front of her face and watched her wince.

My friends did the same in other girls faces, causing one of the little girls to cry. I'd watched the tears roll down her face with a satisfied grin before nodding at my girls to move on to phase two of our operation. I scanned the yard until my eyes landed on the same group of boys that these little bullies had just been staring at and waved them over. They'd come slowly, hesitantly, with curious grins on their faces. I smiled at them, hoping to assuage their nerves, and they had indeed picked up the pace.

"Hello boys," I said, throwing an arm around the one that seemed like the leader of the bunch. "I'm sure you all know my little sister, Camille."

They'd eyed me warily and nodded reluctantly.

"But did you know that these girls here have been bullying her, secretly?"

The boys had all shaken their heads, then turned to eye the girls suspiciously.

"She's lying!" the girl I had just been threatening proclaimed.

I'd spun around on her, jabbing a finger mere millimeters away from her left eye, causing her to stumble backwards, trying to get away from me.

"You shut your trap," I'd said, and she'd glared back at me with a mixture of hate and fear.

I'd turned back to the boys and took a second to appraise each one of them one by one, making sure to catch each of their eyes for a second or two. I moved a bit closer to them and lowered my voice as if I was confiding in them.

"Now, I don't about you guys, but I can't stand bullies."

I scanned their faces again, and each of them nodded at me slightly.

"Since I'm in middle school I can't be here every day to make sure these girls aren't messing with my sister, so I'm hoping I can count on you all to look out for her for me. Can I trust you guys with this?"

I watch these little boys push out their little chests and nod at me as if they are secret service agents charged with protecting the president of the United States of America, and I grin at them.

They each nod and smile at me. And I nod back. Done.

"And you little brats," I'd said, spinning around to the group of girls who'd slowly been slinking away from us. "You stay away from my sister."

"Yeah," Bethany had chimed in. "If we have to come up here again, it's going to be a straight up beat down!" she'd screamed, waving her skinny fist in the air. And I'd wanted to laugh at her bravado, but all of my other friends joined in, waving their fists in the air as well, and I could do nothing but smile and join in.

I'd asked Camille how her day had been when she'd gotten home from school later that day, and she'd beamed at me.

"It was great!" she'd said, throwing her arms around me.

"Thank you so much, Adrienne," she'd said, and I had patted her on the back tentatively, then pushed her away quickly.

"Alright then, don't make it weird okay," I'd said backing away from her, but grinning on the inside.

I bite my tongue, literally. The pressure of my teeth against the soft meat of my tongue serving as a constant threatening reminder to simply not say a single word. I finish helping mama prepare the food. I set the table, I order the kids to go wash their hands, I wipe my powdered hands on my apron, I sit down, I smile politely, I nod, I chew slowly counting before I swallow like the proper lady my mama had always wished I would be. I sit silently, and I watch. I watched my sister cut her boyfriend's steak. I watch my sister flinch at her boyfriend's big laugh, at his hand on her thigh grazing where he thinks no one can see. I watch her hands try to shoo him away unsuccessfully. I watch the way he talks to my kids- dismissive, interrupting, laughing mockingly. I watch the side of my father's jaw clench and unclench as he watches, as he sees what I see. I watch my mama smile and grin and wave emphatically. I watch and I smile, and I nod. But I say nothing.

When it's time for dessert I stand to clear the table. My sister jumps up to help. She scrapes the remnants in the trash, and I rinse and load the dishwasher, just like when we were kids. The timer on the stove dings just as we are halfway through. I carefully remove the cookies from the oven and slide them onto the cooling rack before returning to the dishes. Camille rifles through the dish cabinet until she comes out with a fish-shaped serving dish and carefully places the cookies on it in a neat array. She nods at me and carries the cookies out to the dining room. I grab the almond milk and some glasses and follow behind her.

Her boyfriend is moaning in delight at the taste of mama's chocolate delicacies and talking with his mouth full, but my mama beams all the same. I notice the smile doesn't quite reach her eyes though as I pour homie a glass of milk.

And when the cookies are gone and my children have run off to play, and daddy and Camille's football playing boyfriend have shuffled off to the den to watch sports and drink whiskey and it's just me and Millie and Mama sitting at the table, staring at the intricate design of the tablecloth that was handed down from our mom's mom to our mom and will one day pass down to me, my sister sighs, wipes a tear from her eyes, rubs her temples and says, "I know, DiDi, I know. Stop screaming at me."

CHAPTER FIFTY-SIX

I decided it's time to go see Bethany Brown. I decide it's time to get a real job and pay people back. I decide it's time to go see Jeremy. I decided it's time to take the next step. I pull my notebook out and list each item separately. I number them from 1 to 3 in order of most to least scary. And the order winds up being: Find a real job, see Bethany Brown, go see Jeremy. I do none of the above. I spend a day or two or three waiting for the urge to overcome me. I yell at myself in the mirror, in the shower. My children start doing those glances at each other, where they communicate their worry silently. I get up in the middle of the night and pace, but my little rented cottage is too small for that and seeing the twins sleeping on the couch is beginning to piss me off, so I leave and start taking these long, lonely walks. I pull out a list and write down my accomplishments: TiTi, Darrius, Parris, Mom, Dad, Julien, working on Camille, and I realize I've only touched the people who were always going to forgive me, my family, and I admonish myself for being such a coward.

"Who are you!" I yell into the park air one night, when not a soul is around to hear.

I don't know. The answer keeps reverberating in my ear.

I begin a zombie-like existence, teetering between anger and depression. Anger and depression. What's worse is that I know what it is, I know that I am failing at this. My work at the farm starts to suffer and Miguel pulls me up on it before anyone else dares.

"Adrienne," he says, his voice husky and grave. "I know you're going through something, some sort of spiraling in your head, I can see it in your face, in your actions, is there any way I can help? Is there anything I can do?"

"I'll get it together," I say, and he nods at me, and I take his nod for what it is, a warning.

I get home and I make a list of everything I want and am in the process of building: a stable home with my husband and kids, a business, a way of paying everyone back with interest, some real friendships, a deep connection to my parents and my sister, to give back to the church that saved my life, to make amends with everyone I've ever hurt.

I stare at the list until my eyes ache, I clutch my purple pen until my fingers cramp, and then I write under it all: the courage to do it and get back up, the strength to fall and fall and fall and pick myself up again. Do it, I write, just begin. And then wake up every fucking day and do it all over again.

And so, I pick up the phone and call Jeremy Green.

CHAPTER FIFTY-SEVEN

I AM A GOOD PERSON.

J eremy lives in an apartment with four other people. I know this because I've been there exactly once. I remember the stale smell in the air, like unwashed feet and moldy cheese and wet dog, and I remember wondering how someone so neat, organized, and meticulous with his appearance and his work habits, could live in such a disorderly and disgusting mess. He meets me at a coffee shop over on his side of town, mere blocks away from his moldy cheese apartment, and I buy him an overpriced espresso drink before leading him to an open table pressed up against the window.

"I'm sorry," I force myself to say, simple, straight, to the point, "for everything."

He nods at me, dismissively, "Is that what this is about?" he asks, his voice not bothering to hide his contempt, "because I lost my entire savings and 401K fucking with you, and I'm sorry, Adrienne, but an apology is not going to make that any better. And while I appreciate the face-to-face, I'm not sure I can accept it. You lied to me, to my face, day after day. Promised me that I was good, that everything was okay, and then-" his voice breaks off and I know he's reliving the day that has been chiseled into my brain forever- the day office was stormed with police, when all operations were forced to be ceased, when they started the investigation that uncovered every lie I'd ever made, every false dollar I'd every proclaimed, every deceit that I'd used to cover up the truth.

"I know," I say, and he looks at me with a mixture of surprise and confusion, "I know that words aren't enough."

I want to reach out and grab his hand, but I know that we have never had that kind of relationship. So, I rub my thumb against the surface of my cup instead and continue.

"I want to make it up to you in a real way," I catch his eyes before I say the rest of my sentence, "by offering you a job."

It takes a second or two or three, and I watch as his brain processes the information.

"With you?" he asks.

And I nod.

"You've got to be fucking kidding me, Adrienne," he leans back in his chair away from me and just peers at me incredulously.

"Listen Jeremy," I say, sitting up straighter, "Let's not pretend like we were best buds. I was your boss, and you were my assistant. A damn good assistant, but let's be real, that's where our relationship started and ended. I fucked you over financially more than anything, and I'm here to start making amends in that same sphere by offering you a job."

"And why the hell would I want to work for you, Adrienne, ever again?" he asks with an exasperated twang.

I hold his gaze, refusing to back down, "Because your fucking job sucks, Jeremy."

I nod at him, a gesture telling him that I know where he

works and what he gets paid. He hesitates before breaking eye contact. I clear my throat and don't elaborate. Instead, I watch him, trying to get a read on his response. I'd heard about Jeremy when I'd still been making my rounds trying to find a job of my own. An assistant had sighed at me with pity in her voice when I'd inquired about an interview. She'd said that my former assistant had also called looking for a new job, and that she had tried, and failed, to help him. And then she'd whispered to me in a voice dripping in pity, that she had seen him bussing tables at a restaurant in midtown, and what a shame that was. What a terrible shame. Because this assistant had known Jeremy, had respected him, had seen just how fucking brilliant he was, and knew that he must have been just miserable working such a mindless job.

"You know what I've been doing these past months, Jeremy?" I ask when his silence has stretched on for much too long.

He shakes his head ever so slightly.

"I've been working on a farm."

He slowly turns to look at me then, catching my eyes with a question in his.

I grin.

"I've been working on a farm. Tilling the land, planting the seeds, harvesting, answering phones, ordering supplies, all of it."

"You?" he asks, "On a farm?"

I chuckle at him softly.

"Yes, me," I take a deep breath before continuing, "And it's been good for me. I've been making an honest living. Using my hands to help something just," I shrug one shoulder, "grow."

I watch Jeremy sip his coffee and try to process the information.

"And it's been good for me. I've been able to put a roof over my head, support me and my kids, and process how I came to let everything in my life fall apart. And as great as it has been, I know that I'm not cut out to do this forever."

I lean forward in my chair, pressing my forearms against the table.

"I can feel it, tugging at the edges of my brain, pulling me away from the monotony of my days, searching for more." I close my eyes for a few longs seconds before continuing. "I have to do more. I have to find a way to repay all the people that I hurt, that I stole money from, that I let down. And I think that starting a new company, one that is actually run honorably, is the best way to combine both of those aims. But I also know that I need help."

I smile at him, a small smile, but one that comes from deep inside.

"You were the best assistant that I'd ever had." I swallow hard and force the next sentence out. "And I'd be honored if you'd help me, repay you, by getting you away from your shitty ass job, and back doing what you love, Jeremy."

I lean back in my chair, hoping to break some of the tension floating in the air between us.

"Besides, the faster I can get this company up and running and making a profit, the faster I can pay you back, every last penny that I took from you."

"You plan to pay me back?" he asks, eyeing me curiously.

"Absolutely. We can put it in your contract and everything if you don't believe me." I bite my bottom lip to prevent my voice from shaking as I say the next bit, "I have to pay everyone back. Every last cent. I just have to. I don't think I can call myself a decent human being until I do."

"I'd worked for you for 7 years, Adrienne," he says, spitting the words out at me bitterly, "I came to work for you because you were so passionate, so full of life, so well-meaning, so meticulous. Your products were fucking beautiful and every girl I ever dated, raved about how they were so much more comfortable than any other shoe. It was perfect. I thought I was so lucky. I got to lure ladies with gifts of free shoes, and I had a job I loved with a boss who wasn't bat-shit crazy."

He tilts his head and narrows his eyes at me.

"And then you fucked it all up. Not only did I lose a job I loved, but I lost my reputation. My name was tied to you, and your name was shit. And now you come here with promises to repay me, by asking me to go back to working for you? Don't you think that you have done enough?"

He stands up, looking down on me with disappointment.

"Go back to your farm, DiDi," he says my nickname mockingly, "people like you have no business trying to run a company."

I stand up and call after his retreating figure, "Are you happy, Jeremy? With your life, the way that it is right now?"

He hesitates at the door, hand poised to push it open.

"Come back and do what you love to do." My voice drops several octaves. "Let me make this up to you."

But he shakes his head at me, he pushes open the door, and he leaves.

CHAPTER FIFTY-EIGHT

The next morning, I take the kids to school and I hold a casual conversation with the assistant principal. I tell her that I'm starting a new thing, a Moms Help Moms thing, and ask her if she thinks that it's something that other moms need. She nods vigorously and agrees to let me post my little flyer. It reads simply:

Mom for Hire!
Running late?
Babysitter cancelled and have a hot date?
No time to come up with healthy snacks for the team?
Or bake those cupcakes?
Or anything else in between?
Hire a mom!

I post the flyer with my cell phone number on the bottom and stand back. Day One, I say to myself with a feeling of accomplishment for no good reason at all. Nevertheless, I grin, anyway. I leave the school and head straight over to visit

Gertrude. I find her in the kitchen of the church, brewing a new pot of coffee while she delegates with a clipboard pinned between her body and her left arm. I stand back, in the doorway and wait, working on building my patience. She gestures me over with her chin as she's dismissing her team of cooks and cleaners, people dressed in the gray outfits I once wore, once upon a time.

I ask her if I can help, and she waves her hand at me dismissively.

"Just tell me what you've come for," she says, rolling her eyes at me, "You're always so needy."

She says the last word, with a playful sarcasm, but it makes me pause. A lot of truth is said in jest, and I realize that I have only come around in the last few months asking for help. When have I bothered to be around just because? When have I offered my services? I haven't had much to give. But those are excuses. Time is always available. Time is priceless.

She begins walking, but I don't follow. I watch as she walks and wait for her to notice that I haven't moved. She gets all the way to the door before she looks back, eyebrows raised, expectantly.

"No really, Gertrude, how can I help you?" I ask, seriously.

"Give me a second," she says a playful smile dancing on her lips as she waves me over, "let me think of something," she gestures her head over at me.

I walk over to her slowly, shaking my head at her effervescent grandmotherly grin. "You're right," I say as I draw nearer to her outstretched hand, "You have done so much for me. Found me a job, a place to stay, supported me in getting my husband back, and all I keep doing is asking for more and more and more. What can you do for me?" I shake my head. "I don't want to be that kind of person anymore."

I reach her and grab hold of her gaze so she knows my level

of commitment, my sincerity. She nods at me and I take her hand, finally. She grasps it tightly and for once I note its fragility. She is an old lady. Strong and determined. A woman you can depend on. A woman who has really lived and has the wisdom you expect from an old lady, but rarely come across. I can only hope to one day be half the woman she is. I nod at her, as she begins to guide us down the maze of halls, at once so familiar, and yet also still quite foreign. How does one get to be like her? Start today. Start now. I straighten my back to match her perfect posture, and revel in the guidance she is providing me.

"So how can I help you, my love?" she asks, clutching my hand to her chest and rubbing her thumb along the back of it.

"I'm starting my own business," I say, flatly.

She nods.

"I put in my two weeks' notice at the farm."

She nods again.

"I'm moving out of the cottage in 30 days."

She nods. She waits for me to continue, but I don't.

She waits a few seconds longer before she speaks.

"I'm glad you have realized that it is time for you to move on, Adrienne. Do you need my support in getting your business some legs? Do you need help finding a new place? Or did you come here just to hear me tell you what you already know-" she glances over at me mischievously, "that you are capable of anything."

I smile at her, and I know she can feel it even though she doesn't turn to see it directly.

She pushes through the front door of the church and the fresh air assails me. I take a deep breath and let the air into my lungs, let it work its magic on reinvigorating me.

"I don't need any of those things." I say, grinning at her, "I'm moving in with my sister, and I think I already know how to find all the help I need with getting started, I just need a vehicle. I'm thinking of a very reliable mom-car, but I can't afford much. I've only been able to save about twenty-eight hundred dollars. I was wondering if you knew anyonewho'd be able to help me out. I could even set up a payment plan or something. I'm good for it, Gertrude." I bite my lip, hoping she doesn't dig deeper, or ask why I can't just take out a loan or something.

She doesn't answer for a long while, just guides me towards the back of the church where her small garden grows, ironically beside a playground for the preschool housed in the basement of the facility.

"I may know someone," she finally says, "But it's an old lady. She bought a van a few years back in the hopes of being able to help out with her grandkids, but that was before she got sick. The medication she's on makes it hard for her to drive much, so it's been pretty much sitting in her garage collecting dust. I'll talk to her. See if she's willing to sell it or go into a payment plan with you, like you said."

I throw my arms around Gertrude.

"But I must warn you," she says, patting my back as she hugs me tightly, "she might want a little bit something more than just money from you."

I grin at Gertrude. She is the old, white, granny I never had, and I tell her as much. She laughs at me.

"Come on, grandchild," she says with an eye roll, "help me with my gardening."

And so, I pick up a hoe and begin to weed.

CHAPTER FIFTY-NINE

The year I started high school was the year I started spending Friday afternoons and evenings with Bethany Brown. Every Friday, like clockwork. It became our routine. A bestie tradition. Sometimes we went to the movies. Sometimes we rented a movie. Sometimes we caught a bus and headed to the mall. Sometimes we hung out in one of our bedrooms and did nothing at all. I got my first real boyfriend sophomore year, and he tried to impede on our Fridays. He didn't last long. Fridays were for Bethany Brown. Bethany Brown and me. We would hold hands as we walked home from school, practically skipping we were so giddy. As soon as we'd gotten far enough away, out of earshot from boys who wanted to steal our time and grab at our bodies and girls who thought we were too close to each other and wanted more ammunition to write smack about us on the bathroom walls, we would start talking.

We didn't always get a chance to talk much during the week. We were busy. I was taking honors level classes and forcing myself into as many clubs and extra-curricular activities as I could possibly find the time for. On top of all that, I ran for the track team. Bethany spent most of her time reading chick lit, and chasing boys, along with playing both softball and basketball. During our free time we liked to go to the park. Bethany would read or chat aimlessly about the fine minutiae of her days- the boys she was currently into, the girl who looked at her weird, the proper way to shave one's legs, while I spent the time sketching strangers in the park, trying to see something in them that I couldn't see in myself. Searching. I'd spent hours talking Bethany's ears off about my struggles with feeling aimless, with being pretty good at a bunch of things and not quite excellent at anything, with not having a passion to pursue, with my strong desire to be a success without knowing how to achieve any aspect of it.

Despite our weekend gab sessions, there were things that somehow or for some reason we just didn't share. So, it wasn't from Bethany herself that I heard about the boys, it was from a bunch of giggling juniors, chatting loudly while I was peeing in the girl's room. Apparently, from what I could gather, four jocks were basically rotating through her. Each one got a go at her for a month or so, pretending to be in a relationship with her until he gets tired of her, then passing her on to the next one. And this had been going on for months because, evidently, Bethany gave exceptionally good blowjobs. And since she was dealing with teenage boys, despite their best efforts, they had let what was meant to be private slip quietly out.

It had taken me longer than I'd expected to say something to Bethany. There was something painful about dealing with the experience that I'd tried to avoid for as long as I could. But every day that went by, my guilt grew and grew until I felt over-whelmed by it, like I was drowning in it, and I felt like I would explode in a puddle of shame if I didn't say something.

It was on a Friday, sitting cross-legged on my bedroom floor when I'd finally clasped her hands and held her gaze and told her that people were talking about how Aaron, Brian, Robert, and Tyrone were taking turns dating her.

And at first Bethany had just nodded at me, "I know, Adrienne," she'd said forcing a smile, quickly followed by a shrug, "They each take turns dating me for a month or so as long as they keep their big fat mouths..." her voice trailed off as she'd realized the severity of the situation.

I'd raised an eyebrow at her, "Everyone knows, Bethany. Everyone's talking about it."

Her bottom lip quivered as she tried to force back an array of tears. "But they promised. They, they promised me."

"They're assholes, Bethany. Stupid fucking assholes," I'd said, pulling her in close, giving her permission to cry. I'd felt her body collapse against mine, and I gently rubbed her back. Up and down, up and down, trying to press some of my love into her skin, reducing the pain that she was now engulfed in.

"Everyone's going to think I'm a slut," she'd finally managed to choke out in between sobs.

And I didn't know what to say. She was right. That's exactly what the giggling girls in the bathroom said.

"It's bad enough to go down on one boy maybe, after dating for like a year or something, but four? That's just disgusting." A thin girl had said, making a face as I'd come out of my stall.

"Of course it'd be Bethany Brown, that girl's boobs are entirely too big for her to have been born with a single brain cell. I mean, I heard she let them run a train on her once too."

"Just once? I mean, if you're gonna date all four of them then you might as well have orgies too."

And at that, I'd had enough. I'd spun on my heels and stormed right up into the girls' faces.

"Y'all better watch your fucking mouths," I'd said, damn near growling as I'd eyed each one of them in turn. They had looked vaguely familiar, but I was having trouble placing them.

The last girl I'd glared out had looked like she was about to back down, but then, she'd broken eye contact, glanced at her friends, pushed her chest out and responded with an edge in her voice, "You're that girl's friend, aren't you?" she'd snarled, looking me up and down, "Not my fault that skank's a cumbucket. I suggest you take that up with her."

And before I could even think to stop myself, my hand had come to life of its own volition, darting out and slapping that girl directly across the face so quickly that she hadn't recovered by the time I'd stormed out of the bathroom, the door slamming behind me like thunder clapping down the hall.

Remembering this encounter, I knew we had to act fast, or my dear bestie would become a pariah. If that girl was bold enough to call Bethany a cumbucket to her friend's face, then who knows what others might have been soon willing to say directly to Bethany.

No. I couldn't let it go down like that. And so, I came up with a plan. That very night I called her softball and basketball friends and convinced them to help a teammate win. Then I'd texted the very four boys who had put her in this position and told them that they owed Bethany for opening up their stupid mouths, and they readily agreed especially after I'd threatened to spread some pictures of micro penises around and say that it was theirs. By Monday morning everything was set.

So, on that Monday morning we met with Bethany's teammates in front of the school, and we all walked in together. There were at least ten of us, marching all together with serious looks on our faces and with Bethany leading the way. We stomped through the halls relentlessly, pushing anyone who didn't move fast enough out of our way. Practically demanding someone to say something to us. Soon enough a guy fake coughed the word "slut", and we all stopped in our tracks. We headed right for him, surrounding him on all sides, and started raining insults on him all at the same time.

It sounded something like this, coming from ten girls at the same time: "You got something to say, Ugly? You mad cause you have a small penis? Who's a slut, your mama? You even know how to spell the word slut? You heard of Lorena Bobbit? Your breath stinks. You ever even had a date? Who are you? You ain't nobody."

"Alright!" Bethany finally yelled, which was our cue to stop attacking the boy, who was at that point cowering in front of us, looking like he was about to cry.

Then she got in his face, pressed her index finger under his chin and said in a low, creepy voice that literally took hours to perfect, "We coming after anyone who tries me, spread the word."

And that was our cue to chime out with our chant, "Cause Bethany Brown ain't no one to fuck with!"

Then she blew him a kiss, spun on her heels, and we continued our procession through the school, guiding Bethany to her first period class.

I heard someone whispering a little too loudly, asking how we could keep this up throughout the day. And I'd just grinned at them, because my plan had just begun.

Bethany had classes with at least three teammates each period. The teammates in her class were to surround her in the classroom, leaving no space for anyone to come at her during class. Then, in between each class I had a different one of the 4 boys that started this whole conundrum, waiting outside her room with a dozen roses, ready to escort her to her next class. I had mostly been banking on the fact that no one would dare call her a slut while on the arm of one of the very guys that she had been accused of slutting it up for, but just in case, she was also greeted by at least 3 of her teammates, who marched behind her and the selected boy, guiding her to her next class-room. It hadn't been hard to find at least a handful each period, her teammates plentiful and super willing to be helpful. This was just another game to them, and they all liked to win. By the end of the day, we had caused more buzz in our defense then the original drama had stirred. Instead of being known as a slut, Bethany Brown had become a girl no one would dare mess with.

"That girl Bethany? Her squad don't play. Y'all would protect me like that if people were talking crazy about me too, right?" I overheard one senior saying as we'd made our way to the front door at the end of the day.

By the end of the week, no one would dare call Bethany anything but beautiful. We even had a premier spot in the year-book on the friendship page, a bunch of Bethany's teammates and me holding her up as she laid across our arms with a bright grin on her face, her hair glowing in the sun: Bethany's Crew, and she was the boss. Because although I came up with the plan, it was love for Bethany Brown and her big-heart and bright smile that made her teammates decide to fight for her. It wasn't me.

I had been always jealous at the love that she inspired from everyone. Even the boys. Two of the four stupid jocks that had opened their big mouths, still to this day, as far as I know at least, talk to Bethany consistently, checking on her to make sure she's okay, and even sending her money.

Bethany has always lamented the fact that she has never gotten married, but everywhere she goes, people fall head over heels in love with her. It's infuriating to say the least. I'd complained about it one day, feeling particularly shitty about the lack of invitations I'd gotten to an upcoming dance.

"Adrienne, the people are nice and all, it's nice to be loved, like genuinely loved but, you know you're my only real friend, right? Everyone's cool. And I love them all. But you and me? We got that never-ending true shit. We got that kind of love that middle aged white women write books on. You and me," she'd said, putting up her right arm like Wonder Women, dragging out the old chant from when we were ten.

"Me and you," I'd said reluctantly, feeling a bit silly as I put my arm up too.

"Bethany,"

"Adrienne."

And then together, "Unstoppable," and we'd clinked our wrists together.

CHAPTER SIXTY

The phone rings while I'm packing up our meager belongings into boxes scavenged from recycling. TiTi's clothes, the twins' toys, and my toiletries all seem to be fitting into 8 medium-sized boxes. Things: so stupid, so fleeting, I wonder how I used to put so much stock into the ownership of so many things. I picked up the phone absent-mindedly, glancing at the book that Ms. Ida had forced upon me when I'd dropped by her house a few days ago to talk to her about her van. She had handed me a book, requiring me to read it before she'd talk to me. I have still yet to crack it open. My blood boils just looking at the thing. Who does this lady think she is, anyway? Then I get angry at myself for being so self-righteous. Ms. Ida might help me get my life together, all I have to do is read a stupid book. Is that really so much to ask for? I used to read all of the time. I used to love reading. I shove the book off the counter onto the floor before answering my phone.

"Hello," I say, trying to sound chipper and full of energy in case it's a mom trying to hire me.

"AK," and my heart does a little dance.

My husband.

I accept the charges then collapse into the couch.

"I got a date!" he screams in my ear so loudly that I have to pull the phone back from my ear a little bit.

"A date?" I ask, confused, "with me I hope," I say, half-smiling.

"No, silly, well, yes actually. I do have a date with you. My release date, Adrienne. I'm taking you out, to the finest restaurant in the whole fucking world. You and me, we're going to take over the world. I miss you so much. I miss your smell and your lips and waking up to you beside me." His voice starts to crack at the end of his sentence.

I don't realize that I'm crying until the tears land on my jeans. I swipe at my face automatically. "When?" I croak out in a voice barely above a whisper.

"90 days!" he screams in my ear.

And I pull the phone away from me and laugh.

"Well," I say, as my laughter begins to die down, "Guess I got 90 days to get my shit together."

"Yep," he says, laughing along with me.

But as the laughter dies down, I realize exactly what this means. I've got to get to work. I glance back over at the book Ms. Ida gave me, and I sigh softly. Time to suck up my pride and put my ego aside and get the book read so I can be ready to go once my phone starts to ring. I listen to my husband half-heartedly, as I scan the room for my journal and my purple pen. I spot it on top of a box and open it up to the next blank page.

I write:

•Read the book.

•Make the phone call.

•Get the van!

•Spend more time with the kids.

•Come up with something special for my husband.

"AK?" Julien calls, pulling me out of my thoughts. "I can't believe this is actually happening."

"I can't either," I say, staring down at the list before me, trying to imagine the day Julian will be standing next to me, holding my hand, touching my skin. I try to take a mental picture of the image. I try to breathe it in every corner of my mind.

"Julian," I whisper, trying to hold on to mental picture, "I love you."

CHAPTER SIXTY-ONE

I used to tell people that I ran track because I thought it'd look good on my college application. A mindless answer to deflect from my truth. I ran track because I love to run. It made me feel so free. I think it must be how my dad feels when he rides his bike in the wee hours of the morning. The uphill struggle for the downhill release, the rhythmic pedaling that becomes almost a form of meditation- swish, swoosh, swish, swoosh. I feel that same release with the pounding of my feet. Bam bambambambambambam. A steady rhythm with a tempo all my own that I am in full control of. It's all so soothing. I find my old crusty running shoes at the bottom of the hall closet, but I can't find a single running bra. I wonder absentmindedly if they too were confiscated in the bankruptcy. No, I remember vaguely, used undergarments aren't worth anything. Who'd want to wear a bra tainted by someone else's under-boob and armpit sweat? Who'd want to wear my already been lubricated on panties? Absolutely nobody.

I pull out the box I'd squeezed under my bed, the last box I'd never bothered to unpack. I flip the box open and grin down at a handful of sports bras, but when I scoop them up and squeeze them against my breasts, I can't help but notice what's underneath. My life. The scrapbooks I'd put together in moments of nostalgic clarity. The bits and pieces of my children that I'd tried to save and stash away. I drop to my knees, bowing before their glory, and reach for the one closest to me, until I spot the pink one underneath. TiTi, years 1-3. My baby.

I scoot until I am comfortable on the floor, sitting cross-legged, and poise myself before cracking open the book that I know I need to explore. This is what the search for sports bras was really for, at least partially. I drop the sports bras on the floor besides me and let my hands dance on the cover of the book. It's a picture of TiTi at three. Spinning in a pink dress. She wears a tiara on her head, and I can practically hear her voice as she says, "Take a picture of me. Take of picture of me spinning, Mommy." I did as I was told and was rewarded with the image I now caress with my fingertips. This picture had turned out perfect, barely blurry at all, capturing TiTi's real smile, the one she tried to hide from her friends, from herself, from everybody. The one that came out all the time when she was three, but was so hard to capture, encompass, and then be, when a camera was out. This day had been different. This day had been her birthday. And there was always something about birthdays that made it easier to just be happy.

I hadn't been there for that moment. I mean, I had been there physically, but I hadn't really been there- present. I was in the middle of getting my company started. The grind of performing at 120% every day had created a haze in which life outside of work all just seemed unclear, out of focus. All the things I needed to do, and here I was spending a whole day playing mommy at my little girl's stereotypical princess party. Mommy, Mommy, look at me, look at me, I remember thinking in my head mockingly.

I had been slightly irritated and resentful. I remember my mind wandering while singing happy birthday. I remember the day being a blur of pink and screeching little girls and icing. I remember missing it all.

It wasn't until I'd uploaded the pictures onto my desktop, days later, and had clicked through the images that I'd realized that I had missed it all. I didn't recognize half of the things captured in the images filling my screen. There was a magician? A princess Jasmine? Julien had sung a duet with TiTi? Where had I been? In an effort to remedy this gross error, I'd stayed up into the wee hours of the night plopping pictures into an online scrapbook-making website along with highlights from the past few years. A backwards timeline highlight reel. Similar books were also created throughout the years when I had checked out on my children's lives and tried to remedy it with a hardbound collection of glossy stills. Like these books could replace the experience itself. Where is mommy? In her head planning a new design, plotting out a new marketing strategy, trying to come up with a way to finagle more money. I think back to that day in the car when TiTi lied about me.

Who is she? She's not my mommy.

I drop the scrapbook back in the box with the rest and it lands with a slapping sound on top of a book featuring Darrius' smiling face. I pull off my shirt and bra and put on my favorite sports bra from the pile I'd retrieved, then stuff my feet into my sneakers and take off, determined to run until the fog clears from my brain. There's something I'm not seeing. Something just beyond my grasp, beyond my reach, beyond my ability to see with the tentacles of my brain, but I have a sense that I'm close, so close, almost there.

For me, the beginning of any run is always terrible, a terrible form of torture. Some part of my body would protest with a sharp pain. The rest would dully ache. Like a chorus with a lead singer all bemoaning me to just stop moving, just stop, stop, PLEASE. And the pressure would keep building and building, the chorus demanding with more urgency, until all of a sudden the dam would crack and split open, releasing all the pain at once. And my mind would float up out of my body, and I would enter a higher plane where there was nothing but the wind blowing past me and the air in my lungs and the rhythm of my feet slapping the ground. There would be a peacefulness then, a silencing of all the background mutterings of discontent. Maybe this, what if that, if quite possibly- all the nagging inconsistencies would cease, and I would be rewarded with the gift of quiet. Just me and me. Not a single worry. This was how I solved all life's problems. Do this. Move here. Start this. Sit here. All was clear when I was in this space.

I had lost the habit of this practice in recent years. Determining that I didn't have the time required for these kinds of long-distance runs, and instead spent hours pacing my office, my living room, going on long drives, planning and revising, and coming up with contingencies. Was that really a better use of my time? Did anything I'd planned in that way ever work out quite right? There was always an aspect that I had missed, a point that I hadn't seen, a perspective that had changed everything. I had been trying so hard, so hard, to tightly control everything, that I had lost all control, and I had eventually lost my company.

The beginning of this run is a particular kind of torture. I haven't run in years and my entire body rails against me. At least I've managed not to put on much weight, stress and poverty have been a great diet for me. It takes every last ounce of my soul to continue going. My breath becomes ragged, my heart pounds in my chest, a sharp pain stabs my side, but I know that if I can just keep moving forward I will be rewarded with the release of everything, and that clarity will flow to me. The kind of clarity that I didn't know I've been seeking for all these weeks. I focus on the sound of my feet. One, two, three. One, two, three. The pounding not quite rhythmic. My footsteps out of synch. One, two, three. One, two, three. And then, bam. I'm there. The pain is released from me, I find my stride and I run thoroughly, carefree, proud, and steadily. I grin to myself and dig in. The air smells like grass and tiredness, but the noise is finally gone. The voices have finally been hushed, a constant hum that I had gotten so used to.

I run and run and run. I don't know for how long or how far, my body working off of auto-pilot, while I am floating in a sea of nothingness, reveling in the silence. And then it comes to me. In a voice that is not a voice. In a language that is not words. In a thought that is more like a feeling. And I translate this message into the following:

Put your focus where your focus should be.

And suddenly I realize that my priorities are off. It's not about making money or the business, it's not about getting a car, it's about my kids, my husband, and me. For without them, I am nothing. And the further away I place my focus from them the more fucked up everything is and will be. I race back home. A billion thoughts whirring through my head that I need to write down before I lose them. I finally make it back to the cottage with the half-filled boxes and lunge for the journal and my purple pen.

PRIORITIES I put in bold letters at the top of the next clean page.

1.Me. For without focusing on myself how can I be of assistance to anyone else. What do I need to be happy? Eat good foods. Exercise daily. Be present. Love fully.

2.TiTi, Darrius, and Parris. The loves of my life. How can I be the best mom? Be present, make sure they are well-fed and clothed, have a car to transport them safely and a house that feels like home.

3.Julien. My heart. How can I be the best wife? Be present, be open, be honest, be fearless in all that you share, give 100% of you.

Underneath this list I wrote the following sentences:

How does everything else fit? They either serve to assist these priorities or they don't. This is the measure of everything.

I sit back and re-read the page before me and know that no truer words have ever been or ever will be. This business- it's for me, my mental well-being, my peace of mind, my sense of autonomy, but it's also for my children- so they can have better lives every day, a home where everyone has space and a bed, and a safe, warm, and secure way of getting from A to B. It's also for my husband, so he has something to come back to, as a black man now carrying the weight of a felony conviction, his best bet is working for himself again, building this business with me.

I close the journal and glance over at the book Ms. Ida had given me. And view it for what it is, an opportunity. I saunter over to it, pick it up and hold it in my hands. And so it begins, I think as I open to the first page and begin reading.

CHAPTER SIXTY-TWO

Miguel pulls up with his pickup truck and it takes him all of 15 minutes to load up our meager possessions. We, all four of us, squeeze into the front of the truck and drive across town. The ride takes all of 20 minutes and I spend the time humming Disney songs into the twins' ears, one sitting on my lap, the other sitting on TiTi's. I can practically feel the bouncing nervous electric energy jumping off their skin. The little cottage we'd been staying in, while too small and uncomfortable, had become familiar. Where were we headed to now? What would it be like? I try to silence their endless questions with catchy songs. We pull up to a yellow rancher and I notice the kids glancing at each other before sliding out of the truck cautiously. Something about the glance warms my heart. It's almost as if they can read each other's minds. It's expected amongst the twins, but also with TiTi? Although I shouldn't be surprised when I think about it, because although I hate to admit it, even to myself, there were times when I was pretty sure that I was able to read Camille's mind. It was a long time ago, though. Maybe we can get back to that one day. Maybe this will be part of my Camille remedy, not simply to patch things up with her, but to strengthen the bond, build it stronger, make the kind of connection that I didn't know that I always wanted. Maybe.

I shake my sleeping legs out and slowly walk up the winding drive. The grass is cut immaculately. A single bronze statue of an angel stands near the single step to the front door, gesturing us in with a smile. I punch my code into the keypad and the door clicks open. I push it gently and the lights dance to life.

"Welcome, Adrienne," the house says cheerfully as I cross the threshold.

I walk in slowly, tracing my fingers along the glass table that lines the wall.

"Hello," I call out at the silence.

"Hello," the house says back, "how may I help you?"

"Um," I wrack my brain for something interesting, "Can you play some music, please, House?"

"Sure, Adrienne, what would you like to hear?"

I wrack my brain for something child-friendly, but not so child-friendly that it's only bearable to small children. "Alicia Keys," I finally proclaim, "Songs in A Minor" a classic if there ever was one. The house is suddenly filled with the melodious soft voice that always reminds me of my childhood.

"Really, Mommy?" Titi says, rolling her eyes at me.

I ignore her, as Miguel comes in holding a box and asking me where to put it. I glance at it, notice that it belongs to the twins and begin marching off in the direction of their room.

"Follow me everybody," I say, leading a parade down the hall towards where all the bedrooms lie. "This shall be your room, Titi," gesturing to the room to the left. The room is large, but sparsely decorated, with a full-size bed, a night stand, and a body-length mirror. She enters the room tepidly, glancing around in surprise.

"Is this just for me?" she says.

"Of course," I say, throwing an arm around her shoulder and kissing her on the forehead, "a young lady needs her space."

Now the twins are getting excited, I can see them bouncing in my periphery.

"What about us?!" they screech, animatedly.

"Your room is next door," I say, laughing at them as they race out of the room and into the one next to Titi's.

We turn and follow them slowly. Their room is sparsely decorated as well, but the bed is its shining glory. A bunk bed, with a slide. They begin climbing on it immediately.

"Mom...." Titi says cautiously, and I know from her tone of voice that she's thinking that this all seems too good to be true, "where are you going to be sleeping?"

I raise my eyebrows at her several times, then race across the hall, challenging her to follow. I throw open the door and voila! An oversized bed fills up most of the room, but I really picked it because of the big windows and the natural sunlight. My daughter hops up on the bed immediately, she rolls into the center of it and stretches out her arms and grins out the window. I look down at her for a long minute. The curve of her jaw reminds me of her father, and it warms my heart. It used to annoy me that she favored him so much. I mean, my daughter is very much a girl. She has my facial structure, but all the details are her dad. Right down to the hazel eyes and the shape of her nose. And also, as I'm just now noticing, right at this moment, her jawline.

"Mommy," she says, still staring out the window, and I can feel the energy shift, feel the room get several degrees colder, so I hold my breath and hope she doesn't notice my nervousness,

"Are we going to be here for a while? Or is this," she hesitates, "is this just another something temporary."

Stability. My daughter, like all children, is always searching for stability. What is it about children and wanting everything to stay the same? Wanting to know what will happen in the future indefinitely? Wanting to place their parents in boxes. This is the mommy. This is the daddy. Mommy does this, but Daddy does that. When mommy yells it means stop moving right now. When daddy yells it means, time to play somehow. I can't blame my daughter for craving something so natural, but if I'm honest, I resent her for asking for it a bit because it's not something I can provide. At least not right now. And honestly, I'm beginning to think this whole 'provide a safe stable foundation for kids shit' is bullshit. Who's to say that one way of doing things is better than the other? Just because I can't provide my children with one house to grow up in, does that make me less of a mom? Plenty of children have all the stability in the world and grow up fucked up because their parents didn't meet their needs in some other way. And I know I'm not delusional enough to think I can be everything for my children, but I know that I can give them all the love and support in the world. I know that I can give them a solid foundation to build their lives upon. I know that I am enough.

I sit down on the bed next to my beautiful baby girl, then I lay down next to her. I take her left hand in my left hand and cross it over my body then throw my other arm behind her head. She presses her head into my breast like she did when she was a little girl, and a tear falls from my eye before I even know it's formed.

"TiTi, and I want to be honest with you completely from here on out, I think you're old enough to know the truth," she nods, without looking directly at me, "We're welcome here for as long as we want to be, but this is not going to be our forever house. We're guests here. Welcome guests, but guests none-theless, and we're going to have to find our own somewhere to be. I'm hoping I can get the money together to move out eventually, but we're probably not going to stay wherever we move to for that long either."

I take in a deep breath.

"I know I messed everything up, TiTi. I'm trying to fix everything. But your life is never going to be like it once was." I try really hard to not cry and am surprised that I actually succeed, "We are going to be a bit of a work in progress for a while. We're going to have to move and move and change and adapt. I'm going to try to give you and the boys as much consistency and stability as possible, you will all remain in the same school. For example, we put the money up for school a long time ago and that money is completely untouchable, but everything else, everything else is up for grabs."

I decide that this is the moment that I need to just shut up and wait for her to say something, no matter how long it may take.

The silence is so loud that I can hear the seconds ticking by on my watch, but I bite my bottom lip and wait for her response.

"I know that Mom," she finally says, "and actually I'm proud of you."

My eyes start to water, and I swallow hard to hold back the tears, but they start brimming in the corner of my eyes as she continues to speak.

"You went through all this stuff, you lost everything, even us, and for a while there I was pretty skeptical that you were ever coming back, but here you are. You came for us, and you're figuring it out. I respect that. And honestly, Mom, I don't want things to go back to the way that they were, they were... kind of crappy. We had a lot of stuff, but not a lot of... you. I'd rather have you any day than all the money and cars and clothes and diamonds in the world."

She finally turns to me, wipes away the tears that have escaped from my eyes, and kisses my cheeks. She leans forward and presses her forehead to mine.

"Just never leave us again," she says, eyes closed as if shutting herself off from the hurt of it all.

I smile at her through my tears.

"Of course, my love," I say, pulling her head in to rest in the crook between my head and shoulder blade.

I cry silently, and I feel a couple drops from Titi as well. My strong and beautiful little girl.

But after the energy has subsided, and we feel free to return to our own spaces, the butterflies settle in my stomach. Can I be the mom she needs? I don't really have a choice.

TiTi slowly drags herself away from my body, and paddles out towards the bedroom door, but when she reaches it, she turns back to me and says, "So whose house is this anyway?" She leans her body casually against the doorframe, and her mass of curls surround her face in a perfect halo. Oh, this girl is going to break so many hearts when she grows up. A part of me giggles inside excited for the future she has laid out before her.

I snicker at her. "If I told you, you wouldn't even believe me. But listen, she'll be here in about half an hour. Let's get this stuff unloaded so we'll be ready for her when she comes home."

TiTi gives me a 100-watt grin. "Okay, Mom. I got you," she says, before spinning and bounding out of my new bedroom.

And I wonder why in the world I had been wishing for more space, because I miss her the second she's gone.

CHAPTER SIXTY-THREE

I'd managed to acquire a ridiculous crush on a boy I'd never talked to, during Dr. Ferguson's Business Management class my sophomore year. He was a year older than I was, and I'd not known he'd existed since he was a business major and I'd decided to focus on my fashion design courses first before taking any business-related ones. Since he'd participated a lot in class, I'd started to notice him, and as the class progressed, I'd acquired the false idea that I knew him. I began to catalogue his cadence of speech, his viewpoints, his work ethic. On top of all that, he was drop-dead gorgeous. He was tall and chocolate with green-tinged hazel eyes that always had a mysterious edge to them. I used to daydream about licking the dimples carved into the sides of his face. Weeks went by and I could find no reason to speak to him, yet my infatuation grew. I was sure he didn't notice me. He had no reason to. Besides, I would tell myself fighting back the urge to accidentally bump into him on the way out of class each day, he was dating some bimbo. She was always waiting for him in the hall after class. And, of course, she was be-au-ti-ful, at least in the traditional model-esque way. I'm talking skinny and leggy, with huge boobs, and a mountain of cascading (fake) hair and skin that perfect shade of sun-kissed brown. I mean, I was at least cuter in the face, but... only when I smiled.

It was my obsession with this boy and daily fantasies of being the leggy woman on his armthat inspired what would come to be an award-winning shoe design. I would sit on my spot on the lion that guarded the back entrance to the school's library and think of him as I sketched. I was nothing like that girl. Standing at a mere 5'3" and more pudgy than thin and leggy, with a wild mane of curls and eyes that I thought were always a little too squinty. I hated wearing heels. They hurt my feet so badly, I never understood the appeal. But thoughts of Julian changed all that. If I could strut to class in a cute outfit and some heels that didn't kill my feet, maybe he'd finally notice me. And so, I decided to create them. And right then and there, I'd decided to name the shoe after him. My future husband, yes, but at the time, someone I had never even spoken with.

Julian.

CHAPTER SIXTY-FOUR

Julian had been raving about his best friend for months after we'd started dating. Nearly everything out of his mouth was about Curtis. This one time me and Curtis... I can't wait until you meet Curtis! Oh, did I tell you about the time Curtis and I ... It was all he seemed to be able to talk about. And while I loved to hear Julian talk, I had started to grow weary of constantly hearing about some best friend I had yet to meet.

When the day came to meet this amazing Superman-like best friend, I was underwhelmed to say the least. He was three hours late and hadn't even bothered to send a "running late" text, so the food Julien had prepared was overcooked and dry by the time we'd given up on him and eaten. The baked chicken dish was usually my favorite of the limited number of meals that my Julien knew how to prepare. I ate the dry food slowly, forcing a smile as I swallowed.

When Curtis finally showed up to Julien's apartment, we were curled up on the couch, snuggled up comfortably, kissing softly while a hand slowly slivered down into my jeans. My body had been screaming his name when a firm knock sounded at the door. He'd hesitated immediately, his energy pulling back moments before his body followed. My eyes trailed him, tracing the curves of his form, and I'd smiled as he'd readjusted himself as he'd walked to the door.

The moment the door opened, Curtis washed into the room like a tidal wave of energy.

"Man you will not believe the day I had, I've been trying to get this perfect shot for hours. Supposed to be a beautiful day. Gorgeous. A day of all days, a showcase of spectacular beauty. Up in the mountains on a hilltop. But we got there and the conditions were less than ideal. The wind was blowing crazy, the sun would show up intermittently, teasing us with its beauty and then disappear behind a wave of rolling clouds that never seemed to end. We got a few shots, then moved, got a few more shots, then moved, and when it all seemed like it was going to fall apart, when it all seemed lost, I had a brilliant idea." His arms flailed as he talked, gesturing here and there, bags still in his arms, camera slung over his shoulder, eyes wild, voice entirely too loud. "There was this spot that we stumbled upon. This wilderness within the wilderness, this open plain. And I told the girls to go play. To get dirty and messy. To have fun with the day. And we took shot after shot of this. The joy on their faces, Julien. You have to see it. It came out amazing." He dropped his bags on the couch next to me, nodding at me dismissively, and pulled out his laptop. He marched over to Julian, gesturing him to sit next to him at the dining room table, then started clicking through images.

I watched them from the couch. Never taking my eyes off my boyfriend's face, watching him as he lit up, looking back and forth from the images on the screen to his best friend. There was such love there, dosed in a deep admiration. And I'd decided then and there that I'd have to make myself also love

Curtis. I dragged my eyes from my man and forced myself to take in all of Curtis. He was a decent-looking guy, I ascertained. Bright eyed and full of energy. He had great posture and he spoke... with ferocity? That was pretty much all I could tell about the guy, by looks alone.

I have often thought back to this moment, to this day when I'd met the man who would cause me to stray from my Julien. And I remember feeling so underwhelmed by him. He seemed so full of self-importance. My life is so much more important than yours. I am doing things that most mortals only dream of. I am a buzzing bee. Busy, busy, busy. But he also seemed so fucking lonely. Who was he without Julien to worship the ground he walked on? I'd wondered. But then again, I could ask myself the same question. Perhaps it was this thread, this commonality, that drew me to him and him to me. This underlying sense of nothingness. This fear that maybe neither of us are anything without Julien's belief in us.

"AK," Julien had suddenly called out to me, jarring me from my reverie, "Come and see these photos, they are epic and crazy and beautifully unreal."

And I had slowly forced myself up from the couch, I had slowly wandered over to them, I had slowly extended my hand and introduced myself to this person intruding on my moment with my Julien. And he had grabbed my hand sternly, and caught my eyes with his, and said in the same deep voice that I'm sure was meant to cause some sort of stirrings deep in the pit of my belly, and I hate to admit it, but it did.

"So, this is the Princess Adrienne."

CHAPTER SIXTY-FIVE

My sister barges into her own home three days after we've moved in. Her smile dances on her face so effervescent with her arms loaded with gifts for my children. I bite my tongue to prevent myself from admonishing her. I want to tell her to stop spoiling them with things. They have enough belongings, and on top of that they have more than enough things to last a lifetime. All they had was things at one point. What they need now is time and love and compassion, not more things.

But I say not a word. I need her after all.

I've finished Ms. Ida's book and it's taken me on a quest for more knowledge. I have been reading voraciously ever since, trying to find the words to help form the person I am creating myself to be. I spent an afternoon discussing the book with Ms. Ida and she gave me the keys to her van with the promise that we would spend afternoons discussing books once a week and that I would help her with getting her grand-kids as needed. I am mobile now. It's ironic, I guess, because I'm driving the exact kind of vehicle that I'd sworn I'd never

ever own, and yet it brings me so much joy every time I step into it.

Instead of confronting my sister, I slink away to my bedroom. Away from the squeals of my children, away from the cell phone that has still yet to ring with one single Moms for Sale inquiry. Away. I crawl into my bed with my journal and my purple pen, and I write out my dreams.

When the noise emanating from the living room subsides, I slink out of my room and send the kids to bed before pouring myself and my sister an overly generous glass of whiskey and curl up on the couch next to her. She clinks her glass to mine, and I kiss her cheek like that's what we always do. She looks at me a bit confused, but then decides to simply shrug at me. I pause as I take her in. This is my sister in all her glory. She sold me out to the feds, and now she's taking me and in. Life is so... strange. I watch her as she stares at the dancing flames in her fireplace. Our relationship is so wonky. Stretched this way and then that. Pulled in too many directions. But perhaps that's how we grow. You stretch until you form a new shape. I wonder what new form our relationship will take on now, then I wonder what my sister wants too.

She turns her head to me, a grin dancing on her lips.

I listen to her tell me about her long week. One flight after another. Houston, Atlanta, Paris, Miami, L.A., Hawaii. One after another. Bam. Bam. Bam. Bam. Bam. No thank you, ma'am. I catch myself as I begin to envy her ability to be so free. To get on a plane and wind up in a place day after day, and for such short periods of time. A one-night stand in Atlanta. A night of dancing in France. A wild night of partying in L.A. And yet and yet and yet, feeling like something is missing.

She looks at me. I ask her about the football player, and a smile spreads wide across her face.

"I like him," she says.

"And the guy in Atlanta..." I ask, raising my eyebrows at her, while trying not to sound judgmental. I mean, after all, who am I to judge?

"That was just fun, Adrienne. Something to do," her voice drifts off into a dreamy tone as she picks up her phone and starts scrolling, "He was so fine," she says, gazing at an image before shoving her phone in my face. And she's not wrong. His skin is a deep, deep chocolate with eyes that pierce and a smile that says, "I will break your entire heart, but you will surely enjoy the ride." The perfect guy for a one-night stand, but not good for much else.

I nod at her, "He is a handsome piece of man-meat. But if you're trying to make this thing with football player boy work, then you have to stop doing things like him."

She pulls the phone back and places it slowly on the coffee table. "When we get there, I'll be ready to be serious, but I don't know. He feels so constricting, so restricting, and I'm not sure I'm ready to answer to anybody just yet. I'm not sure I ever will be. He feels like a nice house that you would drive by and go, wow, that's a gorgeous home, I bet whoever lives there has a fabulous life, but this isn't the kind of place I think I would ever want to be. Like if you lived there, you'd have to change and be some other person. Someone who held Tupperware parties and cut the crusts off of cucumber sandwiches in order to save calories. I'm not sure I'm that kind of girl or that I ever can be."

I furrow my brow at my sister, confused. "Is that what he's asking you to do, or are you making that all up in your head?" I ask, "Look, if he's not actually what you want, if he's trying to change you and twist you into being someone else that you don't want to be, then don't waste your time, okay? You are perfect as you are, and you deserve someone who will see the best in you. But if you're really not sure, give the man a chance. Ask some questions. What kind of life does he dream of? What kind of path does he want to lead? What kind of thoughts does he think on? What kind of place does he want to be? Ask him. And listen, really listen to his answers. You'll know what to do then." I catch her eyes, they're big and brown and dazzling, even with the tears dancing in the corner of them, and I hate her just a little bit, but I love her a little bit more. "If he's really worth it, you'll know. It will be so crystally clear apparent to you, that you won't be able to keep yourself away from him if you tried to. The trick is, though, Camille, when you know, you have to follow through. Give 110%, go all in, love recklessly and like it will never end. And don't fuck it up with one-night stands with a dude who probably won't remember your name the next day." I wink at her. "Don't be like your big sister. Be better, because you are. Be stronger, because you are. Be braver, because you are. But always be you. And I bet you, that man won't stand a chance."

She grins at me, wiping at her eyes carelessly, unashamed of her tears. I want to hug her, so I push aside my reluctancy and wrap my arms around my sister. Another crack in the wall between us. I lean back and grin at her.

"And now that I've solved all your romantic ills, I need you to help me," I say, grinning mischievously.

She rolls her eyes at me, takes a swig of her whiskey, and leans against the back of the couch, waiting me for me. Ready. I think I'm ready too.

CHAPTER SIXTY-SIX

The first person to become a part of the Adrienne McQueen team was a mousy brunette named Jill, who was always full of way too much energy. She'd snuck up on me one day when back in college while I was sketching on the lion behind the school's library and scared the shit out of me. No one before had ever bothered me there. Honestly, I didn't think anyone ever really noticed me there. That is, until Jill. She had apparently walked up on me while I was drawing intensely.

"Excuse me," she'd said softly.

I'd almost fallen off my lion, I was so shaken by her sudden appearance. My sketches had gone flying and I'd clutched onto the lion for dear life, narrowly preventing myself from cracking my head open on the pavement below me. I'd caught my breath, righted myself and stared daggers down at her. But she hadn't looked up to even notice my glare. Instead, she was picking up my scattered sketches, eyeing each with a critical gaze. When she'd picked up my sketch of Julien, she'd looked up at me.

"It's the only shoe you've done, at least in the one's that I've seen, but... it's stunning" She slides the rest of the images back to me but holds on to my sketch of the Julien. "It practically jumps off the page," she continues.

"You really think so?" I'd asked, neatly arranging the sketches she'd returned to me. Most of them were of skirts, dresses, and coats. I'd had a desire to make things that were dramatic but practical, unlike many of my classmates who, based on their work thus far, desired to make the least wearable "clothes" possible.

I slid off the lion and walked over to the girl admiring my sketch. I glanced at the image in her hand. It was my most recent sketch of the shoe named after the man who inspired it. It had a wide, high heel, straps that crisscrossed in the front and a wide toe base yet was still sexy. At least that's what I'd hoped. After all, this was my attempt at making shoes somewhat comfortable. So many women suffer in silence, developing ugly bunions on their feet after years of wearing nothing but heels. I flat out refused to participate in this trend of torture, choosing instead to live my life comfortably in flats, sneakers, or sandals, depending on the weather. Comfortable and adorable shoes placed no limits on my ability to be me.

Or so I'd thought, until I laid eyes on Julien. He made me want to drape myself in diamonds and lingerie and dance for him in high heels with a feather boa and satin gloves. He made me want to wear skin-tight jeans and a tank-top and heels and serve him beer on a platter. He made me want to do a striptease then drop to my knees and take him in my mouth. He made me want to love him all the days in all the ways and ride him for hours on end. He made me want to wrap my arms around him every time I heard his voice. I was so thoroughly intoxicated in a way I had never been before.

It had been weeks since the end of the class, but even though we no longer had any classes together he suddenly seemed like Visa, everywhere I wanted to be. I ran into him in the cafeteria and while sitting on the quad. I ran into him while walking across campus, humming songs along to the blaring music on my iPod. And every single time he would catch my eye with the same grin splattered on his face, mockingly.

I found myself telling this girl everything as I'd grazed the sketches laid out before me with the tips of my fingers. I'd blinked at myself as I'd finished describing how badly I wanted trace the line of his face, forcing myself to wake up out of a Julien-fueled trance. I wanted so badly for her to understand me. I'd glanced over at her cautiously, hoping she wasn't judging me, but luckily, she was simply smiling at me with a knowing gaze. She had been there before too.

"You start building them yet?" she'd asked, her voice filled up with entirely too much energy.

"Nah," I shook my head as I spoke, "This is a new area for me. I'm not exactly sure how to proceed with making a shoe." I'd darted my eyes at her. "Why?" I'd asked cautiously, wary.

She'd grinned even wider. "I think I might know someone who can help."

"Who?" I'd asked, my blood suddenly thumping hard against my ears

"His name is Gabe," she'd said, a wide grin on her face, "and he's a goddamned genius."

CHAPTER SIXTY-SEVEN

I'm not there when Camille shows up to the kids bake sale dressed fabulously and wearing six-inch stilettos, but from the story she and the kids have told me, I have created the following imaginary scenario:

Camille, Travis, TiTi, Darrius, and Parris all march into the kids' ridiculously overpriced school, each of them carrying trays of my mother's famous German-chocolate cupcakes baked from scratch. She smiles her dazzling grin at everyone that glances her way. Someone escorts them to an empty table. She sets the cupcakes up carefully, some on a tiered tray, others on beautiful hand-painted plates that she's gathered from her trips around the world, but before she's able to finish arranging the display, people are accosting her. What kind of cupcakes are these? Did you bake them yourself? To the kids and fathers, she says simply that they are German chocolate cupcakes, a family recipe that she baked herself this afternoon. But with the moms she employs a different strategy. She winks at them, ushers them away from their families with a conspiratorial grin, and tells them her secret. She's a busy woman, travelling the world doesn't leave much time for cupcake baking. So, the cupcakes were baked from scratch, but not by her. She slides them a card mischievously with a wink. Moms for Hire, she says, her secret weapon. And they do more than just bake. She grins at them and seals the deal with a "you didn't hear this from me".

She passed out only ten cards, very selectively.

And the next day, the calls start rolling in.

Some mamas just have questions. What kinds of services do you provide? Will anyone know? How do we keep their secret? I whisper their answers secretively. Everyone wants to feel like they're in on something. Everyone needs help sometimes. Being a mom is several full-time jobs. Sometimes a little help is needed.

We begin booking events. Bake sales, parties, playdate plans, one wants help with planning an event for her girlfriends. Half up front and half at the time of delivery. One after another and soon I have an actual business with actual customers and actual plans.

"Houston," I say, grabbing my sister and twirling her around the kitchen, "we have a liftoff, we have a liftoff." And I think hope is the word with wings that picks us both up and carries us away.

CHAPTER SIXTY-EIGHT

I miss him when I'm sleeping. My bed is big now and so, so, empty. I am a small thing floating in this sea of a bed, reaching out for nobody. He always slept with me; it was a requirement. Sleep with me, let me feel your presence in my dreams, let me dream of you and wake up to you and wrap myself in your essence. My husband always smells like home. His body is the thing that gives life to the energy in my soul. I'd lost sight of that when I'd started keeping secrets from him. I used to stay up late, tossing and turning, dreaming of Curtis instead of him. His arms, his smell, his touch, his skin, and I would roll over and my husband would be there instead.

And I would be disappointed.

How stupid I have been.

Now at night, I reach out for him and feel nothing but the cold space where a body should be. I have taken to crawling in one of the kids' beds when the ache gets too deep. Love. I rotate between the kids' beds so as not to make one feel more needed or adored than any of the others. My twins, my TiTi, my loves.

And it's fabulously intoxicating, but still does not quite fill the ache that has been left in his wake.

How could I have taken advantage of him for so many years? He was always the sun to my moon, the gravity that never ceased in pulling me in. How could I betray him and lie to him and let him take the fall for me? Who was I then? How stupid can one be?

CHAPTER SIXTY-NINE

Julien had found me one day, sitting on the quad, in deep conversation with Jill and Gabe, planning out the mechanics of the shoe dubbed in his name.

"Hey," he'd said, squeezing his body in between me and Gabe, marking his territory like a dog pissing on a hydrant.

"Hey," I'd said, trying to recoil from him in a nice, smiling, kind type of way. He grinned at my failed attempt.

"And you are?" Gabe asked, leaning over to glare at this interruption.

"Hey man," he'd said, only bothering to take his eyes away from me for a fraction of a second, "I'm Julien."

And I will never forget how Gabe's eyes lit up. His gray-blue gaze had sparkled in the sun, and he'd lifted his eyebrows at him.

"Julien?" He'd asked incredulously, "THE Julien?"

"THE Julien?" he'd said, trying to hold in a chuckle, "I guess someone has been talking about me." He eyed me with a curious gaze as I'd melted into what I hoped was an invisible puddle.

Gabe had opened his mouth to say more, but Jill in her infinite female wisdom, grabbed his arm, and pulled him away.

"Hey Julien," she'd interjected, cutting Gabe off before he could start his sentence, "It was so nice to meet you, but Gabe and I have something super important to do."

"Yeah," Gabe said, laughing at me, as I'd avoided his playful gaze, "Something super important to do over there." He bucked his chin in a random direction. "See you Julien."

I glared at his mocking face as he was dragged away. Bastard, I thought as forcefully as I could, hoping the message was transmitted telepathically.

"So," Julien said, forcing me to turn my head to look at him, "Been talking about me? Only good things, I hope?"

I'd hesitated before speaking. This was our first conversation after all, I didn't want him thinking that I was like stalking him or something.

"Um, I may have noticed you in Dr. Ferguson's class." I said shrugging, trying to sound nonchalant, "Your girlfriend surely loved screeching your name."

"She's not my girlfriend," he said, automatically.

"Well, someone should have told her that," I said, raising an eyebrow his way, "And that someone should have been you."

He grinned and threw up his hands. "Hey, I told her. She knew she was on my team."

"A team?" I'd asked, super confused.

"Yeah," he'd said, laughing, "she made my roster. She was Monday and Wednesday and every other Saturday evening."

"Just the evenings?" I'd asked, laughing at him, "Wow. You're an asshole."

He'd just grinned at me.

"And is that why you've decided to approach me? Need a new player on your team?" I'd tried not to, but my entire body had pulled back from him as I'd spoken, and he noticed.

"I don't think so," he'd said, leaning in to close the distance between us, "I don't think that you're a team-playing kind of girl. I think you're the kind of girl you get serious with and go all in on. I've been watching you. And I know that you've been watching me, there's something about you that makes me want to know more."

He'd reached up as if to run his fingers through my hair, but I swatted him away.

"You're right," I'd said, with a bit more bitterness than I'd intended, "I'm not really into dating so, when I do, it has to be something real." The words had come out without any thought, but the truth of them stunned me. "If that's not what you're looking for then you're not looking for a girl like me."

And there it was. I'd drawn the line in the sand. Before we had even known a single thing about one another. Before he'd even held my hand or taken me out on a date or had attempted to kiss me, pressed his lips to my lips and seen if this thing was anything other than a crush. I'd made my demands. And waited to see what position he'd take.

"For you, Adrienne..." he'd said and I'd felt a jolt when my name had rolled off his tongue. I'd thought of a million questions at once. Had he been asking about me? How had he found out my name? I didn't have a guy waiting for me after class screaming it for all the world to hear, I'd been me, quiet and modest and trying not to stare. But those thoughts had prevented me from hearing the rest of what he had to say.

"Huh?" I'd asked, "What?" Shaking the whirlwind of questions out from the forefront of my consciousness.

He'd laughed at me.

"I said, that for you, Adrienne, I'd be willing to try anything."

And that was it. I was his, from that moment on.

CHAPTER SEVENTY

The first time I was alone with Curtis was two days before the wedding. He had just flown into town and arrived two hours before Julien got off work. I was tasked with picking him up from the airport and keeping him busy until Julien arrived. The two best friends had bachelor esque plans for Julien's last night before the wedding. They planned on hitting up a few bars and maybe a strip club or two. Julien had been strictly warned not to stay out too late or drink too much. We were getting married the next day after all.

I was not at all happy with playing babysitter. I couldn't wait for them to leave so I could spend a night home alone decompressing from all the stress of the wedding. Sure, Camille and Bethany had helped out a lot, but it was still my day and even with all the help in the world, the impending date still weighed heavily on me. I loved Julien with the force of a thousand suns, but it still felt like some sort of death to me. Goodbye Ms. McQueen, hello Mrs. Louden, the name change a symbol of a major shift in my identity. Who was I going to be? Would

Adrienne Louden make a name for herself or would she fall flat on her face in a mask of fear and disgrace? It was yet to be known. I was yet to see.

I pulled up to the airport just as Curtis was calling me.

"Where you at?" he'd said, so casually.

And the casualness had bothered me to the core of my soul. Who was he to speak to me as if we were best buddies? I barely knew the guy. But he'd spotted me and hung up before I could say anything. He'd sauntered over to my car, grinning like a Cheshire cat up to no good, and I had done my best not to glare at him. He placed his bag in the trunk of my beat-up Civic and I'd started our drive slowly. The whir of the engine the only sound penetrating the silence.

"So," he'd said, after about ten minutes, "You don't like listening to music?"

I could hear the grin in his voice, a sound that served to further aggravate me.

"Not at the moment," I finally forced myself to say, after several tense seconds had passed, "I just have a lot on my mind and music clouds it." I squeezed the steering wheel as I stared blankly at the path laid out before me. "I just need a bit of silence.

"Pull over," he'd said, noticing an overlook path, jutting off the highway to our right.

And I don't know what came over me, but I simply listened, simply followed his directions. It had felt so right, had come so naturally that the idea of not listening to him had not even occurred to me.

I turned onto the gravelly lane and parked. My hands gripped the steering wheel and I kept staring ahead, into oblivion. Then slowly, gently, he'd pried my hands free. Held my hands in his until I finally gave in and turned to meet his gaze.

When his eyes met mine something broke deep inside of me. Tears sprang from my eyes. A deep well of them that had been building up, apparently, for weeks. I cried silently. And he held my hands, rubbing circles along the backs of them with his thumbs until the tears finally subsided. He found a napkin in my glovebox and dried my eyes and patted my cheeks.

He then caught my gaze, squeezed my hands and said, "I know this is a tough time for you. I can only imagine doing what you and Julien are about to do. And I'm sure it's absolutely terrifying. But you know what? The terrifying part isn't in the now. It's not in this moment, or even in tomorrow when you're going to walk down an aisle and marry the love of your life. It's in the future. It's in the possibility of making a mistake. Of messing this up. Of a potential heartbreak. But that mistake, that heartbreak, that's only a possibility. It hasn't happened, and after seeing you and Julien together, the way his smile lights up his entire face when you walk into a room, Adrienne, I don't think it ever will. What you and Julien have is real." He raised his eyebrows at me and grinned. "And that's all you have to focus on today. Just focus on right now, and maybe," he grinned at me, "tomorrow too. Picture it." he emphasized, his voice resonating in my ears. "Julien, standing at the end of the aisle waiting for you. Grinning that goofy grin of his when he sees you. That's your end goal. That's the only thing to keep in mind right now."

I'd done as he'd asked. I closed my eyes and pictured myself in my elaborate and over-priced dress, walking slowly, my dad holding my arm, guiding me. But it wasn't Julien I had seen standing at the end of the aisle with a dopey look on his face. Instead, to my own horror and disgust, it had been him.

Curtis.

His brown eyes dancing as he grinned back at me. I sucked in a breath, my grip tightening in his, and pursed my lips.

"Breathe," the Curtis in my car whispered in my ear, as the Curtis in my mind mouthed the same word to me.

Breathe.

And I did.

CHAPTER SEVENTY-ONE

I go to see Gabe first.

I don't know why. Maybe it's because Jill seems like such a high mountain to climb. Too much to handle. Too much disappointment to face at this moment in time. Or maybe it has nothing to do with Jill at all. Maybe it's because Gabe always had the uncanny ability to see right through me. To see the truth of me. To see me for who I really was, am, are. And to accept me anyway. Maybe it's because Gabe is the right amount of close and accepting and not to close that I can manage right now. A friend, a member of my family. But not the best friend, not the closest family.

I don't know why I muster the courage to see him first, but I do know this. Gabe knew what I was doing all along.

He saw through all my lies when I'd come in with the check from Camille, when I'd come in with the check from Jeremy, when I'd been lying to Julien and Jill, when I'd asked for his donation to the cause, when I'd borrowed money from Jill. I'd seen it in his eyes. And yet he had written the check, and yet he had not said a word, and yet he'd always been in my corner, and I'm sure he's in my corner still.

As I knock on his door and wait to see his face, I wonder if his proprietary invention contract had been part of the reason why he had never ousted me for all my lies. He was, after all, the reason why my idea for a comfortable shoe actually came to fruition, and as such he has always prospered from the licensing of his revolutionary technology. Making more money than Jill, Julien, or I ever hoped to see. A millionaire in his own right, what was loaning a few thousand to me?

And yet, and always yet, I knew I owed him more than I could ever repay. I knew I owed him more than any dollar amount that has ever existed or ever will be.

I knew the truth.

And it wasn't losing the money that had broken Gabe's heart. It was losing his family.

I'm surprised when he opens the door. The house is more of a mansion than a home, so I had been expecting a servant, a butler, or an assistant of some sort. Not Gabriel Delgado, the millionaire scientist, standing in an oversized doorway looking disheveled and sad. He glances at me with vacant, empty eyes, then stands aside to let me in without saying a word. I force a smile as I walk past him into his sprawling estate, but then freeze when my eyes take in the space and I realize that it's completely empty. He slowly closes the door behind me, and then starts off down a hallway. I scurry after him, mouth agape and we walk through several completely empty spaces. I follow behind his lopsided gait, taking in his wrinkled jeans and greasy hair, wondering what the holy fuck is actually going on here as he leads me into the kitchen where he sits at an island and pours himself a drink. A heaping glass of red wine.

"Adrienne Louden nee McQueen, what pray tell, is the reason for your lovely visit today?" He grins at me with the sloppy grin of someone already drunk at 10am, and leans towards me, pressing his elbows into the counter. "Is it more money?" He asks, half serious and half teasingly.

"No, Gabe," I say, sliding onto a stool across the counter from him and catching his eye, "You paid me a favor a long time ago and I'm here to pay you back."

I slide a check across the table towards him for two thousand dollars and when he spots it, he begins to laugh.

"I loaned you ten times that amount, Adrienne," he says, through his harsh, bitter chuckle, "Besides, look around you," he gestures around him at the empty, hollow halls and walls, but I keep my eyes trained on his face.

"I bought this house for 22 mil, Adrienne, paid it off in cash, cash!" He looks down at my check with a sneer, then pounds his fist against the countertop next to my measly check, "I wipe my ass with two-thousand dollars each and every day. Hell, this fucking bottle of wine is worth more than that check."

He takes a long swig of his expensive wine, as if to emphasize his point, then swallows hard as he slams the bottle back on the counter. But then he catches my eyes, and I watch as he relaxes a bit. He closes his eyes and rubs a hand over his face before he speaks again.

"I appreciate the gesture, Adrienne, truly I do. I know all that you've been through, and I know that it can't have been easy, even although you deserved every last thing that came to you." He looks down at his hands, staring at his palms as if there is some secret written there somewhere. Perhaps there is. I say nothing and wait to find out what his hands are telling him.

"Consider your debt repaid," he says, picking up the check slowly and ripping it in half, then in half, then in half again, before dropping the pieces on the countertop and watching them fall like confetti.

I nod at him, then stand up to leave, but something prevents me from walking away.

"Gabe?" I ask, tentatively, as if to not scare him away, "what happened to you?"

He opens his mouth as if to speak, closes it, then opens it again, closes it, and shakes his head.

"You don't have to tell me," I say, in a voice barely above a whisper, "but, listen, if you ever need someone to talk to, I'm the last person in this world who would ever judge you."

I stand for a full 30 seconds, before I am convinced that he will not confide in me, but as I turn to leave, he slams his fists on the table, then begins to speak.

"You remember Rebecca, my girlfriend?"

A vague image of a skinny redhead whose hands were constantly roving all over Gabe's bodyflitsacrossmymind, and I nod at him.

"Well, I asked her to marry me, you know that, Adrienne?"

I shake my head at him.

He continues with a slight nod, "Of course you don't. You were dealing with your own bullshit." He turns from me, looks out his kitchen window and my eyes follow his, tracing the outline of city spread out beyond his expansive yard.

"That woman, she did things to me," he says in a low voice, "She made me feel like no one ever has made me feel. Like I could do anything." He sighs, pausing briefly before continuing. "I never wanted to let her go. And after the whole thing with the company, DiDi... I just needed a win, you know? So, I asked her to marry me."

He takes a long swig of his wine, then goes silent for a long time.

"And what happened?" I ask, slowly, when it seems like he is not going to continue on his own.

He clears his throat, finishes his glass of wine and finally says, "Two weeks before the wedding I'd found her fucking some random fucking UPS guy. Turns out that guy was the real boyfriend, I had been just a mark. She was going to marry me just to divorce me, because even with the prenup, she would walk away with almost a half a million dollars." He scoffs. "I have lived here ever since, all alone, in this empty shell of a house, and I spend my days doing exactly this." He begins to refill his glass. "Let me wallow, DiDi, just for a little bit, I promise I'll get out of this shit soon. Just leave me here, let me be, let me wallow in all the tragedy that has befallen me." He raises his glass up into the air, toasting no one.

I walk over to him and place my hand over his glass before he can take a sip. He glowers at me.

"I think you've wallowed enough," I say, easing onto the stool next to him so I can look him directly in the eye.

"Come work with me. I could use a brain like you, and you can use an excuse to get the fuck out of this sad mausoleum, commemorating nothing. Come work with me, get out of this funk, and when you're back to being the fucking genius that I know and love, then and only then, will I consider this debt repaid, you hear me?"

He licks his lips, squares his jaw, then nods at me slowly.

"Understood."

CHAPTER SEVENTY-TWO

My days have started to get full now, busy. Not that they weren't busy before. What with the farm and the kids and making amends and such. But now they are a different kind of busy, a logistical nightmare. I spend each night planning out the next day while standing at the island in my sister's kitchen, sipping a glass of wine. I used to do this exact same thing with my husband. Every now and again I catch myself glancing over at the fridge as if I'd see him there, bent over, ruffling through the fridge. It's as if I can see him standing up with a container of leftovers in hand, flipping off the lid carelessly, and inhaling it over-dramatically.

"Mmmmm," he'd say, "lasagna," and then wave the food under my nose as if the cold leftover lasagna could beckon.

He'd pull out a fork and dig in, eating the food cold as often as he could get away with it, forcing me to take a bite or two.

We had stopped having these planning sessions right around the time I'd started keeping things from him. I'd begun planning obsessively, all day, maneuvering this and that, my mind trying to make the best decisions, the right decisions, the decisions of our lives.

I miss him.

I put the pen down and walk over to the fridge. I run my hands along its stainless-steel face, then pull open one of the doors, and survey its contents. Camille doesn't have a cook like we did, but when she's home, she cooks, and I've been cooking almost every night for the kids, so the fridge is filled with leftovers. I survey each container one by one. Spaghetti (me), salmon and asparagus (Camille), meatloaf (me), baked chicken and roasted veggies (also me), clam chowder (Camille), and when I open the container filled with soup, my heart does a little flutter. I nuke the container (not quite down for the cold leftover vibe) and ease onto a stool and scoot it up against the island. I close my eyes as I take my first mouthful.

"Good?" Camille says, walking into the room and making me jump halfway out of my seat.

I swallow hard before speaking.

"Holy shit, Camille, I thought you were coming home tomorrow," I say finally.

She grins at me, sliding her shoes off her feet before slinking past me to the utensil drawer. She pulls out a spoon, then climbs onto the stool next to me.

"Hey, sis," she says, dipping her spoon into the container of soup. She takes a deep whiff of the soup before thrusting it in her mouth. "I've made better," she says, shrugging, but she continues to dive back in for a second and then a third spoonful.

That's all I let her have before I slowly pull the container away from her.

"Did I say I was sharing?" I ask, a smile dancing on my lips, "There's plenty of other leftovers in the fridge, this soup is mine."

"Come on, DiDi," she whines, sounding like she did when she was nine, "I'm hungry, and you know I can't eat anything super heavy this late, I have to watch my girlish figure." She says with a wink.

"Bullshit," I say, a bit louder than I'd intended, "I call bullshit. You've always been exactly the perfect fucking size ever since we were kids. You couldn't put on weight to save your life."

Camille breathes out of her nose in a huff. "That was then, sis, I can put on five pounds in one weekend in Italy now. That goddamned place with its goddamned bread. Now I have to watch myself much more carefully. I'm not 23 anymore."

And I don't know why, but it's this one simple revelation that breaks down the last remnant of the wall that used to stand tall between us. My perfectly gorgeous sister, watching what she eats? What has the world come to? I shove the container of soup closer to her so she can resume stuffing her face, and I grin at her as I watch her eat.

"Wait 'till you have kids," I say, timing it perfectly so she spits a bit of soup out onto her pristine countertop.

"Kids," she says, baffled as she wipes at her face with the back of her hand, "I'm not sure I'm ready for that, I mean a lot of women get their bodies right back, but... a lot of women don't." Her eyebrows raise in a shocked but also questioning expression. "Is it really as bad as they say it is?"

"Well..." I say, staring up at the ceiling as if the right words to say are plastered up there, just in a tiny font that I'm having trouble discerning, "Pretty much? I mean, unless you're a body builder or a personal trainer, your belly will never be the same."

She looks down at her flat stomach and whimper talks, "Never?"

I shake my head at her, "I mean, a whole human stretches it out for nine months, and it's just supposed to go right back, like nothing ever happened? Not going to happen. I mean, it can, with a lot of hard work, but you'll have a baby then and who really has time to be in the gym all day? I damn sure don't." I take another spoonful of soup into my mouth.

"What about yours," Camille gestures towards her private parts like a small child, then raises her eyebrows at me. "Is that like permanently changed too?"

I sigh at this one. "See this is a topic of contention," I say, gesturing with my spoon, "Some say it goes back to being the same, it was stretched out for only a few hours which is nothing compared to the stomach, others say that it's never ever quite the same."

Camille sits on this for a long moment, before finally speaking. "Well, what do you think, DiDi? You have three kids, did it go back, or is it forever changed?"

I grin, then shrug at her, "I feel like it was modified. Not better or worse, just different. Everything changes when you become a mom, and that's just one of them. Julien always says he likes me better now. After my babies, after my stretch marks, after my saggy belly, my body permanently altered by giving life to his children, it turns him on." I find myself twirling a strand of hair around my finger as I picture my husband coming up behind me, groaning as he sees me standing in the bathroom brushing my teeth in nothing but a pair of panties.

Julien.

Camille nods at me. "So marry the right guy," she says, "and none of it matters. Not the belly or the vagina or the stretchmarks or the saggy titties."

I grin and nod at her.

Precisely.

CHAPTER SEVENTY-THREE

I have less than 45 days before Julien comes home. My heart flutters at the thought. I have been humming carelessly while baking brownies or calling places to organize adult mommy playdates at swanky brunch spots. I have been floating through life. When my phone rings I think nothing of it.

"MFH," I say chipperly, already abbreviating the name of my shiny new company, "This is DiDi speaking, how may I help you?" I've been using my nickname to answer phones in order to distinguish the receptionist version of myself from the version of me that is the owner of a very new and very small company. Not quite sure I'm fooling anyone.

"Adrienne?" a husky, yet high-pitched voice sings into my ear.

I'd know that voice anywhere.

"Jeremy?" I ask, half-laughing, "you ready to join the team?"

"Maybe," he says, voice still hesitant, cautious, wary, "I got your check in the mail," he says, carefully as not to make his voice sound either thankful or surprised, just plain, matter-of-fact, nice, "and I heard some bitches gossiping about their new secret weapon, Moms for Hire. One was telling the other how easy it all was and how no one would ever know that you didn't do the work yourself. When they bake stuff for you, the one woman said, they ask you how well you want it to be made, like on a scale of one to ten, one being I've never baked a day in my life, and ten being I've come out the womb making this goddamned recipe." He laughs. "Is that true?"

I laugh at him, "That's what you want to know? Are we willing to fuck up brownies so moms can pass them off as their own?"

"Yeah, pretty much."

"Well, to answer your question, of course we are. We'll fuck them up in whatever precise way you want us to. We can make things too sweet, too salty, burn them, undercook them. You name it, we'll do it, we live to pass our shit off as your shit. Our plans off as your plans. Save you time and energy and effort, all for a few pennies."

There's a long pause, so long in fact that I call out Jeremy's name, wondering if we'd lost our connection.

"Can I come see you guys in action?" he finally says.

"Sure, Jeremy," I say and rattle off the address to Camille's house, "Stop on by whenever you want to, but we're normally most busy between 9 and 3."

"Gotcha," said Jeremy, before he hung up on me.

CHAPTER SEVENTY-FOUR

I don't know why, but besides Bethany Brown, Jill is the last person I muster up the courage to see. I don't have her money yet (she'd given a substantial amount), but it's more than that. I bite my bottom lip as I drive down her familiar winding street. It is a long, long drive to her house overlooking the bay. I was always jealous of her for picking a place so obscure with its lavish, yet understated beauty. I used to trace my finger along her mahogany banisters, imagining myself as a goddamned queen, waving at my subjects with a delicate twist of my wrist.

"Marry me," I'd said to her, one evening when we'd laid on her couch and binge-watched movies.

I'd placed my head in her lap and looked up at her, sincerely. I'd even grazed her cheek to put the icing on the cake.

"You know you want to, Baby," I'd said, laying it on extra thick.

But she'd looked down at me, and her eyes had caught mine, and she'd stared so deeply, my smile had erased. She had grazed my cheek then, so tenderly, so bemusedly, so appreciatively. And then her face had bent slowly towards mine. She'd kissed me and I'd found myself kissing her back, curiously. She was so soft, so different from my hubby.

When she pulled back, she'd grinned at me.

"If you weren't married," she'd said.

And I'd grinned back at her. I wasn't into girls, but something about her gentle touch had been nice. I could see a future with her if I had never met Julien. It would have been nice. It would have been a great place to exist in this world. I'd grinned up at her and caressed her cheek again before turning back to watch the movie.

"Adrienne," she'd said, in a voice super low and throaty, barely perceptible above the sound of the TV, and yet, I had heard every last word, "I love you," she'd said, and I'd known then, what I know now, that she'd meant it in the same way that I'd meant it when I'd said it to Julien.

"I love you too," I'd said, lightheartedly.

And yet, the moment it'd come out I'd regretted it. Why so light? Why so flippant? Had I said the wrong thing in all the wrong ways?

The thought lingers in my brain as I pull up in front of her sacred space.

Jill. I loved you then, and I love you still, just not in the way that you want, but love you, I always will.

CHAPTER SEVENTY-FIVE

I miss the next two times that Julien calls. I am working, I am busy, I am mom-ing, I am juggling 8,000 things, and I don't hear the phone ring. But now all the world is quiet. The kids are in bed, Camille is out flying the friendly skies, and it's just me, pacing the living room like a caged tiger freshly plucked from the wild. How. Can. I. Get. Out. I stare at my phone, mocking me on the coffee table as it dares not to ring. Who the fuck does it think it is? How dare it refuse to answer to me? Ring damn you, bring my husband to me.

The screen remains black.

I want to pick it up and throw it at the wall, but it's not my wall to damage and I don't have the money to buy a new phone. I owe too many people too much money to waste a single penny on a new phone because I wrecked a perfectly good one in a moment of frustration.

I pick up the phone and check it, wondering why Julien can't feel me telepathically willing him to call me, when my eyes catch the clock on the wall. It's after hours, lockdown in my husband's penitentiary. He couldn't call me if he wanted to. I wonder what it takes to get a cellphone through the security gates but know we mustn't risk it. Not now when he's so close to being free. Not now, when in no time at all he'll be laying right beside me. Not now.

I place the phone down and back slowly away from it.

I want to hear his voice. I scream at the universe inside my head, and a second later, my phone is ringing. My heart flutters in my chest as I inch closer to it, but it's not Julien whose number I see, but Jill's smiling face looking up at me. I wrinkle my brow at it. She must have gotten the note I'd haphazardly scribbled when she hadn't answered her door. I hesitate before reaching for the phone, not quite ready for the conversation laid out before me but knowing that the conversation must be had anyway. Jill, the one who had stumbled upon me and seen something that no one else had seen in me, seen me for the woman I could be. And I had let her down. I'd been glad she hadn't answered the door when I'd stopped by a few days ago, but now, here it is. Time to face the music.

"Hello," I say, voice a bit trembly as I answer the phone, "Jill?"

But it's not Jill' voice that greets me.

"No," a female-sounding voice says, gruffly before clearing her throat, "I'm not Jill, just watching her place and things until her family comes around to claim them. I saw your letter. I figured you didn't know. I'm calling to clear things up." She clears her throat again. "Jill died about 3 weeks ago."

I gasp. "What happened to her?" I ask, pressing my hand to my chest as I try to wrap my mind around all of this. Her smile flashes across my brain. The feel of her hand in mine flits across my memory.

"She killed herself,"'s he says slowly, "She left a note.'"

"Wow," I say, reaching for a chair to collapse in, "Seriously?" I imagine her alone and lonely, and I wonder if there was something I could have done. I've been on this path of reconciliation, why had I waited so long to reach out to her? If I had only said something, reached out to her sooner, done... something.

"Adrienne," she says, after a long pause, "she left something for you. If you want it, I can meet you over at the playground over on 13th street. It's kind of... important. She has something she would like for you to do."

I nod my head, then realizing she can't see that; I clear my throat and agree to meet her immediately. After all, who am I to refuse the last wishes of my dead best friend.

I hang up the phone and a wave of nausea suddenly overcomes me. I barely make it to the sink before the entire contents of my stomach come ripping out of me in violent waves. Over and over until there's nothing left, and yet my body won't stop reaching, reaching for more. More to expel. More to release. More. I dry heave until tears start flowing freely down my cheeks, and I finally stop clenching onto the sink and finally let go. I collapse onto the floor and curl into a tight ball and cry until I run out of tears. And then I just lay there. Spent. Empty. Blinking up at the ceiling.

I hear a voice in my head. Her voice. Soft and gentle, and yet firm.

"Get up, Didi. You have shit to do."

I want to tell her no. I want to tell her to go fuck herself. I want to ask her how dare she lecture me on getting shit done when she just gave up completely. I want to lay on the floor forever and melt into the stone tiles and be walked all over for all eternity. I want to admit failure and defeat.

Butinstead I find myself standing slowly and pulling on my

skippy sneakers. Instead, I find myself clutching the steering wheel tightly and steering it towards the playground on 13th street. Instead, I find myself continuing to go, move, think, be, search for the answers, and simply breathe. Instead, I continue. Because Jill is right. Jill is always right.

I got shit to do.

CHAPTER SEVENTY-SIX

When I was a little girl, my daddy woke me and Camille up really early one morning. He gathered us together and whispered to us that he was taking us on an adventure. We got dressed really quickly, our little stick arms quivering with excited energy, and clamored in the backseat of his Cadillac. My daddy loved to play music from his heyday, still does. Crooning Motown tunes and the early echoes of hip-hop. I remember his deep baritone so distinctly, crooning to Papa was a Rolling Stone, arm bent so the elbow was hanging out the window, breeze rustling through his plaid button-up shirt, vibrating a clear unending joy. I wanted to be him when I grew up. I want to be him still.

On this day he drove for what felt like a very long time to two small, little girls. We started off feeling excited, so excited, jittery with energy. We would catch each other's eyes and grin. Something good was coming and we could feel it. A day to remember.

And it was.

As the minutes turned to hours and my daddy reached for a

new tape to play, Camille and I found ourselves drifting off to sleep. Camille started dozing first. Her eyes blinking ever more slowly until she'd finally leaned her head against my shoulder and allowed the sleep to take over. I had sat there for a few minutes, staring out the window, listening to the slow, deep, cadence of my father's voice, until I'd finally drifted off to sleep.

There's something about a car coming to a stop that makes you wake. I'd awoken to the smell of salt and the soft melodious sound of waves rising and falling, crashing and receding, pushing and pulling back. My daddy was no longer in his place in the front seat, Camille was stirring next to me, she'd grinned as the sounds and smells and sights all came washing over her. The beach. I'd eased open the door and we'd climbed out of the car, hesitant, searching for our daddy. We were in a small unkempt parking lot without guidelines for parking and ours was the only car in the lot. I'd closed the car door and we'd walked around the car to where the pavement met the beach and stared out at the wide expanse of white, white, sand laid out before us, and there he was. Out there, swim trunks on, shirtless, standing right out on the edge where the water met the shore, the waves just barely washing over his toes, staring out at the majestic expanse of ocean laid before him.

I'd stopped Camille from running out to him by instructing her to take off her shoes first. We took our cheap Keds off swiftly and left them right there, lined up neatly on the edge of the pavement, a sock tucked in each shoe. Camille had taken off then, running, her hair blowing in the wind behind her. But I'd savored every single moment. I'd stepped out cautiously onto the sand, expecting it to be scalding hot, but it wasn't. It was a deep warmth that made me feel safe and cared for and loved. It made me feel like dancing, so I did. I danced a dance that came from deep within my belly, spreading out to every inch of me, careless and carefree, headed for Camille and my daddy. By the time I'd gotten there I was breathless, shiny, eyes a glow with energy.

"Daddy!" I'd said, and I'd given him a hug around his waist, pressed my chin to his belly, and stared up at him expectantly.

As a mom now, I know that 90% of the things that parents do with kids have been planned out thoroughly, and yet often wind up being epic failures. But this moment on the beach with my dad was not one of those 90% moments. It was not something that was planned, but something that my father had been called to. It was not a family moment that he was trying to force or create or cultivate, but something that he had been propelled to do in that moment.

He had looked down at me, kissed my forehead, and grinned at me, then gestured with his head towards a duffel bag that I hadn't noticed lying off away from the ocean in a pile of sand.

"Lovebug," he'd said, "your swimsuits are in that bag, you and your sister should get into the water, it's the perfect temperature."

I gave him a hug before running off to get changed in the car.

We spent the day at the beach. Swimming, playing, lounging, attempting to glide on a boogie board, only leaving for a brief half-hour period to go and pick up an extra-large cheese pizza, breadsticks, wings, and an ice cold 2-liter of Coke. He let us sit on a blanket on the hood of his car while we ate, silently, and filled with joy. As the sun started to set, we'd sat together on the blanket in the middle of the beach and watched it. Camille's head rested on my shoulder, my head rested on Daddy's, his big arm wrapped around us both. Camille had wound her hand into mine, and my dad had kissed my forehead, and I drank in every last moment, knowing it would soon come to an end. That my daddy would soon state that it was time to go. That we would soon gather up our belongings, get changed in the backseat of the car, fall asleep on the long drive home, and wake up covered in our everyday reality.

"Can we stay here forever, Daddy?" I'd asked.

He'd hesitated before answering. "No Lovebug," he'd said finally, his voice sounding a million miles away. "It wouldn't be special anymore. Then it'd just be ordinary."

And 'till this day I do believe that that was one of the most profound things that he has ever said.

On the ride back home, Camille and I changed back into our original clothes, just the same as before except doused in sea water with sand caked between our toes. Camille had curled up in my lap, and I had automatically started stroking her hair, mimicking the way that mama used to stroke mine.

Mama.

I wondered if the lovely trip had had anything to do with her, had opened my mouth to ask the question, but something inside me silenced my tongue, so I'd closed my mouth, leaned my head against the door and watched the scenery go by, taking in each building and tree and traffic light. Eventually I'd fallen asleep, only to be awoken, once again when the car had come to a stop. This time, when I'd opened my eyes, my father had still been there, hands on the wheels, shoulders slumped, breath coming in harsh and raspy, but low, so low, my ears had strained to hear the sound at all.

After several moments, he'd pushed his shoulders back, taken in a deep breath, and reached behind his chair to shake us out of our slumber, not realizing that I was already awake. That I had already seen him before he'd put on his "Daddy" face.

"Girls," he'd said, his voice gruff and flat, bending down to get to our eye level as we'd stepped out of the car, rubbing the sleep from our eyes, "when we get inside, I want you to go straight to your rooms and straight to bed, do you hear me? Straight to your rooms and straight to bed."

He'd caught each of our eyes with a firm gaze and waited until we nodded in agreement before nodding back.

"Okay," he'd said straightening up before slowly walking over to unlock the door.

But the door was unlocked. The first sign that something in the house was terribly, terribly wrong. Mama never left the door unlocked; she was paranoid about such things. Would always be reminding us, checking behind us. Lock, twist, pull. Lock, twist, pull, pull.

We followed closely behind Daddy as we entered the house, my sister clutching at my arm, her warm breath dancing on the back of my neck, both of us halfway expecting something or someone to come jumping out at us.

And then we'd seen her: Mama. Curled up on the couch, wrapped up in a blanket like a burrito, rocking back and forth, a low, animalistic broken sound emitting from her. This is the scene daddy had been trying to protect us from, shield us from, had taken us to the beach to hide us away from. Spend a day in joy instead of a day in sorrow- rational. I remembered his words then, and before he could bark at us, I'd grabbed Camille's hand and guided her up the stairs and down the hall to where our two bedrooms remained, just as we'd left them, side by side. I'd slid into my room without saying goodnight, suddenly in a rush to curl up in my bed. The sand between my toes suddenly felt uncomfortable, unwelcome, unwanted, so I'd swiped at my feet with a clean pair of socks before sliding a nightgown over my head and crawling into bed. I'd lain there for all of two seconds before the questions had started to parade across my forehead: Is she okay? Is she crazy? Did something happen to her? Would she ever be the same? What if she never is the same? What then?

My door had creaked open, and Camille had wandered in, wearing her nightgown and dragging her favorite stuffed pig.

"Didi?" she'd asked, standing in the doorway, "Can I come sleep with you?"

And I had simply pulled back my sheets, not saying a word at all, and she had climbed into my bed and we had held hands, in an intertwined web, facing each other, breathing each other's air as we drifted slowly, slowly, off to sleep.

I asked my daddy about this day once, years later, when I had grown and had my own kids and dreamt of taking them there. It had been so quiet, so secluded, such a wonderful day, and I'd wondered if I could replicate such a moment in time. Not copy him exactly, but make my own good memories. But my dad had pretended like he didn't know what I was talking about. Had sat there and stared at me, almost unblinkingly, daring me to pursue this conversation further. A conversation neither my sister nor I had ever dared to speak of since, out of fear that the magic from the day would be gone, disappear into thin air, be replaced by nothingness. And so, I'd backed away from the subject, shifted the conversation, and never broached the topic again.

I guess I'll have to find my own beach. I guess I'll have to make my own memories.

CHAPTER SEVENTY-SEVEN

When my thoughts wander while cutting off the crusts of the twin's sandwiches, I imagine what Julien's days look like. I place myself in his body, picture myself standing in his shoes, shuffling across a dingy cafeteria floor, head down, doing his best to try not to stand out. Dulling his edges. Muting his shine. I imagine him spending his days in the library, reading, learning something new, escaping to another world. I imagine him playing chess or basketball or jogging around in a circle. I imagine him lying in a creaky bed with a thin mattress below some bald guy who snores, wishing he could stare up at the moon. Wishing he could hold me in his arms.

When I ask him about it, I say something like, "What's it like for you in there?"

When he answers me, he says something like, "Fine, I mean, it's whatever."

I wonder if he'll tell me the truth when he can stop daydreaming about me and actually hold me in his arms. I wonder if there are just some things I may never know. I'm pretty sure that even if he tells me, there will always be this space, this place, this lack of knowing between us that wasn't there before. And I know that it will always be my fault.

CHAPTER SEVENTY-EIGHT

When I arrive at the park, the woman is already there. She is a broad woman with a wide frame squeezed onto a swing. I realize, as I walk up to her, that I never even got her name.

"Are you waiting for me?" I ask, as her gaze meets mine, "My name's Adrienne."

CHAPTER SEVENTY-NINE

"Adrienne," Jill startles me from my sleep by screaming in my ear. I'd glared daggers at her through my sleep crusted eyes, and whined about how she had ruined a perfect dream where I had been riding a unicorn through the clouds while the sky rained glittery raindrops all around.

"It was a good dream," I'd said, turning away from her and rolling into a ball.

"I have a surprise for you," she'd said, her voice dripping in enthusiasm.

"Do you?" I'd said after a long pause, turning towards her slowly, and peering at her from one half-open eye.

She'd simply grinned and nodded, bouncing on her toes, flat out ignoring my irritation.

"Get up," she'd said exasperated with me.

I'd glanced over at the clock on my nightstand, blinking until my eyes focused on the time displayed there.

"It's 5:15, no self-respecting college student would show up and wake up another self-respecting college student at 5:15 in the morning. Which leaves me to believe that you are not Jill at all, but some sort of android sent to replace her, kill me when I'm least suspecting, and run off with my shoe designs." I'd clutched Jill and pulled her close to me, staring her in the eyes intensely.

"Are you a human being?" I'd asked, and she'd giggled at me.

She'd grabbed a pillow and thrown it at me, "I'm a person," she'd said in a robot voice, while laughing, "Now can we get a move on, please, I want to show you something that's a bit time sensitive. So... get your stinky butt up."

I'd groaned and fallen back against the bed, arms outstretched, then shuddered all over as if hit with a taser.

"Oh my god, Miss Melodrama," she'd thrown the pillow at me again, "Be ready in five minutes or I'm leaving your ass and you'll never see me again." She'd tried to make her voice sound harsh, serious, final, but all she'd actually managed was to sound a bit like a small child whining to her mommy about getting a lolli.

I'd sighed, then obediently hoisted myself out of bed, thrown on my day-old clothes from yesterday, then marched out to the living room where Jill was waiting impatiently.

"This better be worth it," I'd said as she'd grabbed my hand and dragged me from the dormitory.

She didn't really say much, just entwined her fingers in mine and lead me to the college shuttle.

Jill pushed me on board first as if to insure I wasn't going to run off at the last minute. I'd stumbled onto the bus, catching myself just before I'd fallen headfirst into the crotch of the bus driver, a young man who I instantly recognized as one of Jill's business class buddies. I was sure they'd all make rich and successful men when they graduated, but until then, they were painfully awkward and frankly a bit uncomfortable to be around. At least that's how I'd felt.

Jill bounded onto the bus, shouting the bus driver's name and giving him a fist-bump. The bus driver, a very clean-cut, looking Asian boy, named James, apparently, welcomed her with a silly grin on his face.

"Can you take us to the spot?" she'd asked.

"Course, Jill, anytime," he'd said, closing the door and signaling before pulling the bus away from the curb, "And you know, very rarely do I get anyone looking for a ride this early so... maybe I can hang with you guys for a bit?"

Jill and I both shook our heads simultaneously. I started to wrack my brain for a suitable reason for him not to go, but Jill beat me to the punch.

"That's not true, James, you just told me, what was that, like 2, 3 weeks ago, that you picked up some crying, distraught freshman, around this time? You never know who may need you. Don't undermine what you do," she'd said, sincerely, "Besides, this here is my best friend in the whole world, and I have something special I want to share with her. So maybe we can hang next time, okay?"

"Okay," he'd said, sounding a bit deflated.

I elbowed Jill playfully, then leaned down to whisper in her ear, "I think James wants you, baby."

"Yeah," she'd said shrugging, "I know. We hooked up a few times."

I'd leaned away from her then.

"But I thought you were..." I'd let my voice trail off into oblivion.

She chuckled at me and finished my incomplete thought, "Strictly pussy?" she'd whispered, one eyebrow raised.

I'd hesitated before answering, then shrugged and nodded at her. "Yeah, pretty much," I'd said, with a nod, "those are the only people I ever see you ogling."

"Yeah, well, I am, mostly, but not always. Why you trying to put me in a box, DiDi?" she'd said playfully.

And it's only then that I noticed that Jill was a bit off that morning. She'd been a bit fuzzy around the edges. A bit too bright eyed and bushy tailed for the hour of the day. And I instantly switched to super protective, gentle DiDi and slide my hand into hers before resting my head on her shoulder. I wanted to ask her what happened. I wanted to give her a hug and beg her to tell me. I wanted to kiss her cheek and remind her that she could trust me with any and everything. But I screamed at myself in my head, forcing my lips to stay closed. To let the chips fall as they may. To hear her out when she was ready to talk to me.

James dropped us off at the park and I followed her as she wound up a curvy hill until we reached the peak. She plopped down in the grass, and I slowly did the same. She pointed at the rising sun, and I grinned. The sunrise is always a marvel to behold, and it has always been so rare for me to take the time to relish its beauty. I stared in awe at it, and I mentally bowed down before its glory, so immersed that it had taken a few minutes for me to realize that Jill was crying.

She cried silently, her body shaking gently with each wave of sobs. My heart broke at the sight. I quickly shifted so that I was facing her, then leaned forward and pressed my forehead to hers, telling her without saying a word that I was there for her in whichever way she needed me to be.

It took a few minutes, but Jill eventually calmed down. She eased her face into the curve of my neck and breathed slowly until her body stopped shuddering and her breathing became rhythmic and steady.

"It's my grandmother," she finally said, "She passed away last night."

Realization flooded over me. The bags under her eyes, the trip to her spot. This was how Jill asked for help.

"Jill," I'd said, rubbing her head softly, "I got you." And I could feel the soft smile stretching out and spreading through her body as she collapsed further into me.

CHAPTER EIGHTY

When the woman on the swings looks up at me, I see that she has eyes as bright as the Caribbean Sea. She's a tall lady with an oversized frame, with her long hair pulled back into a low ponytail, and a face that looks like it's accustomed to smiling big and wide and bright. Her entire energy feels full of joy. I wonder if Christmas is her favorite holiday and have to actually bite my tongue to force myself not to ask.

She gestures towards the swing next to her and I grin as I walk over to it, memories of the nine-year-old version of me flooding back into my mind. In the game of who can swing the highest, I would always win. I was fearless as a child. What happened to me, I wonder as I begin to sway in the swing gently.

I await the woman whose name I never asked, to fill me in on personal details about a former friend of mine who I had considered family before I'd fucked her over and destroyed her life.

She starts speaking slowly, "My name is Margaret," she tells me, turning in her seat to look at me.

"I was Jill's on-again, off-again partner for the past," she breathes out in a whistle, "7 years or so."

"Wait," I say, thrusting out a hand in her direction, palm forward, "How were you Jill's partner and I never heard of you."

She shrugs, "You know how it goes. We would mess around and be serious for a bit, then taper off. We never really got around to deciding anything formally. Never had the exclusivity conversation. Just let it go the way it went. Looking back, I should have said something, I should have done something, I should have found a way to be more open and honest with her, then maybe she would have found a way to be more open and honest with me, and maybe she'd be here with us right now, having a different kind of conversation altogether." She shrugs again, but I can see the strain in her eyes.

"Tell me how it happened," I say.

She clears her throat, and her voice takes on a strained cadence as she begins to speak.

"We hadn't talked in a month, maybe two... she worked so hard sometimes. Really buried herself in her work. Head in the clouds, laser focused. She'd stop answering my calls and texts and I'd just wait for her to come back. To reach out to me. To text me late at night, like, 'Margaret, come and see me.' But instead of that late night text, I got a phone call from the police. Jill was found dead in her home and the note was written out to me. It was four pages long. She apologized for keeping me at such a distance, then the rest were explicit directions for how she wanted me to carry out her last wishes. How she wanted her funeral to proceed, how she wanted her belongings distributed, and how she wanted it to all be managed by me." She taps the box in her lap. "This one is just for you. I tried to get ahold of you, but all Jill's numbers for you weren't working.

Out of Service. None of her other friends knew how to reach you either."

She reaches out, moving the box towards me, propelling me to take it from her. I grab it with both hands, my purple nail polish glinting in the moonlight as I recognize it as a Julien shoe box. I hug the box to my chest and it feels weighty, but I'm well aware that it could all just be in my head.

Margaret nods at me.

"I haven't been able to get in touch with Gabe either," she says, "His numbers work, but his mailbox is full, and he never answers the phone."

"I know how to get in touch with Gabe," I say.

"I had a feeling that you would," she says, and I hand her my phone so she can plug his number in it. She hands it back to me after she's done.

"Should I open it now?" I ask, raising my eyebrows at her, "or is it something... private."

"It might make you cry," she says, then hesitates for a long moment before continuing, "I went through all the boxes she left behind, and yours, yours might make you cry." She stands from the swing slowly, easing her body up and out in one smooth, and graceful movement.

"Make sure you have Gabe call me," she reminds me, with a half-smile as she begins to walk away.

"Is this all?" I ask, trying to quelch the rising tide in my gut, "Isn't there anything else you need to tell me, or that," my voice drops low, to that of a little girl, "you need some help with?"

"Nope," she says, without looking back, "you have all that you need now, and so do I."

I roll my eyes at her cryptic words as I watch her walk away from me. When I see her climb into an old green pickup truck and start the car, I finally look down at the box in my lap. I take a deep breath and decide to face my future and my past.

Jill is gone. This is all I have left from her. I take a deep breath and prepare to lift the lid off of the shoebox, but then I notice which shoe box this is. It's the box of a red Julien, size 7. Jill's favorite pair that she called her "go get 'em" shoes. A tear manages to snake its way down my cheek and splattered on the box lid as I picture her strutting around the office, with a grin on her face, ideas dancing across her eyes, and the pair of shoes on her feet that used to be housed in this box.

Jill. My Jill.

I take a deep breath and open the box. Insides are only three things. A letter, folded neatly on heavy cardstock paper, a framed photograph, and a Ziplock bag full of what appear to be ashes. I assume the ashes are Jill's remains, so I look at the other two items and grab the letter first. I open it slowly. I read the letter: once, twice, three times. Hoping to let the words wash over me. And then I cry, just like Margaret said I would.

Here's what the letter said:

Didi,

You weren't the greatest friend in the world, but, man, did you have your moments. Remember when we stole that street sign off of 5th? Or when we stayed up all night watching scary movies and slept in a pile on the floor all day, missing all of our classes? I often wake up smiling after reliving those memories. Remember when we started a company and you betrayed me? I often wake up crying when I dream about that. But that's not what this is about. This isn't some sort of blame game where I sit around blaming all the people that I have loved and who have loved me for what I have decided to do. No. The first thing I want to say, Adrienne, my bestest best friend, is that this is not your fault. I have struggled with depression my whole life, and it has been a hard life for me, but I have lasted as long as I did because I found people like you and Gabe. You two were my island in the middle of the sea. You two were my crew. And I love you to infinity for that.

But no one can save anyone else. I was meant to save myself. But, Didi, the truth is that I no longer want to. I've fought the fight for a good long while, and I'm ready to go back to the place where we all go and come from and belong.

So, don't think me weak for making this decision. The me that I am when you are reading this letter is a me that is eternally happy and free, something that I have struggled every day to find and be.

I think that this is why people have children. They are something tangible to tether them to this life. This life that is so beautiful and horrible all at the same time.

I know that you know what I'm talking about Didi. I know that you have been down for a while and may still be there. At the bottom. At a place that feels alone and alien and empty. But know this, even there I am with you. I am always with you. I am always there.

I have left you with half of my fortune. On the back of the picture frame in this box is a certified check made out to you for whatever is left of half of all the money I have left in this world. Money has always been so important to you. May you use these coins to build something beautiful.

I only have one request. I only have this. That you and Gabe find a way to scatter my ashes somewhere where things are living and being and growing. That you two come together and be the two that once were three. That you and Gabe continue in our family.

I love you. I always have. I always will. I love you still.

Jill

.   .   .

When I stop crying, I pick up the picture frame and stare at it. It contains a photo of me, Jill, and Gabe. It's from our college days. We are arm in arm in arm, grinning up at the lens. So young. So carefree. So much opportunity.

I kiss the glass, right in the middle, right in Jill's grinning face, and know the photo will hang in a prominent place. A place where all can see my best friends and me. My other rocks, my other family. And I send a thank you up to Jill wherever she may be. Thank you, Jill, for blessing me with the many moments that you have given me.

Thank you.

CHAPTER EIGHTY-ONE

I take the kids to school, sit in a PTA meeting, and then shuttle Ida to see her grandson's awards ceremony, before I finally park the minivan back in front of my company's head-quarters- my sister's house. I open the door to a flurry of activity. Gabe is at work building an elaborate diaper cake for an upcoming baby shower and my mom is icing a tableful of cupcakes. I walk over to her and rest my head on her shoulder, breathing in her familiar scent.

"You need help, Mom?" I ask, wrapping my arms around her waist like the little girl I will always be to her.

"Child, please," she says, shooing me away. "That boy that used to work for you showed up a few hours ago," she gestures her head to the living room, "he's in there organizing and taking phone calls. Said you offered him a job, so I put him to work."

"Boy?" I ask, eyebrows raised at her, quizzically.

"I'm sorry," she says, shrugging while maintaining eye contact on her perfect icing job, "I guess he is grown. He's young though. Twenty-somethings all seem like children to me. Red-headed fellow with a lot of energy, talks a mile a minute."

"Jeremy," I say, realization dawning on me.

She doesn't reply, so I wander over to the living room and find him sitting, perched on the couch, pen in hand, scribbling furiously into my planner.

"You need me," he says when he finally spots me standing there, "and I, unfortunately, need you too."

CHAPTER EIGHTY-TWO

His eyes met mine, and I could see all the pain and the thoughts and the desire he was trying to hold back.

"Didi," he'd said, "kiss me," he'd said.

And so, I'd moved in, and so I'd moved closer, and so I'd given him everything I'd promised not to.

CHAPTER EIGHTY-THREE

I t is one week before my husband comes home. And so, I
hop in my van, and I force myself to drive across town and
sit in front of the place that she lives. Bethany Brown. I grip the
steering wheel and look at the door that used to be such a
welcoming place. I grip the steering wheel and imagine the look
on her face when she opens it and sees me. Anger? Disgust?
Disgrace? Hurt? I don't know. I grip the steering wheel and
fight the almost overwhelming urge to throw the car back into
drive and drive until I can't go anymore. An image flashes
across my mind. But it's not even really an image, it's more like
a feeling. The warm, settled feeling of certainty.

I picked up her envelope. My letter. Her repayment.
Repentance in paper. Is it enough? Is anything ever enough or
too much or the solution? Can any action really negate
another? I ease open my car door and walk across the street to
her home. I stare at the door and raise my hand to knock, but it
never comes down, it never falls against the wood, it remains
there, poised, perfectly set to knock, but unmoving.

Instead, I open my hand and press my palm to her door,

and stare at the brown up against the bright red, focus in on my purple polished nails, and think back to the conversation I had with Getrude all those months ago, when I'd hit rock bottom. The day I'd begun this quest towards redemption. I'd started with the most important people, and ended with the hardest. Then I imagine Bethany's face when she opens the door. The glare of fury. The dead eyes. The screaming anger. The fighting rage. Maybe? Or maybe a hug. A tear. A squeeze. A look towards forgiveness. Or maybe somewhere in between. Maybe we will never talk again. Maybe we fix everything and wind up stronger in the end. Maybe we remain cautious friends afraid to be open and honest with each other. Maybe.

I bring my fingertips to my lips, kiss them softly, then press them to the door. I open her mailbox and slide the envelope into the metal box that bears her last name. I glance back at the red door one more time, and then I walk across the street, get in the van and drive away.

CHAPTER EIGHTY-FOUR

When I was a little girl, my mama pulled me and Camille aside one day for the "talk". She'd described our vaginas as flowers that we needed to tend to, to nurture, to take care of, and to protect. She'd placed her hand over her own box and said that when we were older, much, much older, and very much in love, that we should come and talk to her about whether or not it was time to let some worthy gentlemen touch our gentle flowers. I remember reaching for Camille's hand, hers squeezing mine so tightly. I remember thinking I could read her thoughts, and them being the same as mine. No one will ever touch me there. No one.

The years went by, and I started getting boyfriends. One after another in quick succession. They all said the same things. Adrienne, please. Adrienne, don't you want to see how it feels? Adrienne, don't you think that we should just give it a try? No. No. No. The voice would come up from somewhere deep inside me, shouting profusely and insisting that I listen.

I graduated from high school with my hymen intact, despite having too many boyfriends to count. But college was a different story. I was suddenly thrust into a world that looked a lot different from me. I was suddenly one of the 8% of black students in a school that was mostly white. There were no more whistles when I walked by. There were no more folded papers slipped onto my desk. There were no more giggling girls sliding into the cafeteria bench next to me to ask me to guess who sent them. There were only averted eyes and silence. A silence so loud it was deafening.

I told myself that I didn't miss it, didn't miss the constant attention, the coos in my ear, the hands inching up my thighs, the parade, parade, parade of boyfriend after boyfriend. Guy after guy. But there's something to be said for being wanted. I'd never really done anything to call boys' attention to me, they just were always kind of there. A part of the atmosphere. Some boy asking me out, grinning shyly at me over a shared milkshake, wiping his hand off on his jeans before sliding his fingers between my own. Some boy carrying my books and ushering me safely to class. Some boy picking me up at the end of the day, driving me home, leaning in for a kiss. Some boy proclaiming his undying love for me in verses of poetry, lyrics to a song, while lying on the hood of his car as he traced and named the constellations for me. Some boy picking me up in his mom's car with the music blaring as we drove fast on the highway just for the thrill of it all.

And then all of a sudden it was gone.

I would walk around campus and no one would catch pace with me and try to start a conversation. I would walk through a classroom and no eyes would follow me, tracing my every move. When it was time to join up for group projects, I found myself matched up with a bunch of giggling girls, not a single boy in sight. When it was time to go to lunch, I found myself often eating alone.

It wasn't a big deal, I told myself. The attention had always annoyed me, hadn't it? Besides, I was focused on my artwork, my designs, my education, and becoming a millionaire by 35. I didn't have time for boys, anyway. And telling myself that worked for a while, but eventually the lack of male attention, whether I was ready to admit it or not, started to wear on me. And after the first year, I honestly started to feel less... sexy. I mean, I had never really thought of myself as the "sexy" type. My standard outfit consisted of a pair of jeans, a graphic tee, and matching sneakers, with my hair pulled up into a sloppy bun, or cascading all around in a crazy mess of curls. I would say that I dressed cute and comfy. But while Camille had that whole, hot girl who doesn't try to be hot thing going for her, I always thought that I possessed my own kind of understated beauty. The kind that at first glance is not particularly over-whelming, but that pulls you in and makes you wonder, delve deeper, want to know more. Plus, I have always been unapolo-getically me, and I guess boys tended to find that sexy?

Well, at least the ones that look like me did.

One day I'd found myself analyzing my figure, tracing the lines of my face, questioning my height, my weight, my choice of hairstyle. Maybe I wasn't actually pretty. But I caught myself, and then I'd gotten angry. I'd pulled on my Chucks and headed out. I'd stomped across the quad, sketchbook in hand, and I'd sat down in the middle of it all and looked. I'd looked for boys. No boys had walked up to me and nervously asked me what I was doing on a Friday night since I'd started college, but perhaps I'd overestimated them. I usually didn't pay much attention to boys, they'd mostly come up to me, but I could picture every single one I'd said "yes" to. Name all the boys I'd dated and sketch the lines of their faces from memory. Hand-some devils that made me swoon. There smiles so irresistible when they'd ask me for a moment of my time, please. Had I seen that here? Had any of these college boys who seemed to see right through me, given me butterflies? I didn't recall. But maybe I just hadn't been paying attention. And so, I'd decided to try. I stared at each boy as he'd passed by, tried to catch his eye, grinned at him. Some of them noticed me, smiled back, then glanced away shyly. Many of them did not see me. I'd sat there for an hour or two or three and not a single one of the boys who'd walked by, moved me. There was not a butterfly to be found anywhere inside me.

So, I'd grinned and gathered my stuff, and walked right off campus. And as I'd stepped past the overly landscaped grass and out into reality, I felt a shift inside me, a weight lifting off of me. I caught a bus heading downtown and got off right in the middle of the heart of the city. I'd wandered around until I'd found the busiest street I could find, leaned against a wall, and I'd watched for boys. This watching was a bit harder than the watching on the quad. Half of the people walking by on the quad were boys my age. But here, in the middle of the city, most of the people walking by were grown. I didn't want to catch the attention of some married dad, or some mid-life crisis-having divorcee. I wanted to find a boy, near my own age, that gave me butterflies. A few younger teens rolled by on skateboards, saying "hey beautiful" to me as they rode past. One winked and asked if I'd wanted a ride. I'd just grinned and let them continue on their way. But then there was nothing. Businessmen and women in suits with stern faces and eyes that didn't glance around. Mom's ushering their children in and out of cars and revolving doors. Elderly people waiting at the bus stop. I'd slid down against the wall, butt propped up by my heels so I wasn't actually sitting on the dirty sidewalk floor. I'd dropped my backpack in front of me and fished out my sketchpad. And then I'd started to draw. I drew furiously. People walking, the flow of a dress, the face of a child tugging at his mother's hands- no, Mommy, Mommy, no, let me go. I drew the buildings, immensely looming up above me. I drew the feel of the place, the energy. And as I drew, I felt myself coming back to me.

"Excuse me, miss?" a voice said, startling me out of my intense trance.

I looked up at him, wild and crazy and confused. It took me a second to pull myself back out of my own head and realize that a human being was attempting to talk to me.

"Yes?" I asked, taking him in. He was a delivery guy, wearing the distinctive brown UPS garb, but he had a bright smile and eyes that twinkled and his skin was just a lovely shade of cinnamon.

"I'm sorry, I didn't mean to interrupt," he'd said with a half-smile in his voice, "but you just looked so intense and fully invested in what you were sketching, I just had to ask if I could get a peek."

I'd grinned at him, letting my hair fall in my face, then nodded and stood so the poor man didn't have to keep stooping down to talk to me. I'd handed him my sketch book, glad to share, although a bit apprehensively. The sketches felt so personal somehow, but I'd released the notebook to him anyway. He'd taken it from me slowly, and I'd watched his eyes dart around the page as he'd taken in every line.

"You are very talented," he'd said, handing the book slowly back to me as if he didn't want to let it go.

I'd thanked him and clutched the book to my chest.

"Look," he'd said, glancing back at his truck double parked in the street in front of me, "I've got to get going, but I'd love to see some more of your work, maybe over coffee or something, if you're down?"

And there they were, the butterflies. And suddenly the

world was right again. And as I'd grinned and given this hand-some devil my phone number, I vowed to never allow other people to make me second guess myself again.

Too bad that lesson is something that I've had to continue to learn, time and time again.

CHAPTER EIGHTY-FIVE

I walk in the door to find none other than Jeremy with his arm around a crying TiTi. So I stand in the doorway for a second, listening in on their conversation. They're sitting at the island in the kitchen, Gabe is pacing the living room nearby talking on the phone on a headset, but every now and then he mutes the phone in his hand in order to interject a comment or two. TiTi, apparently, is upset about a boy. Jeremy is consoling her in a soothing voice. Telling her how silly boys are, how stupid and slow they can be, how beautiful she is, and how she deserves better.

"Listen TiTi," he says, making her look him in the eyes, "I don't know you that well, I just started working for your mom and coming around here, but from what I have seen of you I can tell that not only are you absolutely drop-dead gorgeous, but you are smart, funny, and witty. You're not some ditzy bimbo only worried about her hair and nails. You're passionate and full of life. Any guy would be lucky to have you."

She grins at him. "You're just saying that," she says.

"Why? Because I work for your mom?" He asks, confused.

The twins spot me and run up to give me a hug, blowing my cover. Jeremy looks over at me as TiTi answers his question.

"No, because that's just something that old people say," she states with a shrug.

"What?" Jeremy asks, confused, "Let me tell you something, TiTi, nobody, and I mean nobody, goes out of their way to compliment someone if they don't mean it. Most people would rather say nothing at all than to give someone some fake praise."

"You should listen to Jeremy, TiTi," Gabe interjects, pulling his headphones off and joining us in the kitchen, "this time he is actually making a pretty valid point," he says, winking.

"Whatever," Jeremy says, dismissing Gabe's sarcastic retort, "The point is that I'm not just saying positive things to you dismissively or because I feel obligated to do so or just to be nice, I'm saying it because it's just true." He winks at her and offers her a silly grin. "And now that your mother's here I'm sure she'll take over and do a much better job than I ever could, adieu mon amour," he says, and actually does a full bow, theatrically, before walking away to return to work.

I shake my head at Jeremy, then turn to Gabe and raise my eyebrows. He gestures with his head towards my daughter, answering my unspoken question by telling me to turn to the source. My first-born child.

"So," I say, pulling up a stool and sitting close to her, "What's up?"

She sighs a heavy sigh. "There's this boy at school," she starts very slowly, "and mom, he is so hot."

I grin at her. "Oh really? Describe him for me."

She picks up her phone, "Oh I can just show you," she says, but I place my hand over hers and shake my head. "You don't want to see what he looks like?" she asks.

"Yes, I do, but I want to hear you describe him for me first."

"Ohhhh," Gabe says, also pulling up a seat at the table, and I grin at him because this scene is reminiscent of the time before I fucked up my life. When Julien and I would be cooking and Gabe and Jill would be sitting around, munching on chips or grapes, drinking wine while we talked around the island of our kitchen. Moments that I have always treasured. He catches my eye and for a moment there we are, sharing the same thought. A tear begins its crawl down my cheek, and I quickly swipe it away. Julien is missing, still in prison, but the tear is for the one who will never share a moment like this with us again.

Jill.

I refocus my attention on my daughter. She is biting her bottom lip, eyeing us cautiously, before she finds the courage to speak.

"He's tall and thin with deep chocolate skin like a dark chocolate candy bar. And when he talks to me, he like listens with his whole self, with his whole being and his whole body. And he has a smile that lights up his whole face. And when he laughs, he makes everyone want to join in." She catches my eyes and raises her eyebrows. "Is that a good description?" she asks.

"Yes," I say, "And now you can show us the picture."

She grins, picks up her phone and scrolls through her pictures. She finds the one she wants to show us so quickly that I know she has spent a lot of time staring at it.

"Here," she says, handing me the phone.

And the image is of a dark-skinned boy, perched on a stool. His skinny arms dangling as he laugh-smiles at the camera, his entire face a glow in mirth, just as my daughter described. The boy has a presence to him that comes across even in this one image. A self-assuredness that coats his skin.

"Very handsome," I say, as I pass the phone to Gabe, who glances at the image and nods.

"You described him perfectly," Gabe says, before passing the phone back to TiTi.

She takes the phone back, grins at the image, then locks her phone and places it back on the island.

"So, what did this handsome young man do to my fabulous daughter?" I ask, and then watch as TiTi's shoulders slump, and she kind of caves in on herself.

"I thought he was going to ask me to the dance next week," she says slowly, clearly trying not to cry, "but instead, I just found out that he's going with Wendy."

"I see," I say, looking at my beautiful daughter sitting before me- so grown, so vivacious, with the sad puppy dog face she got directly from her father. I grab her face and force her to look me in the eyes, but I hesitate before I speak. Julien was the first boyfriend I ever actually cared about. Everyone else was just something to do. But the way that she describes him, the twinkle in her eyes, it doesn't remind me of fantasies for her father, but instead for the one who never should have been. So, I sigh, and finally find the words to say.

"I don't want to tell you that you're beautiful, although you are. Or that he doesn't deserve you, although he certainly does not. Or that this will only make you stronger, although I'm sure that it will. Right now, I'm going to give you permission to be upset. Listen to all the sad songs, cry and yell and scream until you are tired and empty. Then I want you to find a mirror and look yourself in the eye and say, 'He doesn't want me. He chose somebody else. And that's okay.' Then close your eyes, accept it, and let it go. Feel all the energy you've been holding onto, all the hurt and pain that you've been clinging to, evaporate from your body. And then find something else to obsess about. Do something you've always wanted to do. Focus on the ones that you love and work on making every moment with each of them beautiful." I place my forehead against hers and ask, "Can you do that for me, my gorgeous little sweet pea?"

And she swipes at her eyes and she nods and she hugs me. She grabs her phone and runs off to her room, and a moment later we hear Adele blasting down the hall. I look over at Gabe and grin.

"That was pretty good," he says, pushing his chair back to walk his lopsided walk over to me.

He throws his arm around my shoulder, and my smile is already fading as my face presses into his body.

"I miss Jill," I say, leaning into his familiar scent, always a bit woody like the bark of a tree.

"You and Jill and me. One and two and three. Always friends. Always will be."

And I love Gabe so much, so, so, so, much, that my heart expands in my body, so I weave my arm around his waist, and he rubs my back softly while I cry.

CHAPTER EIGHTY-SIX

The day after my daddy took us to the beach, I'd woken up early. So early. The sun was just beginning to think about dancing across the sky, so everything was tinged with the faint light blue of an early morning day. But mixed in with the typical sounds of an early morning summer day, was as sound that didn't belong. It pulled at me. And I knew instantly that the sound in question was emanating from my mother. That there was something that I needed to hear or see. Something that I needed to do or that she needed from me. Something that would bring her back, snap her out of this reverie.

So, I'd crept out of bed careful, as not to wake my sister. And I'd crept down the hall slowly and slinked down the steps. And inch by inch I'd crept towards her, sitting in the same spot that she'd been in all those hours ago, still rocking. The moans had become mixed with some sort of gurgle. And so, I had sat down at her feet and called her name.

"Mama. Mama can you hear me? Are you okay?"

And slowly, slowly, she turned her head to look down at me. Her face was blank, her eyes were dead, but then suddenly it contorted into rage, and she grabbed my hands within her hands, so tightly, too tightly. I was scared, but she was my mama, and I knew intrinsically that I need not ever show fear of her, not in this way, because she is my mama, and she would never hurt me. I forced my body to stay still, to allow her to hold me, so tightly, too tightly. And she moved her face down, down, down, close to me.

And she'd said, "DiDi, you listen to me, do you hear me, girl?" her breath was stale and hot, but I forced myself not to turn away as she shook my fists.

"You listen to me," she's said, her voice cracking as tears started falling from her eyes, her bottom lip quivering.

"You never depend on nobody. Not your friends, not your family, and damn sure not no fucking man," she'd spat a bit when she'd said the word 'man'. "You only depend on yourself. You always make sure that DiDi is good. You do whatever you have to do, but you make sure that you look out for you. Do you hear me girl?" and I stared into her red, red eyes, took in her sunken face, but I couldn't respond. So, she shook my hands again. "DiDi!"

I'd nodded my head then, a tear falling from my eye.

"You are not going to end up like me. You never are going to be like me. You promise me. You will take care of DiDi."

And finally I'd found the strength to speak.

"Yes ma'am," I had never said the word ma'am before in my life, but if there was any time a ma'am was appropriate, I knew that it was then.

My mama had nodded her head at me, then released my hands, and slowly pulled back into herself and away from me.

"Go now child," she'd said, as the rocking started up again.

CHAPTER EIGHTY-SEVEN

I t's the middle of the day when I open my sister's front door and find Bethany Brown. She is holding my letter in her hand and biting her bottom lip. I stand there silently, taking her in from head to toe, looking for any evidence of her reason for coming. She is standing tall and proud, but her almond-shaped eyes look a bit sunken in, like she has been up late for nights on end.

"Hey, Bethany," I say, trying too hard to sound casual.

"Hey Adrienne." She looks me in the eye for a long second, and my stomach sinks. The feeling of dread, like the moment before your car crashes into a wall, envelopes me.

"Got your letter," she says, shrugging her shoulders in a gesture that attempts to be casual but fails.

"And?" I ask. I don't mean to sound rude, but it comes off that way, a bit snippy.

"I saw you that day actually," she says to my feet. "Saw you pull up; heard you climb up my stairs. Saw you walk away."

I don't say anything.

"Can I come in?" she asks.

I take a deep breath and step aside. As she walks past me, I catch a whiff on her scent- her favorite flowery perfume mixed with her very essence, and a wave of agony flows over me. I miss her. My oldest, dearest, closest friend, who was always supposed to be there for me. The same one who also betrayed me.

Bethany.

I close the door behind her and follow her into the living room. Jeremy is making phone calls. Gabe is building a science project. My mom is baking a lasagna and a few dozen cupcakes. I usher Bethany past them and onto the back patio before my mother can spot her and say something, I really don't need her throwing her two cents in on this. I gesture Bethany towards chairs in the somewhat shady part of the yard and watch as she fiddles with my letter in her hand.

"I want to know why," she says finally, while placing the letter on the wicker coffee table between us.

"Why what?" I ask, slinking back into my chair and wrapping my arms around my body.

"Why you lied to me, Adrienne. Why you used and manipulated me. Why you kept coming back time after time asking for just a little bit more, promising that I'd see a double return on my investment. Again and again and again." She swipes at a stray tear on her cheek.

I use this moment to interject, "I didn't even borrow that much from you, Bethany."

"It's not about the money, I would have helped you however I could. It's about all the lies. You lied to me. You, my best friend since the beginning to time. Why didn't you just tell me?"

I am breathing heavily. Her words have landed like a weight on my chest, each word falling there and then dropping into the pit of my stomach. I want to say, I'm sorry Bethany. But

I hear the words playing in my head before I blurt them out and they sound hard, brittle, jagged, and I realize that I am angry, seething, raging mad at the woman standing before me, and that any word that comes out of my mouth right will be laced in that anger.

So, I say nothing.

She leaves space for me to think, to organize my thoughts, to frame the words inside my mind carefully, and I simply try to breathe slowly, in and out, in and out, 1, 2, 3. But I don't feel myself getting any calmer. Yes, I took her money. Yes, I lied. But I was lying to everybody, myself included. She, on the other hand, abandoned me before she even knew I'd lied. She'd left me when I'd confided in her. Judged me and pushed me out of her life.

"Adrienne?" she asks, and her voice is lower, softer, tinged with a layer of fear.

"I didn't tell you," I say, slowly, methodically, trying to force the anger out of my words, "because I didn't even tell myself. If I told you. It would have become real. And I would have had to face up to the truth. That my kids hated me. That I was fucking up my marriage. That I was in love with my husband's best friend. And that I was stealing money from everyone who loved me. Denial is why, Bethany. And denial is a hell of a drug."

I stand up, so angry I'm shaking, and then I start pacing. Back and forth, back and forth, until I get into a rhythm that reminds me of the first time I'd called Camille. I'd just gotten out of a meeting with Julien. His eyes droopy and sad as he stared right at me and told me we'd have to stop work on the new product line. That we couldn't find the funds to fund it. That we should probably scale back and focus on building up the foundation of our company, improve the brand, streamline and dig in so that we focus on making what we do really well, even better, and nothing else.

I'd heard him, but I hadn't heard him. Not really. We were supposed to be expanding and reaching more people, not shrinking and trying to make lemonade out of lemons. I retreated to my office, closed all my blinds, told Jeremy to hold all of my calls, and I'd paced the room. Back and forth, back and forth, trying to come up with something on my own.

And I'd finally looked at myself in the mirror hanging on my wall, and I'd asked myself three questions:

1.Who are you?

2.Who were you born to be?

3.What kind of company are you meant to lead?

And then I'd made the fucking phone call to steal money from my baby sister, crossing my fingers and praying on a hope and a dream.

"I'm not like you, Bethany," I say, spinning around to face her, and opening my arms wide as I speak, "I was destined for greatness. Not some boring, mundane, everyday life in a cute little house with my safe fucking husband and kids that resent everything I do. My name is Adrienne Destiny McQueen Louden and I wasn't meant to be kowtowing to anything or anybody. Especially not you."

"Yeah, Adrienne," she says, standing up and shaking her head to me, "But at what cost? You were never one for a quick fix before. Why then? Why me?"

"I was losing everything alright! My fucking kids hated me, I was cheating on my husband because I never thought I deserved him," I chuckle a bit crazily, "I damn sure was right about that. My sister was never around, and let's not forget that you weren't around for most of it either, Bethany. Let's not forget that you just fucking up and abandoned me when I poured my heart out to you. Let's not forget that you weren't there to tell shit to."

I watch her as she slowly sinks back into her chair, places

her head in her hands and softly sobs. If we were Adrienne&Bethany, I would have gone over to her, I would have pulled her into my arms, I would have rubbed her back while she cried. If we were Bethany&Adrienne, I would have said something to make her laugh, reminded her of something we did silly in the past, wiped the tears from her eyes and cursed whatever it was that made her cry. But we aren't. I am Adrienne, slowly finding a way to be a better Adrienne, and the woman sitting before me is no longer my friend.

As I watch her calm herself down, I realize the reason I didn't knock on her door. Everyone else on my list was someone I'd hurt in a selfish attempt to save my company. But Bethany, she'd left me. And why? Why were my life choices such an affront to her? Why did she give so many fucks? How could you abandon me so?

I wanted to ask her, but something inside me told me to wait. Instead, I take my seat and sit stoically, listening to her trying to gather herself, awkwardly, as if she's a stranger on the train crying next to me.

She finally calms down, sits up and wipes her eyes overemphatically. She clears her throat, and I turn to her, knowing my response before she even says a word.

"You're right, DiDi. I shouldn't have just left you like that. It's just," she sighs and pushes back her shoulders, "you had everything that I wanted, and you were just so flippant about it. Took it all for granted. Your fucking gorgeous husband, your beautiful kids, your world. And you set me up with the guy you're fucking on the side? It was just such a huge slap in the face to me. I just don't get it, Adrienne. Everyone always said I was so beautiful, I was everything any guy could want or need, I was the whole package, but it was always you with the guys throwing themselves at you. Guys would fight each other to get a chance to go out with you. And then you found Julien. A man so perfect he inspired a million-dollar shoe, and you even took him for granted." She sighs and catches my eyes. "Just take a second, Adrienne, and imagine what it's like... to be me."

This I don't have to do. I have done it before, many times throughout our lives. I did it when I made up Bethany's Crew. I did it when I ditched my boyfriends to hang out with her. I did it when I was ignoring her fucking phone calls and being a shitty friend. I never let go of what it was like to be Bethany Brown.

"Bethany," I say to her, shaking my head slowly, "I always imagine what it's like to be you. I spent our entire friendship imagining what it's like to be you. I'm not sure you've ever done the same."

"What do you mean?" she asks, staring daggers at me, "I always place myself in your shoes."

"No, you imagine what it would be like if you were you with my life, not if you were me. There's a big difference between those two, Bethany. When I imagine being you, I put myself in your perspective based on all the things I know about you. When you imagine being me, you just envision yourself in my circumstances. You don't actually place yourself in my mental state, in my body. If you did, you wouldn't have abandoned me after I confessed my deepest darkest secret to you. You would have tried to give me guidance. You would have tried to help me."

She looks at me, then down at her hands. Looks at me, then down at her hands. She doesn't look at me again.

"There's a reason I didn't knock on your door that day, Bethany. There was nothing left to say. I needed you, and you couldn't see past your own bullshit ass insecurities to be there for me. I'm sorry I took your money. You'll be getting all of it back as soon as I can get it to you, incrementally. But this, this friendship, it's over."

And with that, I guide Bethany Brown back through my sister's house and watch as she drives away in her sports car, wondering why I feel so empty.

I hope she's happy. I hope she's free. I hope she becomes everything that she's ever wanted to be. But I also hope that she stays far, far, far the fuck away from me.

CHAPTER EIGHTY-EIGHT

When I first met Gabe he looked me in the eye so deeply that I thought that he had fallen head over heels in love with me. Or was infatuated with me. Or just wanted to fuck me really badly, whatever.

Jill had convinced me somehow to go meet him in his dorm room, and I was dreading it. Boys' dorm rooms always smelled like a mixture of feet, armpits, and Cheetos, a side effect of their general disregard for proper hygiene. But when we opened the door, I was surprised to find that this boys' dorm room smelled faintly of pine and pizza, a weird mixture, but not quite unpleasant. The room was neat and orderly, with books stacked up in piles on desks and laptops showing a slideshow of rivers and waterfalls and forests and lakes, poised, waiting to be woken up and put back to work. Gabe gestured towards his side of the room and Jill plopped down right on his bed, while I slid into the chair at his desk. Immediately, he walked over and grabbed my hand. He held it tightly within his and stared deeply into my eyes. I stared back at him, quizzically. The boy was tall, but also muscular, with his brown hair falling in curls around his face.

"What are you, reading my aura or something?" I'd said, cocking my head at him.

"Yeah," he'd said, rubbing his thumb across the back of my hand.

"What are you reading?" I'd asked playing along with him.

He squints his eyes and looks at me quizzically. "You are a hard thing hiding in a seemingly soft shell."

I bit my bottom lip to prevent myself from saying anything.

He continues, "You are a creature who is very supportive and very emotional and very free, but who curtails her emotions and cages herself."

I'd tried to look away from him, but he'd squeezed my hand tightly the second that my eyes attempted to leave his. I took a deep breath before reluctantly allowing my eyes to reunite with his.

"You are afraid of love. You are lost. You are swimming against it. You are definitely a virgin."

And with that, I'd snatched my hand away from him.

"Dude," I'd said, "Fuck is wrong with you?"

"You're among good people," he says throwing up his hands and grinning at me "Your people," he says nodding at me, "Because I definitely want to join you two."

He had taken the same hand that had just held mine to his mouth and bitten down on the knuckle of his index finger. And despite the fact that he had outed my virginity to Jill, I found myself grinning at him and shaking my head, already feeling some hint of the connection he was describing. A pull like an invisible thread connecting the three of us. An indelible bond. And I had just met him.

"Something beautiful or terrible will come out of our

union," he'd said, grinning at me mischievously, "I look forward to it either way."

And that was it. It was like we all became instant friends right then and there. And Gabriel was my Gabriel. My best friend. The second part of my triad. The other half of my soul. The one who made me finally feel full and happy and whole.

"I wish for something beautiful," Jill had said with a wide grin, grazing my shoulder as she walked past me to the bathroom.

"And I wish for something terrible," Gabe had said, grinning wickedly at me, although I knew as soon as he'd said it that it was something that he didn't really mean.

I'd waited for Jill to finish peeing before I'd said where I stood on the matter at hand, "I wish for something beautiful and terrible both," I'd said smiling through a laugh, "I wish for us to be legends."

CHAPTER EIGHTY-NINE

My daughter bursts into the house with a big smile, rushes over to me, and throws her arms around my neck, pulling me in for a tight hug. Her hair smells like lavender and honey, and I revel in the wave of love that comes cascading over me.

"What's up, my little bug?" I ask, as she pulls away from me, clutching my shoulders at arm's length with a wicked grin on her face.

"Mom," she says, waiting until I meet her gaze, "he asked me out! He asked me to be his girlfriend!"

I shake my head, a bit confused, "The same boy as before or... a new boy?"

"Same boy," she says, her face all a glow, "I listened to you, I let it go, and he came after me!"

She is damn near screaming at this point, and Jeremy and Gabe whoop from the other room. I just shake my head at them and refocus on my beautiful daughter who is turning into a beautiful young lady. And as I listen to her describe in excruciating detail how the boy who had just broken her heart had come up to her after school, pulled her aside, and apologized for not asking her to the dance instead of Wendy. He'd told her that he was head over heels for her, and that he had only asked Wendy because he knew that she would say yes, and he liked TiTi so much he was scared of being rejected by her. Then, apparently, he'd asked her to be his girlfriend.

My eyes go wide in my head. I grin at her and wonder how I can guide her in this next stage of her life, when I am no good at managing relationships myself. For a split second my mind wanders to Curtis before I can shut him out of my mind.

I half listen to my daughter as I am teleported back to a moment in time. Our first time.

CHAPTER NINETY

I t was the night before my wedding. Curtis was staying with us until the big day, and I finally decided to stop tossing and turning in bed and get a glass of milk or a drink or to take a walk or something. I was so young. Fresh out of college, in the throes of starting a new company, and here I was about to get married. It felt so big and overwhelming, I couldn't sleep.

I'd bypassed the kitchen completely and headed out to our oversized deck, taking in three big, deep, breaths, hoping the fresh air would rejuvenate my soul. I'd been so immersed in my own thoughts that it'd taken me a while to even notice him standing there. And he'd been there all along. A silhouette pressed against the pale moon sky, ignoring the sounds of my soft, sad cries. I walked up to him and pressed my fingertips to the back of his neck, ran my hands along the back of his head. I don't know why. His short hairs tickled the palm of my hand, and I fought every single cell in my body to keep my other hand in its place, preventing it from sliding down his chest, down, down, down, to the places I must never go.

I told myself in my head to go, go, go, that this was all

wrong, no, no, no, but something in the very center of my chest kept pulling me forward. I inched closer, bit by bit, until the sound of my breath became ragged, until my mouth was inches away from his skin, until I could see my exhalations moving the hairs on the back of his neck. And then I'd stopped. I'd let my hand drop. I took a step back and away. I began to turn away.

But his hand reached out and grabbed my waist.

And I. Was. Undone.

The rest happened all in a blur. His fingers in my hair, his lips pressed to mine, so fierce, so incessant, his tongue on my neck, in my ear, his fingers sliding down my oversized pajama bottoms so easily, so effortlessly, and then the ecstasy when he pushed his fingers inside me.

When it was all over, I could feel his cum sliding out of me as I pulled up my panties and backed away from him, an over-whelming feeling of remorse flowing throughout me at who I was and what I had done and who I had done it with. My soon-to-be husband's bestie. How could I? How could he? I didn't realize I was crying until I saw a tear hit the floor. I'd swiped at my eyes and backed away from him, and he had turned away from me, I'd assumed from feeling the same rush of shame as me. I'd turned and run into the house. Up, up, up the stairs, as quiet as a mouse and into the shower of the guest bathroom so the sound wouldn't wake Julien, my love, my heartbeat, the one who I had just betrayed.

I'd gotten into the shower and scrubbed and scrubbed and scrubbed, until I realized that soap would not be able to cleanse me of this affliction. Then I'd sat down right there in the shower, under the waterfall, not even caring that I let my hair get wet, and wrapped my arms around my legs and cried and cried and cried.

I don't know how long I was sitting there. I don't know much at all. But eventually, the door slid open and slowly he had crept in the shower with me, wrapped his arms around me, and pressed his forehead to mine.

"There's nothing to be afraid of," he'd said, and his words caused me to sob even harder, "It's just you. It's just me. And we can do anything."

And I'd wrapped my arms around Julien and let him wrap his arms around me.

A lie. A lie. A lie. A lie. The first one of many.

CHAPTER NINETY-ONE

We decide to wait until Julien gets out of prison. We decide that he needs to be there. Gabe and I will share our bits of her with him. Gabe and Julien and me will hold a ceremony at the sea and send Jill off to a peaceful resting place. But today I am taking a day off. Today I woke up off and missing something, and so after I drop the kids off at school, I just keep driving. I head upstate to where the roads are long and windy and meandering, and I can drive with the windows down, with the wind blowing through my hair, with the sun on my face- fully in this moment, fully in this space. I pull over randomly and spot a hiking trail that I instantly know that I must take. And I follow it to another and another and another, until I wind up on top of a rock that sits on top of a hill. And I sit down there for a while, taking in the world all around me, feeling like something small and forgettable in the midst of something so big and grand and spectacularly beautiful. And I allow myself to think of all the things I've done, all the people I have hurt, one by one. My mom. My dad. My sister. TiTi. Darrius. Parris. Gabe. Jeremy. Jill. And Julien, my love. I think of Jill's smile and wonder if I could have saved her. If I had faced her sooner, would she still be here, smiling at me on this day? I think of my mom and her frown, and I wonder if I took her words that day when she was broken down and beaten, way too seriously. I think of my dad, and the look in his eyes, and the determination in his soul, and I wonder if I will ever be half as amazing as he has always been and always will be. I think of my babies and wonder if I will ever be enough for all of them. I think about Jeremy and Gabe and how the light has slowly been returning to their eyes. I think about my year spent fighting and trying to survive, and how I did, and how I turned it all around, and how I was never meant to do anything less.

And then I think about him, Curtis.

I think of his smile and his tight angry face. I think of his love, then I think of his hate. And I realize that there is no other way that I ever could be. Me and him. Him and me. Never, in a million years, could we ever be anything real. And so, I release whatever last bits of him resided in my heart and my mind and my soul, and I feel the tiny wisps leave from the corners of my body, and I watch as they fly away from me. Leaving to join the other dreams of what never was and was never meant to be.

And now I am done crying. I sit up and wipe my face free of this wetness, and I finally allow myself to think of my heart-beat. I smile and laugh at the sun, and all I can think about is that he's almost home. Almost home. Almost home. And somehow the void in the center of my chest that I hadn't even realized was there becomes a little bit smaller, and I exhale, finally feeling a bit of relief from the bitter pain. So steady that I had almost become it and it had almost become me.

CHAPTER NINETY-TWO

I had marched into the room in thigh high boots and pressed my palms against the table, looking in the eye of each individual on my marketing team one at a time.

"Tell me," I'd said, pushing off from the table, and parading myself before them, "What do you think of me right now? What is my look saying to you?"

"Slut," I'd heard someone mutter softly, and I thought it was Gary, the moderately chauvinistic prick that I never should have let Gabe hire.

And I should have known then, I should have known then, that I was dead ass wrong. That the type of woman looking to buy expensive shoes that are sexy while also comfortable isn't looking to wear thigh-high boots. I had missed the mark and forgotten who our customers were. Women who wear thigh-high boots aren't worried about comfort. Besides, to be honest, it was our least comfortable pair of shoes. Even Gabe couldn't get his heart into the shoe enough to make it work. Nevertheless, we had pushed it out half-heartedly. Maybe you're right Adrienne, they had all told me begrudgingly. I could see it being a hit. Maybe. Yes. Definitely. All of us ignored the fact that, while parading around like a peacocking idiot, someone had called me a slut in the boardroom of my own company.

Someone had called me out on my bullshit.

And the worst part is, that I didn't even have the gall to face him. Call him out and confront him, have an open and honest conversation about why he said what he did. See if there was anything I needed to consider, anything I needed to change. That's the type of boss that I was when I created my company. That's the type of boss that I want to be. That's the type of boss that I am now. No more peacocking and ego stroking. Just real. Just open. Just honesty.

CHAPTER NINETY-THREE

The closer it gets to the day Julien comes home, the more nervous I get. I find myself having difficulty making decisions, muttering to myself, losing myself in thought in the middle of the day, taking long showers just to feel the water cascading over me. Reveling in the rhythmic sound and warmth surrounding me.

I woke up early one morning from a nightmare. The details elude me, but leave me with a lingering sense of fear, sorrow and apology. I decided to get in my car and go for a drive. This time I find myself at my childhood home. The light is on in the kitchen as I enter slowly, confused at the sight of my mom cooking at 5 in the morning.

"Mama?" I ask, as I drop my keys on the counter.

She looks up at me from the bowl of batter she's beating by hand with a level of dexterity that I know I will never possess, and a feeling of overwhelming sadness comes over me. I rush to her before she even attempts to speak, and I wrap my arms around her waist.

My mom hesitates, but then slowly she's dropping her

spoon into the bowl, and wraps her arms around mine. She squeezes me tightly.

"What's wrong baby?" she asks in a voice so soft and sweet that I almost don't recognize her.

"Mama," I say. "I'll never be like you; I'll never be as good a mom as you."

"What do you mean?" she asks, "You're a great mom. I see the way you're raising TiTi and the boys. You know exactly what to do. You know exactly what they need." She rubs my back and asks me where these comments are coming from.

"I can't do this," I say, gesturing towards her kitchen, her mixing bowl, her apron, her hair done up in a chignon even though it's 5 a.m.

She chuckles at me softly, "Girl, I thought you knew there's more than one way to be a mama. The way that you mom is perfectly fine."

"Mama," I say, trying to not sound exasperated, "Don't lie to me. There was a whole period of time when I didn't even have my kids. When I didn't even feel like I was worthy of seeing them. When they were here, with you. You took care of them so well. And there's a part of you, I know there is, don't lie to me, that thinks that maybe I should have never taken them back. That maybe with you is where they belong." A single tear escapes from my eye despite my best effort to keep it in.

And with that, my mother pushes me away. She turns around to look me straight in the eyes and says, "Adrienne McQueen, you're right. There was a time when I thought that you should not have your children. I am your mother, and you gave them to me because you knew that was what was best for them at the time, but I also knew that I was just holding on to them for you."

She cups my head in her hands.

"I know I gave you a hard time. But that's because it's what you need to grow. And at the end of the day, that's my job, Didi. Even now. Still to this day. A mother's role is always to give her children what they need to be the best that they can be, and you," she pauses to grin at me, "were born a bit soft for my liking so I raised you to cultivate your strength. And look at you! Stronger than ever and doing more than I've ever dreamed of."

I start crying because my mother has never spoken to me in this way, and I am overwhelmed by her openness.

"Mama," I say through my tears, "what if I'm not enough? What if I haven't changed enough? What if I fall back into my old ways?"

She laughs at me.

"Adrienne McQueen," my mama says, turning back to her cupcakes, "Let me finish icing these cupcakes, you go fix us a pot of coffee, and then I'll tell you a little bit more about you."

Something warm lights up inside me as I begin making the coffee.

When the cupcakes are complete, I pour two heaping cups full of coffee and follow my mother into the drawing room.

"Didi," she says, after taking her first small sip, "did you know that the day you were born you came out in the world so angry with your face scrunched up tight as a fist?"

She balls up her own fist as a demonstration

"The doctor gave you to me, and I swear you looked right at me. I know they say that babies can't see but so far, but I swear you looked at me like you could really see me. You looked at me with the same knowing gaze that you carry around with you to this day."

She grins at me.

"I placed you right here," she says, pointing to the space between her collarbone and chin, "you curled up right there and went right to sleep. And I watched your face relax with each breath."

"I never heard that story before Mama." I say, not hiding my awe.

She smiles at me over her cup.

"So angry," she says, "always so angry. Just angry at the world. Angry at yourself. It's like you just get angry and react. But Adrienne, sometimes you just need to take a moment and breathe Baby. You got this. You always have."

She places her cup on the table and curls her feet up in the chair underneath her.

"Nobody's ever accomplished anything without failing some. Did you learn from your mistakes?"

"I don't know..." I say, looking away from her, ashamed, "I hope so." I finally say in a small voice.

My mind wanders. I think about how I never heard this story, the story of my own birth. All my mama's stories had been about Camille. I swallow and gather up the nerve to ask her about it.

She sighs before speaking.

"You and your sister are two very different people with two very different needs. I told Camille all those stories so she would see that she is capable of anything. But you, you didn't need that. You were always standing up for everyone around you, which is a fine quality, I guess, but I was always concerned that you were giving too much of yourself. I wanted you to keep some of you, for you."

"You think I gave away too much of myself?" I ask more to myself then to my mother, but she answers anyway.

"Yes!" she says a bit exasperated, "Listen, when you were three, there was a girl about your age crying at the playground. She was just wailing. And you went over to her and gave her a hug, and handed her your favorite stuffed animal- you remember the little blue bunny you had?"

I shake my head, no, a bit flabbergasted by the story she's telling me.

"Well, you used to take it everywhere."

"Until that day, with the little girl?"

My mother laughs at that.

"You think I was going to sit there and let you give your favorite toy away?"

I smile, laughing at her, trying to imagine my mother watching me passively give some little girl my favorite toy- impossible.

"Nope, I walked over to you and that little girl and I told her that she could hug my daughter's bunny for 30 more seconds, and then she had to give it back."

"Oh wow," I say, "only 30 seconds?"

"Yes, that was more than enough," she says indignantly, "And I told you, that day, that you don't have to go giving bits and pieces of yourself away, not for anybody."

She leans over to rub my knee with a smile, then sighs.

"I think you learned that lesson a little too well, maybe, because you don't have to go taking things from people either."

I swallow hard at that last comment.

"Now, you have both of these tools, ready to use whenever you need. Two sides of one coin. Strength and fragility. You need both to live authentically, are you hearing me?"

"Strong and fragile?" I ask, my brain processing, "Like glass?"

My mom grins at me.

"Like the finest China in all the world."

CHAPTER NINETY-FOUR

The day I married him was an emotional rollercoaster that I barely remember riding. The only thing that really stands out to me during that entire day, was walking down the aisle.

My dad by my side, guiding me. My best friends are all there to stand beside me. And Julien.

I caught his eyes as I walked. So many emotions being transferred between us in an instant. He was crying, he was so happy, and it warmed my entire heart. I wanted to run to him. I wanted to sprint down the aisle and jump into his arms. I wanted to wrap my entire body around his and stick my tongue down his throat. I wanted to go dancing in the sun with him holding my hands. I wanted to be his forever.

So forever his, I am.

CHAPTER NINETY-FIVE

I see him.

I see him a moment before he sees me, leaning against the old van with sunglasses on, pretending I'm starring in a classic movie.

The gates open and a small group of men meander out. Julien is in the back. I wait for the small crowd to part so I can witness him in all his glory, and oh, what a sight he is to behold. He spots me immediately and walks towards me, confident as ever in the same $4,000 suit they'd sentenced him in. Oh, this man, I think, swallowing as I force myself not to run to him, he does something to me. I shift my hands from my pockets to my hair to my waist, because I'm suddenly not sure what to do with them as I watch my husband grin as he walks over to me.

I want to tell him to run if he wants to. I want to tell him that we only have one life to live so feel all your feelings and stop hiding behind fear. I want to tell him that I love him, and I'll always be here. But I say nothing. Because, after all, who am I to judge? Who am I to tell him what to do when I am sitting here doing the same thing? Trying to figure out what to do with my hands and just standing in one place when every piece of me wants to run to him and jump into his arms and wrap my legs around his waist. Who am I to judge when I'm a hypocrite myself?

He reaches me, finally, and he hugs me tightly and I breathe him in, the scent of his skin, and we stand there for a long moment, swaying ever so slightly, me crying on his shoulder silently, him kissing my hair.

And it is Julien, my Julien, my love. And he is finally free. And here and with me. And everything is right in the world.

We don't say much on the drive home. Julien holds my hand, gently rubbing his thumb over my skin, sending tingles down my spine. And I sneak glances at him every chance I get.

Julien, my Julien, mine.

CHAPTER NINETY-SIX

When I pull into the driveway of my sister's house, I sit there for a second, clutching his hand in my lap. I know what lies in that house, waiting for us inside. A houseful of our friends and family all waiting to surprise Julien with a welcome home party, but I want to take this moment for just him and me. I bring his hand to my lips and kiss his knuckles and fingertips. And the tears fall freely.

"Julien," I say, "I'm sorry," I say.

And I can hear the smile in his voice as he speaks, "I forgave you long ago. You my love, my heart, my soul."

And he turns my head to face him, and he kisses me, full-on and passionately. His tongue sliding gently into my mouth, his taste so familiar it triggers an ache deep inside me, and I groan. Suddenly I regret this party, wish it was just him and me and a hotel room, fucking like rabbits and whispering to each other under the covers into the wee hours of the night.

But I know that we've stayed in the car long enough. And I know that the show must go on. And I know that everyone is waiting for us.

I slowly extricate myself from him and remind him that his children are waiting.

And although he says, "Fuck those kids," he also reaches for the door handle, grinning.

I roll my eyes and follow him out. I follow him up the walkway to the house, but fall back, so he can get the full experience of the surprise. The sound is deafening, and I watch as he gets swallowed into the sea of people. I slink sideways circling the perimeter, letting my husband feel the full effect of all the people who love him and have missed him. I lean against the wall and watch as the children bombard him, clinging to him like he's been gone all their lives. Watch as he gallantly manages to carry a twin in each arm while TiTi tugs on his hand.

I just grin. And watch.

Everything is finally working out. Everything is finally getting fixed. Everything is finally coming together perfectly.

"DiDi," a voice whispers in my ear, and I jump, taking in a sharp breath. I know this voice. I know this man. How dare he be here now.

"You know you're not welcome," I say through clenched teeth.

And I turn to see Curtis' smiling face grinning at me.

"Well," he says, his voice Cheshire cat sweet, "I was invited, after all, by Julien's parents, and who am I to disappoint them? Besides, I thought it would be a great opportunity to see my favorite mommy..." He leans in close to get a good whiff of me.

I take a deep breath, pull myself away from his touch, and glare at him.

"Curtis," I say, through gritted teeth, "You better get out of here before Julien sees you. I don't know what you're trying to accomplish, but I'm telling you right now, if you mess this day up for my husband, I will personally see to it that you never see the light of day again. Do you understand?"

"Of course," he says, but he moves in closer, bringing his lips to hover inches away from mine.

I gasp, as I feel the pull of him, an urgent tugging sensation from my mouth and crotch to his. An intoxicating feeling so surprisingly powerful, that I freeze in it. Eyes darting from his eyes to his mouth and back. The pull calling out to me.

I know that it would only take one word, one small gesture, one fraction of a sign, and Curtis would take me. He'd guide me away into a bathroom or something, somewhere and push himself deep inside me, and, to my horror, a part of me is begging me to let him.

Do it, the voice pounds in the back of my head. Just do it.

I take a step back from him instead.

"Let me show you out," I say, lowering my eyes from his and guiding him to the nearest exit.

He follows me obediently, a smirk dancing on his lips.

I open the side door for him since it's the one furthest away from Julien's sightline.

"Have a lovely evening," I say, tilting my head towards the door as I hold it open for him.

"You know where to find me," he says, as he walks by me, his fingers dancing along my waist for the briefest second as he passes, "I have missed you, Didi," he says, turning in the doorway.

I close the door on him before he can say anything else, I lock it with a flourish, then take a deep breath, plaster a smile on my face, and try to push Curtis out of my mind as I search the room for the love of my life.

I caught his eyes, finally. He's in a corner of the room, the kids still draped all over him, his college roommate standing nearby, talking at him loudly, but he's looking right at me.

He saw.

He holds my gaze for a beat too long, forces a smile, then looks away.

I feel panic flush my body. What did he see? What did it look like from where he was sitting? What the fuck am I going to do? I force myself to breathe. I didn't do anything wrong. I rejected Curtis and sent him home. Julien and I have gotten through much worse than this, we can get through this too. I tell myself this, over and over as the night wears on, and the party continues all around me. But the words don't sink in. They don't feel real. And I can't help but wonder if Curtis will be something I always have hanging over me and my relationship with Julien. A dead body clinging to my feet, dragging behind me, preventing us from ever being truly happy.

CHAPTER NINETY-SEVEN

I pull into the driveway with a van full of bouncy children, talking incessantly, and the knowledge that my husband is waiting inside the house with Gabriel, Jeremy, and my mommy, causes me to feel a wave of panic. I throw the car into park, step outside, and feel the world spinning on its axis all around me. I don't know how to live in all this happiness. And my mind starts to go down its rabbit-hole of disbelief. Something bad, something bad, something bad is going to happen to me. But TiTi comes over, she threads her fingers with mine, and smiles at me. And I rub my thumb across the soft skin of the back of her hand, and she grounds me. I take a deep breath and now I'm here, right here, right now, in the moment, breathing this air, standing in this space, ready to just take one step after another and another until I find myself home.

CHAPTER NINETY-EIGHT

"It's time," she'd said climbing into bed with me.

"No," I'd said, curling further into a ball, shaking my head profusely, "I'm, not ready."

"It's time, DiDi," she'd said, rubbing my belly, pressing her face into my hair, so her lips were near my ear, "Your contractions are a minute apart, she's coming, it's time to bring her out into this world."

"No," I'd said, irrationally, tears springing into my eyes as I gritted my teeth and tried to ignore the wave of pain spreading from my lower back around my entire belly, making me want to push down, push her out, if only just to ease the agony.

I'd let the contraction pass, and then I could feel it, Jill's hands on me, rubbing, rubbing my belly so steadily. It had been Jill. My mom was to meet us at the hospital. Bethany was on her way. Julien was there, he was always there, pacing, gathering things, monitoring the time, the intensity, creating a fucking graph on his computer for the future baby to see. But it was Jill, just Jill and me. Jill in my ear guiding me, comforting me, a steady constant to steer me.

I felt a wave of gratitude wash over me, and I'd started to cry.

"Jill," I'd said between sobs, clutching at whatever part of her body was most near, "thank you so much. Thank you. Thank you."

And at that moment, I wished that one day, she would have kids too. It was for purely selfish reasons. So, that day I could return the favor and be the voice in her ear, the hand on her belly, a constant steady thing for her to lean into.

But Jill never had kids. And I never got to pay her back in this unexplainable way. And now I never will. I wake up often, in the middle of the night, mind filled with moments like this, pillow drenched in a pool of my tears. So much she never got to experience, so much she never got to live.

Jill. I miss you. I love you. I always will.

CHAPTER NINETY-NINE

I asked my mother for a moment of her time one late afternoon. She is placing a cake in the oven, humming a soft, familiar tune, and looks quizzically at me. After a moment of thought she simply nods her head and follows me out to Camille's backyard. She sits in a cushioned chair and I pace nervously, trying to gather up the courage to ask the question that has been plaguing me for over twenty years.

Start, just find an entry point. Start somewhere.

And so, I do.

"Mama, do you remember when I was little, you told me not to depend on anybody," I ask slowly, cautiously, "especially not a man?"

My mother looks at me for a long time, searching the depths of her mind.

"I'm sorry, Adrienne," she finally says, "I don't quite recall..." Her voice trails off as if asking me for clarification.

I take a deep breath and force myself to speak. "It was when you were really upset. Crying and sitting in the rocking chair for days, do you remember that?"

Her face flushes, and she looks away from me. "Ah yes, that," she says, flatly with a dry chuckle of unease.

I move to sit next to her. Silent. Waiting for her to speak in her own time.

She pats my knee.

"That was when your father decided he was going to leave me," she says frankly.

I gasp, but force myself not to speak.

"He came to me one day, and he said that our lives were too boring, too predictable. That he couldn't breathe. That he couldn't take it anymore, and that he was ready to leave."

I bite my bottom lip, finding it hard to imagine my father saying this. He always seemed so... steady.

"I fell apart spectacularly." She forces a grin at me.

"For days, maybe weeks even I just fell apart. I felt like the floor had caved in beneath my feet. For I had never imagined, not once, a life without him since the day we were married. And yet, that's exactly the reality that was being forced upon me." She shakes her head, as if pushing the memories from her mind.

"Eventually, your father threatened to take you girls away with him." Her voice cracking as she speaks.

She grabs my hand.

"Something snapped back into place then. I got up, I took a shower, I told him that he'd have to pry my children from my cold dead hands, and then I... crawled into bed with you."

She grins at me.

"You probably don't remember this, but for weeks I used to take turns sleeping with you and Camille. I'd place your little hand in mine and trace your lines until I fell asleep."

She traces the lines in my hand as she speaks, and a faint memory raises to the surface, the touch so familiar to me.

I look up at my mother wide-eyed, amazed that so much of her lives inside me.

"But Daddy never left," I finally say, shaking my head.

She smiles. "No, your father never left. I don't know why either. I never wanted to know. I always liked to think that it was watching me fall apart and pick myself up that made him see me, us, our lives in a different way. But I don't actually know why, Didi. I don't know why he chose to stay. And I don't want to know. What matters is that he stayed. What matters is that I knew we'd be okay if he left. What matters is that we all came together to cherish each other and hold one another up. What matters is that we continue to do so to this day."

She lets go of my hand and turns to face me.

"I don't remember telling you not to depend on anyone, Didi. I see that comment has left a mark on you, and I am sorry for that. Instead, I want to say this," she runs a hand along the side of my face and I press my cheek into her palm and close my eyes.

"Some people are worth the risk."

CHAPTER ONE HUNDRED

I go to see Curtis at his studio downtown, and he opens the door with a wide grin.

"Decided to take me up on my offer after all?" he asks, gesturing for me to come inside.

I walk past him, making sure not to let any parts of me graze any parts of him, then I walk up the flight of stairs to his studio. I find my eyes looking around, taking in the new stills lining his walls, noting the things that have changed and the things that have stayed the same. Feeling the strangeness of my being here, again.

"This is weird," I say, half-sitting on a stool.

He chuckles at me, as he leans against a wall and stares at me, drinking me in.

"I don't get you," I say, feeling unnerved by his eyes on me, "I go to see you months ago, wanting answers, and you dismiss me, telling me to go back to my family-"

He cuts me off.

"That's a bit reductive, isn't it?"

I roll my eyes at him.

"Reductive or not, Curtis. You told me to focus on my family. And then you just show up at Julien's homecoming party? Seriously?"

He walks towards me, slowly, and I simply watch him, cocking my head at him curiously. He stops just an inch away from touching me.

"Don't you miss me, Didi?" he says, looking at me as if he can see into my soul, the same look that used to make me melt right into his arms, into his bed, into his heart, "Don't you stay up late at night, just dreaming about you and me and us together?"

His voice, his words, they trigger memories inside me. Didi, I love you. Didi, I miss you. Didi, just stay here with me, let me breathe you in, I love the smell of your skin. Didi...

I shake the words out of my head and force myself to remember the other words too. Didi, I don't want you. Didi, really, what did you think was going to happen? Didi, you've got to stop living in this fantasy world where you and I are a thing. Didi, go home. Focus on your family.

I chuckle at him. Then I stood up to grab my purse from where I'd dropped it on a crate, thinking somehow this would be a longer conversation than it clearly needs to be.

"I used to miss you," I say, turning to look at him, as I throw my purse over my shoulder.

I catch his eyes, but something inside me won't let me stay there, looking directly at him, so my eyes drift to the brick walls to the left of his head before I continue.

"I used to spend hours dreaming of you and me and the life we would live. And, Curtis, if that's what you had chosen, I'm sure we would have been happy. But it's not. You could never choose me. So, I let that dream go. I have new dreams now. Some are good. Some are bad. Some are mundane and boring. But none of them involve you."

I start walking towards the door.

"I'll see myself out, Curtis," I call behind my shoulder as I start prancing down the stairs.

And I thought I'd feel happy, like a weight lifted from my shoulders, but instead I feel quiet and still. I don't look back when I drive away, but I know that I will never see Curtis again and it doesn't make me feel happy or sad or angry. I just feel like me. And know that he is no longer a part of my spirit or my heart or soul, and damn sure no longer part of my body. Finally.

CHAPTER ONE HUNDRED ONE

There is a conspiratorial conversation between Gabe and the twins that makes this Saturday the day that we say goodbye to Jill. We each bring our boxes and our hearts and meet at the top of the hill of Jill's favorite park. It's clear that the twins were the ones running this show. They start the ceremony by talking about Jill and her brilliantness. How she really listened to them when they talked, how she made the best chocolate chip cookies ever created in the history of time itself, and how they will miss her and her cookies forever.

They each pull a chocolate chip cookie out of their pocket, toast one another with them, then raise their cookies in the air and shout, "For Jill," before devouring them whole.

They then take a handful of ashes and do and little dance while spreading her ashes around. They remind me of Charlie Brown characters dancing to Schroeder's musical numbers. So young, so carefree. They remind me of leaves gliding on the power of the wind in the middle of autumn. They remind me of a young me.

Then it's TiTi's turn. There is a slight shake in her hands as she begins speaking of Jill as her cool auntie, who was always so patient and listened so carefully. Of how she was a sounding board for TiTi when she felt like she couldn't talk to her mommy. Of how she had always looked forward to seeing her get old, because she just knew that she'd be the kind of quirky old lady with a penchant for dancing and baking cookies and covering up for young whippersnappers who were always breaking the rules.

"Let them be," she'd always imagined Jill saying, "they're just children. Life will have its way with them soon enough. But for now, let them be."

And then TiTi starts crying as if only now, she has realized that Jill will never get to be that silly old lady. She takes a moment to gather herself, then wipes her eyes with the backs of her hands and grabs two handfuls of Jill's ashes and scatters them in the wind. I watch her as she stands stoically, a young lady, her spine straight, her tears silently trickling down her face, and I wonder if I have done her wrong by exposing her to so much reality at such a young age or if she will continue to stand this strong, this carefully carefree.

Gabe stands up to go next. He pulls out a foldable chair and stands for his keyboard, and bends over it. "This is for Jill," he says before he begins playing, a song we all know well, but with a slowed down melody.

It's "See You Again" by Wiz Khalifa and Charlie Puth. The twins jump back into the spotlight to help him out with the rap verses, taking turns to rap different lines. And this is when I break. When Gabe hits the chorus for the second time, I lose it. My mind swirls with images of all the things that I will never get to do with Jill. Things that she and I were always supposed to do. Grow old and drink hot cocoa laced with whiskey. Come together for an afternoon walk in the park over times long gone and times that have yet to be. And I'm crying so hard, that when the song ends, Julien volunteers to go next, instead of me.

I miss the beginning of what he says, but I gather myself just in time to hear the gist of his story. And it's a story that I've never heard before. It was a few days before our wedding, and he was starting to feel antsy, like a mirror reflection of my own uncertainty. He knew I was the one for him, but he was starting to feel unsure that I truly felt that he was the one for me. He looks at me then, catching my eyes, and mouths an apology that I quickly brush off, wiping the last falling tear from my cheek. It was then that he'd decided to go see Jill. He asked her if she thought that we were making the right decision. If he and I were really meant to be. And he pauses, swallowing back his own tears, taking in a deep breath to compose himself before continuing. He tells us how she had said his name and held his hand and told her that I had never looked at another man the way I looked at him. That we were indeed meant to be. That I had been obsessed with him from the moment I'd first laid eyes on him, and that I was obsessed with him still. That was Jill. She always knew the thing that needed to be said to inspire, to propel, to make you believe. She was the rock of our whole team, and she was the most insightful human being that he has ever seen.

And with that he nods at me. And I know that it's my turn. I stand slowly, feeling dizzy from all the crying and from the weight of this moment, then propel myself forward to stand before my friends and family.

"Jill," I say, my voice cracking, "was my best friend. I may have had other close friends, but Jill, she understood me. Without her, I'm not sure any of the good things I've ever done would have ever come to be. She saw me, through all the bullshit and lies and fronting, she saw me. And I, in turn, saw her."

I take a deep breath, close my eyes, and swallow in the world around me.

"The last time I saw Jill, the last time I laid eyes on her, was right after I'd lost everything."

The memory comes to life in my mind as I speak.

"I'd lost my house, I'd lost my husband, I'd lost my children, I'd lost my entire family, my friends, my respect, my integrity. But Jill, Jill had come to me."

I feel the tears welling up in my eyes and I try to fight their fall, unsuccessfully. I continue on despite them, trying to hold my voice steady.

"I was a lost, broken shell of a human being, and she'd come to me. Despite all I had done to her, despite all the havoc I had caused in her life, despite all the lies, she had come to me, and taken me by the hand, and pressed it to her chest," I intertwine my hands and press them to my chest for emphasis, "and she'd said, 'Didi, come with me, I think we can find a way to save each other,' but I didn't understand."

I break down into sobs that cause me to keel over at the waist, bending under the pressure of my biggest mistake.

"I didn't understand that she needed just as much help as I did. That she was drowning just as badly. That she was looking to me to be the branch that she leaned on while I leaned on her. Her and me."

I stop, take a deep breath, reliving the moment that I failed my best friend.

"And I didn't understand. I thought she was patronizing me. Offering to be my savior. I took it as an act of pity."

I shake my head at myself, looking off into the distance away from the loving eyes of my family, as I try to find the courage to continue to speak.

When I do, my voice comes out harsh, broken, raspy.

"I was just so broken. Too broken to even accept a helping hand. Even from her."

My lip quivers and it takes everything in me to fight back the sobs.

"Instead, I'd snatched my hand away, I'd glared at her, and said, 'I don't need you to save me, Jill.' I'd practically spat it at her. I was so angry."

My voice shakes as I say the last three words, and I swallow hard back against a wave of uncontrollable sorrow.

"I didn't understand," I say, through a quavering voice, "that she needed me too."

I take a deep breath and gather myself, then stand up straight and look up at the sky all around us, knowing that Jill is somewhere in this universe, smiling down on me.

"I'm sorry, Jill," I say, finally. "I'm sorry I let you down. I'm sorry I didn't understand. I'm sorry I couldn't save you from you like you have always tried to save me from me. I'm sorry."

And with that I pick up the last of Jill's ashes and scatter them in the wind.

Go, Jill, go. Be free.

CHAPTER ONE HUNDRED TWO

It is a random Sunday, and my life has fallen into simple patterns of contented beauty. My alarm goes off in the early morning hours, and I hesitate before getting out of bed because my husband's arm is around my waist, his hand lightly cupping my breast and the feeling is pure heaven. But I sigh and slide out of the bed because I know that my dad is waiting for me. I speed across town and pull up right in front of my dad's house just as he's finished checking the tire pressure, and grin at him as he shakes his head at me. My dad has no qualms about leaving me behind, he's done it before, because who am I to fuck up his morning ride, even if I am his daughter?

I couldn't agree more.

We ride down a path that I have never been, up a slow, but steadily mounting hill and arrive at the precipice just as the sun begins to rise, as usual. I pull out our travel mugs of coffee, the pastries mom baked for us last night, and the protein bars that dad forces me to eat even though they taste like moldy ass. On the ride back I zigzag down the hill, arms outstretched, grinning as my hair blows in the wind, and I'm ready to take on the rest of my day.

I give my dad an oversized hug before heading home to make an overly ambitious breakfast for my baby sister, her boyfriend, Gabe, his new girlfriend, and my family. I lay out all the ingredients for the pancakes and the twins take turns mixing the batter and then trying to best each other at making their pancakes the perfect size, thickness and golden shade. TiTi has been working on perfecting the fluffiness of her eggs, and Julien has the bacon down pat. I am in charge of French toast, as usual, while Camille mixes mimosas, and Travis makes the hash browns. Gabe and girlfriend waltz in right on time with fresh fruit from the farmer's market.

Before we dig into the meal laid out before us, I ask the twins to pull out two more chairs because we are expecting some very special guests today. Everyone looks at me, eyebrows raised, mimosas held comically in the air, as they freeze. I catch my sister's eyes, as they twinkle mischievously, and I just shake my head at her. The doorbell rings, and I go to answer it.

"Father Fred!" I say, gushing with pure joy as I encircle him in a big bearhug.

I haven't seen him in a while and I hadn't realized how much I missed his face, his smile, his energy until this exact moment. Gertrude stands behind him clutching a big bouquet of flowers and a batch of freshly baked cinnamon buns that smell heavenly. I let go of Father Fred to wrap my arms around her neck and breathe in her familiar scent. I relieve Gertrude of her flowers and cinnamon buns and usher them in. The twins squeal at the sight of the cinnamon buns and everyone greets Father Fred and Gertrude warmly. By this time, everyone has heard about how they have helped me find my own strength, how they each and both simultaneously have thrown me the rope that I used to pull myself out of the deep dark hole I had fallen into, so they are welcomed into the fold like family.

Father Fred leads us in prayer before we eat.

CHAPTER ONE HUNDRED THREE

E verything is working out and yet, I keep waking up in the middle of the night, planning and re-planning. Pacing the living room. Wandering the streets. Crying in the dark away from everybody. I hide it from everyone, but eventually he notices. And he is waiting for me when I slowly creak open the door to our bedroom. His face is lined with sadness and anger, and I swallow hard because I already know what he is going to accuse me of. Of course. Of course. What else could he think, given our history?

"I'm not cheating on you," I say, preemptively, "I'm just, I've just been having trouble sleeping."

I bite my bottom lip and ease onto the bed next to him. I wrap my arms around his waist and lay my head on his shoulder. I let the words spill out in a tumbled mess.

"I have these dreams, these nightmares. That everything falls apart. That I make another colossal mistake. That I destroy everything and everyone's lives. That I fuck everything up and lose you and the kids and my family and friends, and that this time there's no forgiving. There's no forgiveness. They're done handing out second chances because they already gave me one and I squandered it."

My voice has dropped low, so low. And I feel as if I'm slowly drowning, but I continue, because he needs to know. This is how we do better. This is how we grow.

So, I continue.

"And I fall and I fall and I fall some more, and this time I don't get back up again, babe. This time, there is no redemption. This time, I make it my permanent residence."

I'm crying silently, and while I don't care about the tears, the mound of snot pouring from my nose requires attention, so I shift to grab a tissue off the nightstand, while I wait for my husband to say something.

He watches me in the dim light of the night and waits for me to blow my nose before he responds.

"Didi," he says, stroking my back and guiding me to look him in the eyes, "I know we have been through a lot this year, but you're going to drive yourself crazy if you keep thinking like this. Life is risk. There's always a chance that any one of us can mess it all up, but we can't let that stop us from living. You just have to take it one step at a time, one day at a time. And every day you just have ask yourself if you did the best you could. And if you did, you vow to do it again the next day. And if you didn't, you vow to do better the next day. You just have to be vigilant, AK. Wake up every day, look yourself in the mirror and own up to who you are, what you have done, and who you have become. Own it, accept it, live with it in the forefront of your head, and shape your days around that knowledge. That's the only way to be."

I hear him, and I nod at him, and I curl back into bed, clutching his fingers within my own, but his words feel hallow to me, harsh, impossible. I fall asleep, but I don't sleep well, and when I wake up, I decide to give my husband's advice a try.

What's the worst that can happen after all?

I wait for TiTi to get out of the bathroom, then hug her tightly when she emerges, a cloud of steam billowing out around her. Her eyes twinkle, so young and innocent and full of hope. I kiss her cheek. I caress her face, and I watch her bounce off to get ready for school.

So, it is my daughter who is on my mind when I face my reflection in the mirror.

"You failed her," I say to my reflection, "You failed her and Darrius and Paris. You failed them as a mother."

A tear falls down my cheek, but I don't bother to brush it away.

"You failed them," I say, my voice cracking, "You dropped them off at your parents' house one day and you didn't come back. You pretended that you were doing them a favor. You were protecting them from seeing how you failed them so epically. But you were just trying not to deal with them, not to face them, not to look them in the eyes and explain to them what you did. How you betrayed everyone you loved. How you stole their money and lied about it. How you destroyed your company and got their father put in jail. You did all that. And you could do it again."

I grip the sink, bent over it, sobbing as I think about how I could lose it all again. As I accept it.

And then a thought comes to me through the shadows of my mind.

But today, today, I have everything I have ever wanted, and today, I have all the power to keep it that way.

And as I wipe away my tears and gather myself to make the most out of this day, one name keeps banging around in my brain.

Bethany Brown.

CHAPTER ONE HUNDRED FOUR

When Bethany Brown had her heart broken sophomore year, she showed up at my dorm looking pathetic, puffy-eyed and smelling like a whole bottle of vodka. I'd pushed her into a shower, washed her hair, and combed it out slowly, wrapping it in bantu knots, while I waited for her to start talking. As I bust out our trademark container of vanilla bean ice cream, she'd started blabbing.

The guy she had been dating had been lying to her. He had a girlfriend. She lived on the other side of campus in a sorority house. And when the girl had found out, she and all her sorority sisters had started slut-shaming her. Gathering together in bunches and chanting "slut" at her in the cafeteria, shoving her when they walked by, dropping notes in her lap that said things like, "Bethany Brown has ten STDs" or just simply the word "Bitch."

This had only been going on for a couple days, but it was getting to her, driving her crazy, so she'd stolen a bottle of Vodka and boarded a bus directly to me. And she'd lain in my lap and she'd cried openly and freely, that ugly girl cry that girls only allow themselves to cry when they are all alone or with their best friends. The kind where her face got all scrunched up and a double chin magically appeared out of nowhere and the snot fell from her nose in a thick cascade that built a bridge between her open lips which were emitting an animalistic sound that came cracking out of her in bursts and stops.

I'd wrapped my arms around her shaking body and wound her fingers in mine and told her exactly what I knew that she needed to hear. That she would go back to school on Monday with her hair done and her head held high and an aura of "Go fuck yourself" around her. That I would blow off all my classes if need be and go with her. That we'd kick anyone's butts who dared lay a finger on her. That we'd spend all weekend coming up with a thousand comebacks. That all she had to do was show them that she was fearless and a bad bitch and they'd leave her alone.

And she had listened, and she had nodded and she had stopped crying, but the worried expression had not faded from her gaze.

"What is it?" I'd asked her, squeezing her hand more tightly, "Tell me," I'd said, my voice low and steady, trying to convey the level of sincerity that I'd felt.

"It's just," she'd said, taking a deep breath, "I feel like I just keep making the same mistakes over and over and over again. And I'm starting to feel like it's me. Like I'm the problem. And if I keep on going down this path, then I'm just scared that I'm going to wind up alone and lonely, with no one to love and nobody to love me. And," she hesitates, her voice cracking as she tries to hold it together, "I'm scared, Didi."

And I'd wanted to laugh at her. It had taken everything within me to hold the laughter in. My silly, silly Bethany. But I knew immediately, that laughing at her at that moment in time would have been detrimental to her self-esteem. So instead, I'd taken a deep breath, swallowed the laughter, and responded to her like she was the hurt little girl that lives inside us all.

"Bethany Brown," I'd said, "you know that that will never happen, because at the very least, you will always have me. As long as I have air to breathe, I will be by your side. And I will always, always, always love you. No matter what crazy fucked up thing you do. I will always be here for you."

What a liar the future has made of me. If I could go back, what would my eighteen-year-old self say to me?

Get your shit together, Didi.

CHAPTER ONE HUNDRED FIVE

I want to take Camille with me. I want to take Julien or TiTi or Darrius or Paris or Gabe or my daddy. I want to take Jeremy or my mom or Gertrude or Father Fred. But instead, I take Jill with me in my heart, and I gather up all my willpower and go and see Bethany.

I ring her doorbell, and I stand there for an eternity, but she doesn't open the door. She isn't home. I sit down on her steps and lean my head against her red door and vow to wait right there for however long it takes for her to come home. My mind drifts as I sit, and I wait. I wonder if maybe I should not be sitting and waiting, if I should come back another day, if maybe she's on vacation or spending the night with a new boyfriend. But something inside me tells me to stay. To sit. To just rest here against Bethany Brown's red door. That I was meant to be just right here, right now, at this moment in time.

I think about Father Fred and Gertrude. I think about how I haven't seen Miguel in a while and vow to set up a lunch date or something. I think of TiTi's smile. I think about my twins and of how much they've grown in such a short period of time. I think about my mom and me cooking in my sister's kitchen. I think of following my dad up hill after hill. I think of Gabe and his heart. I think of Jeremy's relentless determination. I think of letting Curtis go. I think of Julien's eyes when he decided to believe in me. I think of Jill laughing, her head thrown back, her full body involved. And then I think just her name, just her name, just my best friend's name.

Bethany.

CHAPTER ONE HUNDRED SIX

I'd like to tell you that Bethany Brown came then. That she'd tapped me on my arm and pulled me out of my reverie. That I'd apologized for how I'd treated her that day when she came to see me. That she'd wrapped her arms around me and pulled me into her house and we'd spoken for hours, for days, for weeks, and months intermittently. But that's not what happened.

She'd come after quite some time and sat down on the steps next to me and asked me why I was there. She'd listened to my apology. And I'd told her how I had promised to be there for her always, but that I never thought she'd bail on me. That she had hurt me so deeply that I had not been able to see anything but the hurt, and so I had failed her in return.

And she had apologized to me. She had hugged me, wrapped her arms around my shoulders while I cried, while I begged her to forgive me.

"I forgive you," she'd said, hugging me again, more tightly this time.

She'd wiped my tears with her hands, looked at me with her

cold, dead eyes, and she'd said, "I forgive you, Adrienne, but we can't be friends. What we had has been broken, and I never want to see you again."

She'd reached in her bag, pulled out a small travel-sized packet of tissues, and handed it to me. She'd kissed my cheek, she'd caressed my face, and she'd stood up and walked into her house without so much as a goodbye.

And maybe I'll find a way to fix it. Maybe I'll find a way to atone like I have done for so many others that I have wronged. Maybe I'll wear her down into submission by being purely relentless, by refusing to let her go. Maybe I will. But one thing that I do know is that Bethany Brown is right. What we had has been broken. There are things that are done that may not be undone. It may be able to be fixed, it may be able to be repaired, we may be able to build something new and beautiful out of the remnants of broken pieces. But it will never be the same. And maybe the kindest thing I can do to her, for me, for the both of us, is to simply to let her go. Maybe that's how I love her always and forever. I hold her in my heart, right there in the middle, right next to Jill.

I carry you with me. I carry you in my heart.

Maybe.

ACKNOWLEDGMENTS

I want to start off by thanking my dad for always believing in me. From when I was little and scribbling on tons of yellow lined paper, to bragging about my stories to get me into the Honor Program at Loyola, to telling everyone he knows about the publication of this very novel, he has always been my loudest and proudest cheerleader. And I have always and will always be grateful for it. I love you, Dad.

Mr. Derrick J. Witherspoon, what would I do without you? Always my first reader, always cheering me on, while also holding me accountable, always yelling at me to just do the thing already. Thank you for always believing in me, for helping me puzzle through things, and for always standing in my corner. It may seem like I take you for granted, but I fully appreciate everything you do. You mean the world to me. I bow down before your glory. I love you always.

Malachi and Malcolm. Thank you for inspiring me to be the best version of myself, and for reminding me that I should be writing when I'm sitting in front of my laptop and scrolling through my phone. You two are the loves of my life. Always remember that there is nothing you cannot be or do or have.

Steve Azeka, for someone who is "just" my birthday twin's husband, you have been one of my strongest supporters. Thank you so much for forcing me to send you my book, for always asking me about the process, and for quietly holding me accountable to finally finish my edits. I have so much appreciation for you. Thank you from the bottom of my heart.

For all my first readers: Lee Cohen, my bestie for LIFE; Carol Jean, my gorgeous and vivacious auntie; Cecilia Webb, the amazing lacrosse player; Jill Klieger, the fabulous interior designer; and a special thank you to Lori Brown, who not only took the time to read my story, but also gave me valuable advice when interpreting my publishing contract. Thank you for taking the time to read my ramblings. I appreciate and love you all.

For my photographer, Julia Maylszko, who shines brilliantly inside and out. For Ming-Huei Fisher, her consultant, who has a magnificent creative eye. And for Maceo Morgan for holding the light. Thank you so much for giving up your lunch to photograph your silly teacher for the jacket of this book. You are rockstars.

And lastly, of course, I would like to thank the team at Running Wild Press/RIZE for making this process so easy. I'd especially like to thank my editor, Laura Huie, you have been an amazing partner throughout this revision process. Your words of encouragement helped me face my edits without fear. I am eternally grateful and thankful for all your help.

AUTHOR BIO

Niki Dominique lives in Harlem with two of the dopest boys on the planet. She spends her days teaching, her nights writing, and the moments in between, running from the thoughts in her head. She tries to find moments to shift her perspective by focusing on finding or making joy in every second of every minute of every day. *Shades of Purple* is her first novel.

RIZE publishes great stories and great writing across genres written by People of Color and other underrepresented groups. Our team consists of:

Lisa Diane Kastner, Founder and Executive Editor
Mona Bethke, Acquisitions Editor
Rebecca Dimyan, Editor
Abigail Efird, Editor
Laura Huie, Editor
Cody Sisco, Editor
Chih Wang, Editor
Pulp Art Studios, Cover Design
Standout Books, Interior Design
Polgarus Studios, Interior Design

Learn more about us and our stories at www.runningwild-press.com

Loved these stories and want more? Follow us at www.runningwildpress.com, www.facebook.com/running-wildpress, on Twitter @lisadkastner @RunWildBooks @RwpRIZE